Bigfoot: Echoes in Stone

Shadows in the Timberline: Book 2

by

Ethan Blackwood

Copyright © 2025 Ethan Blackwood
All rights reserved.
No part of this book may be reproduced in any form without written permission from the author.

Chapter 1: Echoes in the Concrete Jungle

The insistent, low hum was the first thing Elise registered, a sound that resonated not just in her ears but deep within her sternum, vibrating along nerve pathways still raw from subterranean silence and resonant calls. For a disorienting moment, she wasn't standing behind a lectern in a brightly lit University of Washington lecture hall, bathed in the artificial daylight pouring from fluorescent tubes overhead. She was back in the oppressive darkness of the cavern, the air thick with the scent of damp earth and ancient stone, the immense, shadowed forms of the Stick-shí'nač materializing from the gloom, their collective hum a physical force that seemed to bend the very air. Her hand instinctively tightened on the edge of the lectern, knuckles white, her breath catching in her throat.

"Dr. Holloway?"

The voice, young, slightly hesitant, pierced the bubble of memory. Elise blinked, forcing the cavern walls to recede, the glowing moss to fade, replaced by rows of expectant undergraduate faces staring up at her, bathed in the mundane glare of the overhead projector. The hum wasn't the guardians; it was the projector fan, whirring diligently as it displayed a detailed diagram of *Cercopithecus mitis* skeletal structure onto the screen behind her. Just a fan. Mundane. Safe.

"Sorry," Elise managed, her voice emerging rougher than intended. She cleared her throat, pushing her glasses higher on her nose, a nervous tic she'd developed since returning, her fingers brushing against the faint, almost invisible scar near her temple where Nora's hurled axe had miraculously *not* connected during the chaos in the sanctuary. "Lost my place. Right. As you can see from the relative length of the ischium compared to the pubis, the pelvic girdle in *Cercopithecus* is highly adapted for quadrupedal locomotion, particularly evident in the… the arboreal subspecies…"

3

She tried to regain the thread, forcing her eyes to focus on the slide, on the familiar bones and Latin names that had once formed the bedrock of her professional life. Six months. Six months since she and Nora had stumbled out of the Olympic wilderness, smoke-stained, half-starved, haunted, only to be intercepted by Kestrel's anonymous agents and fed back into a world that had no inkling of the impossibility they had survived. Six months of trying to stitch the frayed edges of her old life back together over the gaping wound left by AO Hollow.

It wasn't working.

The lecture hall felt like a cage, the tiered rows of seats rising like canyon walls. The projector's hum continued its low thrum beneath her words, a constant reminder of other, deeper resonances. The scrape of a chair leg on the linoleum floor sent jolts of adrenaline through her, mimicking the sound of rockfall in the Crevice. Even the faces staring up at her felt alien. These students, bright-eyed, concerned with midterms and weekend plans, existed in a reality utterly incompatible with the one she now carried within her. Their world was one of textbooks, peer-reviewed journals, observable phenomena. Her world now included nine-foot-tall sentient beings who built subterranean villages, communicated through infrasound, and left eighteen-inch footprints by creeks haunted by missing persons.

She fumbled through the remainder of the lecture, her explanations mechanical, her mind straying constantly. She saw Boone's grim face reflected in the window glass, heard Levi's pained breathing in the silence between her sentences, felt the crushing weight of Graves' secrets and the icy presence of the Kestrel woman from the debriefing room. The non-disclosure agreement she had signed felt less like a legal document and more like a physical restraint, a gag woven from veiled threats and the overwhelming burden of an unbelievable truth.

When the bell finally released them, the sudden surge of chatter and movement felt like an assault. Students gathered their backpacks, laptops snapped shut, voices rising in casual conversation as they shuffled towards the exits. Elise gathered her own notes with trembling hands, avoiding eye contact, desperate to escape the confines of the room, the proximity to unsuspecting normalcy.

"Dr. Holloway? Are you feeling alright?" A young woman paused near the lectern, her brow furrowed with genuine concern. Sarah, one of her brightest primatology students. "You seemed a little… distracted today."

"Fine, Sarah. Just fine," Elise lied, forcing a tight smile that felt brittle, unnatural. "A bit tired, perhaps. Didn't sleep well." An understatement of epic proportions. Sleep offered no escape, only fragmented nightmares – falling stones, chilling roars, the glint of intelligent eyes in utter darkness, Levi's final, resolute gaze.

"Okay," Sarah lingered for a moment, clearly unconvinced. "Well, uh, that article you recommended on gibbon pair-bonding? Really fascinating comparison with siamang social structures. I had a couple of questions about the methodology, if you have office hours later?"

"Yes, of course. Four o'clock," Elise confirmed automatically, grateful for the return to familiar academic ground, however briefly. "Happy to discuss it."

Sarah smiled, relief washing over her features. "Great! See you then." She hurried off, merging back into the river of students flowing out into the damp Seattle afternoon.

Elise watched her go, a pang of envy hitting her. The simple, uncomplicated passion for knowledge, the belief in discoverable truths within established frameworks… she remembered feeling that once. Now, her own framework was shattered, her understanding of the world irrevocably warped. What would Sarah think if she knew her professor, the expert on Old World monkeys, had spent weeks being hunted by creatures straight out of folklore, had witnessed impossible architecture beneath the earth, and carried secrets that could rewrite biology textbooks and potentially ignite global panic or trigger a ruthless cover-up?

Packing her worn leather briefcase – a comforting anchor to her previous life – Elise stepped out of the lecture hall into the bustling university corridor. The noise, the bright lights, the sheer mundane density of people felt overwhelming after the profound silence and isolation of the valley. Every face seemed like a potential watcher, every overheard snippet of conversation a possible coded message. Paranoia, Kestrel had called it during the debriefing. Understandable trauma response. But Elise knew it wasn't just paranoia. The feeling of being observed was too persistent, too specific. The subtle glitches that plagued her life since returning felt too targeted.

Her work laptop freezing whenever she strayed too close to researching Kestrel Foundation subsidiaries or accessing satellite imagery archives of the Olympic Peninsula. Static on her phone line during sensitive conversations, brief though those attempts were. The flicker of streetlights as she walked beneath them on her way home. The utility van parked across the street from her apartment building for three days straight, supposedly fixing a 'cable issue' that none of her neighbors had reported. Coincidences? Perhaps. But the pattern felt chillingly deliberate. Kestrel wasn't just enforcing silence through legal agreements; they were likely ensuring it through active surveillance. We know what you saw. Stay silent, or be silenced. The woman's calm voice echoed in her memory, devoid of inflection but heavy with implied threat.

She bypassed the elevator, taking the stairs down three flights, her footsteps echoing loudly in the concrete well – another sound that sent phantom shivers down her spine, recalling the descent into the Crevice. Outside, the ubiquitous Seattle drizzle had returned, casting a grey, melancholic sheen over the campus buildings and the slick pavement. The air smelled of wet concrete, exhaust fumes, and distant coffee – the familiar scents of the city that now felt alien, inadequate compared to the rich, complex perfume of the old-growth forest, the sharp tang of ozone near the hidden sanctuary, the terrifying musk of the creature's nest.

She pulled the collar of her trench coat tighter, hunched her shoulders against the damp chill, and began the walk back towards her apartment in the University District. It was usually a pleasant walk, through leafy streets lined with Craftsman houses and independent bookstores. Today, every corner felt like a potential ambush point, every parked car a possible surveillance vehicle. She found herself constantly scanning rooftops, alleyways, faces of passersby, her hand instinctively hovering near the heavy canister of bear spray she now carried illegally in her oversized purse – a useless talisman against Kestrel agents, perhaps, but a deeply ingrained habit from the valley, a desperate need for some form of defense.

Halfway home, she stopped at a small café, needing the warmth, the caffeine, the illusion of normalcy. Sitting at a small table by the window, cradling a steaming latte, she watched the rain trace patterns on the glass, blurring the world outside. She pulled out her phone, intending to check her university email, scroll through harmless news headlines. But her fingers hesitated over the icon.

She hadn't tried contacting Nora directly since sending the postcard months ago. Respecting her silence, respecting the boundaries Nora likely needed to re-establish with her own world, her own community, felt paramount. But the isolation, the weight of the shared secret, was becoming unbearable. Did Nora feel watched too? Had Kestrel approached her again? Or had they deemed her less of a threat, protected by her cultural context, dismissed perhaps as an unreliable witness prone to folklore? Elise desperately wanted to know, needed the connection to the only other person alive who truly understood the reality of AO Hollow.

Resisting the urge, knowing any electronic communication was likely monitored, she instead opened her personal email account, the one she used for non-university correspondence, the one Kestrel theoretically shouldn't have access to, though she no longer trusted that assumption. A handful of messages waited – junk mail, a notification from her bank, a newsletter from a conservation group... and one from an unfamiliar address, a generic string of letters and numbers from a supposedly secure proton-mail server. The subject line was blank.

Her heart gave a sudden, heavy thud. Kestrel? Or something else? Her hands felt suddenly cold, clammy. She hesitated, hovering her finger over the message. Opening it could be clicking on a phishing link, confirming her email was active, perhaps even triggering tracking software. Ignoring it felt impossible.

Taking a deep breath, she tapped the screen, opening the message. It contained only three words:

Echoes persist. Vigilance required.

No signature. No context. Just those five words, chillingly ambiguous yet undeniably resonant. Echoes persist. Was it a warning? A threat? A coded message from an ally? Or simply Kestrel, subtly reminding her that the past was not buried, that her knowledge remained a liability, that vigilance – their vigilance over her, and perhaps her own necessary vigilance – was required?

Elise quickly deleted the message, her mind racing. The phrasing felt deliberate, echoing her own internal experience, the way the valley haunted her waking thoughts and sleeping nightmares. It felt less like a direct Kestrel communication – those tended towards bland corporate speak or implied legal threats – and more like... something else. But what? Who else could possibly know enough to send such a message? Aris Thorne, the Kestrel pathologist who had warned against further engagement? Had he gone rogue? Or someone else from the shadowy fringes of Project Backwoods, perhaps? Or was it just Kestrel playing mind games, using psychological tactics to keep her off balance, reminding her she wasn't safe, wasn't forgotten?

The uncertainty amplified her anxiety. The feeling of being watched intensified, no longer just a general paranoia but a focused scrutiny. She finished her latte quickly, the lukewarm liquid doing little to soothe the knot of fear tightening in her stomach. Leaving the café, she scanned the street more intently than ever, searching faces, noting license plates, feeling the invisible net closing in.

The rain intensified as she reached her apartment building, a drab brick structure that usually felt like a safe haven but now seemed like just another part of the cage. She fumbled with her keys, glancing over her shoulder, convinced a shadow detached itself from the rain-slicked entryway of the building opposite. Just the rain, she told herself. Just shadows. But the conviction felt hollow.

Inside her apartment, the familiar space felt alien, potentially compromised. Was the faint static on the landline still there? Was the Wi-Fi router blinking erratically again? She resisted the urge to sweep for bugs – she wouldn't know what to look for, and finding one would only confirm her fears without offering a solution. Instead, she performed her nightly ritual: checking the deadbolt, wedging a chair under the doorknob, drawing the heavy blackout curtains, creating a small, defensible pocket within the encroaching city.

She ate mechanically, reheated leftovers tasting like sawdust. She tried to work, opening her laptop to review Sarah's questions about gibbon methodology, but the words swam before her eyes, meaningless. The image of the Stick-shí'nač adolescent curiously examining the quartz crystal superimposed itself over the graphs of primate social interaction. The sound of the elder's roar drowned out the memory of gibbon calls.

Later, lying sleeplessly in bed, staring at the familiar water stains on her bedroom ceiling, the city sounds outside – sirens wailing in the distance, the rumble of traffic on wet pavement, the muffled bass from a neighbor's stereo – felt like a thin, fragile membrane stretched over a vast, terrifying silence. The silence of the Hollow. The silence of Kestrel's conspiracy. The silence demanded of her.

Echoes persist. Vigilance required.

The cryptic message pulsed in her mind. It confirmed her deepest fear: escape wasn't truly possible. The valley, Kestrel, the hollow truth — they were indelible parts of her now. She had survived, yes. But survival was just the beginning. The real struggle — the fight to stay alive, stay free, and somehow navigate the crushing weight of the secret — was only just starting. And the watchers, human or otherwise, were closing in. The concrete jungle offered no sanctuary, only a different kind of wilderness, with its own predators lurking in the shadows.

Chapter 2: Dead Ends and Door Bolts

The cryptic email burrowed under Elise's skin, a persistent irritant beneath the already raw surface of her nerves. *Echoes persist. Vigilance required.* Was it Kestrel tightening the leash, a reminder veiled in poetic ambiguity? Or was it something else, a phantom reaching out from the conspiracy's tangled web? The uncertainty was almost worse than overt threat. It amplified the feeling of being watched, turning every shadow into a potential observer, every technological glitch into a possible sign of intrusion.

Sleep remained elusive. When exhaustion finally claimed her, the respite was brief, shattered by nightmares that dragged her back to the dripping darkness of the caves or the terrifying, luminous expanse of the hidden sanctuary. She saw Boone falling into shadow, heard Levi's final, desperate sounds, felt the ground tremble under the elder's roar. She woke gasping, heart pounding, the scent of moss and fear phantom-real in her sterile apartment air. The echo of the creatures' resonant hum sometimes seemed to linger, a subsonic thrum just below the threshold of hearing, making the floorboards vibrate, or perhaps that was just her own pulse hammering against the mattress.

During the day, she tried to maintain the façade. Lectured on primate evolution, graded papers on biomechanics, attended faculty meetings where debates about curriculum changes felt like absurdist theatre. But the focus wasn't there. Her mind kept circling back to the impossible truth she carried, the weight of the secret pressing down, making concentration feel like wading through thick mud. She caught colleagues glancing at her with concern, noticed the slight hesitation before they asked how she was *really* doing. She deflected with practiced vagueness – the trauma of the expedition, the wildfire, the lost colleagues. The official story provided a convenient shield, but it felt increasingly flimsy, transparent.

The small anomalies continued, too frequent, too specific to be dismissed as mere coincidence. Her office computer at the university began experiencing bizarre slowdowns whenever she tried accessing certain geological databases related to the Olympic Peninsula, or attempted searches using keywords like "uncharted drainage basin," "Project Backwoods," or even the name "Aris Thorne" – the Kestrel pathologist from the Goliath autopsy report. Pages would hang indefinitely, search queries would return inexplicable "server errors," or her entire system would require a forced reboot. The university IT department found no malware, blaming network traffic or aging hardware, but Elise knew better. It felt like sophisticated digital walls, specifically erected to block her inquiries, monitored by algorithms far beyond standard university security. Kestrel wasn't just watching her physical movements; they were policing her access to information, subtly reinforcing the boundaries of her confinement.

The final straw came a week after the cryptic email. Returning late from the lab one evening, exhaustion making her less cautious than usual, she let herself into her apartment, tossing her keys onto the small entryway table. As she shrugged off her damp coat, a faint discrepancy caught her eye. A tiny smudge of mud, almost invisible, on the pristine white baseboard near the doorjamb, right where the chair she wedged under the knob usually rested. She hadn't noticed it that morning. She was meticulous about cleaning, especially since returning, needing the illusion of control over her environment. Had she tracked it in herself? Possible, given the perpetual Seattle damp. But something about its position, low down, slightly smeared, felt wrong.

A cold dread washed over her. Moving slowly, deliberately, she knelt down, examining the smudge. It wasn't just mud; there seemed to be tiny fibers embedded within it, dark, synthetic. Then she scanned the area around the doorframe, her eyes sharp, the scientist's observational skills kicking into high gear, fueled now by adrenaline. And she saw it. A minuscule scratch on the metal doorplate near the lock mechanism, almost imperceptible unless you were looking for it. Fresh. Another tiny fiber, caught on the splintered edge of the scratch.

Someone had been here. While she was out. Someone skilled enough to bypass the deadbolt and likely the chair wedge without leaving obvious signs, but perhaps hurried, or just slightly careless, leaving behind these minute traces. Kestrel. Confirming her suspicions, checking if she'd brought anything back, planting new listening devices? The thought made her skin crawl. Her sanctuary wasn't safe. It never had been.

Panic threatened to overwhelm her, a suffocating wave urging her to run blindly out the door. She fought it down, forcing herself to breathe, to think rationally. Running wildly would achieve nothing, likely lead her straight into their hands. She needed a plan. She needed to disappear, properly this time. Staying silent wasn't enough; her very existence, her knowledge, was a threat Kestrel would eventually feel compelled to neutralize. The surveillance, the glitches, the likely intrusion into her apartment – they weren't just warnings anymore; they felt like the precursors to more decisive action.

That night, sleep was entirely forgotten. Fueled by black coffee and a desperate, cold clarity, Elise began systematically erasing herself. She started with the digital footprint. Using encrypted browsers accessed via public Wi-Fi hotspots miles from her usual haunts (changing locations constantly), she deleted social media profiles, closed unused online accounts, scrubbed cloud storage. She knew it was likely futile against Kestrel's resources, but it felt like a necessary ritual, severing ties. She backed up her essential, sanitized academic work onto multiple encrypted thumb drives, then reformatted her personal laptop's hard drive, wiping it clean. Her university computer would have to wait – tampering with it directly might trigger immediate alerts.

Next came the physical world. She gathered cash, withdrawn in small, random amounts from different ATMs over the preceding weeks, a paranoid precaution that now felt prescient. She packed her go-bag – not the one from the expedition, but a new, anonymous backpack purchased with cash. Inside went durable outdoor clothing, sturdy boots, a basic first-aid kit (replenished after the expedition), water purification tablets, high-energy food bars, a reliable compass (hoping it would work away from the valley's influence), detailed paper maps of Washington state and the Olympic Peninsula, and her small, essential field notebook. Finally, heart pounding, she retrieved the waterproof container holding the memory card and the logbook page from its hiding place. This, the core of the truth, the reason for her flight, went into a hidden pocket sewn into the backpack's lining.

She moved methodically through her apartment, destroying anything that could easily trace her movements or intentions. Credit card statements, bills, old journals, research notes related to Kestrel or the Olympics – all shredded, then soaked in water, reduced to illegible pulp. She kept only essential identification documents, tucking them away securely. She considered leaving a false trail – booking a flight she wouldn't take, sending misleading emails from a burner account – but decided against it. Kestrel was too sophisticated; clumsy misdirection might only confirm their suspicions faster. Better to simply vanish as cleanly as possible.

The hardest part was leaving behind the remnants of her life, the tangible connections to the person she had been before AO Hollow. Books accumulated over years, photographs holding cherished memories, research materials representing decades of work – all had to be abandoned. It felt like another kind of death, an erasure of her past self. But survival demanded it.

As dawn approached, casting long, grey shadows across the city, Elise took one last look around the apartment that was no longer hers. It felt hollowed out, stripped bare, reflecting the state of her own life. She left the key on the table, pulled the hood of an anonymous dark rain jacket over her head, hoisted the unfamiliar backpack, and slipped out the back entrance, melting into the pre-dawn anonymity of the awakening city.

Her first challenge was ditching her car. Driving it would leave an electronic trail Kestrel could easily follow. She drove several miles across town, parked it on a quiet residential street where it wouldn't immediately attract attention, wiped down the steering wheel and door handles, and walked away without looking back, merging into the flow of early morning commuters heading towards bus stops and light rail stations.

Public transport felt safer, anonymous. She rode a bus across town, paid cash, transferred to another line heading south, away from the Peninsula initially. She kept her head down, hood up, avoiding security cameras where possible, constantly scanning faces, looking for anyone paying undue attention. Every suited man, every person talking too intently into a phone, felt like a potential Kestrel agent. The paranoia was exhausting, but necessary.

She spent the day moving, never staying in one place too long. A few hours in a sprawling public library, hunched over maps in a quiet corner, planning a tentative route towards the Peninsula that avoided major highways and population centers. Lunch was a quick, cheap meal at a nondescript diner in a different part of the city, paid for with cash, eaten near the back exit. Another bus ride, then another, gradually circling back towards the Puget Sound ferry terminals, but choosing a smaller, less busy route, aiming for one of the islands first, a place to potentially disappear for a day or two, throw off immediate pursuit before making the final jump to the Peninsula.

Throughout the day, she resisted the urge to use any public computers, any traceable phones. Her burner phone remained off, its battery removed, tucked deep in her pack. Contacting Nora's intermediary was the next critical step, but it had to be done carefully, at the right time, from the right place, using the pre-agreed, low-tech method. They had established it during those brief, hushed conversations after the Kestrel debriefing, anticipating this possibility: a specific, innocuous message left within a particular, commonly found guidebook (a birdwatching guide, Elise recalled) shelved in the reference section of a designated small-town library on the Peninsula itself. A long shot, relying on the contact checking regularly, relying on the message not being discovered by others, but infinitely safer than any electronic communication.

As the afternoon wore on, the strain began to tell. Lack of sleep, constant vigilance, the gnawing uncertainty – it created a physical ache behind her eyes, a tremor in her hands. She found herself experiencing micro-flashbacks more frequently now, triggered by mundane things. The rumble of a passing truck became the sound of falling rock in the Crevice. The fleeting glimpse of a tall, dark-coated man disappearing around a corner morphed momentarily into the silhouette of the Stick-shí'nač on the ridge. The city, which should have felt safe through sheer population density, felt instead like a hostile wilderness of concrete and watchful eyes, every corner potentially concealing a threat.

She caught her reflection in a shop window – pale face, dark circles under haunted eyes, hunched posture – and barely recognized herself. The pragmatic, confident scientist was gone, replaced by a hunted fugitive. The transformation was chilling. Kestrel hadn't just silenced her; they were actively dismantling her, forcing her into a desperate, reactive existence.

As dusk began to settle, she found herself near the ferry terminal for Vashon Island. It felt like a plausible intermediate step – close enough to Seattle to be unassuming, yet offering a degree of separation, a place to potentially lay low for a night before heading further west towards the Peninsula library and the designated contact point. She paid cash for a walk-on ticket, joining the sparse line of commuters and island residents waiting for the next departure.

Standing on the ferry deck as the vessel pulled away from the Seattle skyline, the city lights glittering like cold jewels against the darkening, rain-bruised sky, Elise felt a profound sense of severance. She was cutting ties, burning bridges, stepping fully into the unknown. The wind whipped strands of hair across her face, carrying the salty tang of the Sound. She scanned the receding docks, the other passengers on deck, searching for any sign she had been followed. Nothing obvious. But Kestrel was good. Subtle. Patient. Were they already aware of her departure? Were agents waiting on the other side?

She clutched the railing, the cold metal biting into her fingers. The vast, dark water churning below felt symbolic. She was adrift, navigating treacherous currents, with dangers lurking both behind and ahead. Ahead lay the Olympic Peninsula, the source of her trauma but also potentially her only sanctuary, her only ally in Nora. Ahead lay the daunting task of retrieving the buried evidence, of confronting the Hollow Truth. Ahead lay the Stick-shí'nač, their hidden world, their inscrutable intentions.

Behind her lay Kestrel, relentless, powerful, determined to maintain their secrets at any cost.

Echoes persist. Vigilance required. The words resonated with new meaning now. The echoes weren't just memories; they were the consequences rippling outwards from AO Hollow. And vigilance wasn't just paranoia; it was the fundamental requirement for survival in a world where hidden giants guarded ancient secrets and shadowy organizations erased inconvenient truths. Her life as Dr. Elise Holloway, primate biologist, was effectively over. Her life as a fugitive, a keeper of impossible secrets, a potential catalyst for world-altering revelation or catastrophic conflict, had just begun. The ferry plowed onwards through the dark water, carrying her towards an uncertain future, towards the looming shadow of the Olympic mountains, towards the next chapter in her terrifying descent into the hollow ground.

Chapter 3: The Watchers

Vashon Island drifted into view through the ferry window, a smear of dark green against the bruised grey canvas of the Puget Sound sky. Elise huddled deeper into her anonymous rain jacket, pulling the hood low, trying to blend into the sparse collection of passengers making the mid-morning crossing. Most were island commuters returning home or delivery drivers, their faces etched with the familiar indifference of routine. Elise envied them their normalcy, their apparent lack of concern about unmarked vehicles or cryptic emails signaling impending doom. For her, every shadow held a potential watcher, every mundane interaction felt like navigating a minefield.

The near-miss on the ferry deck hadn't happened. No jostling stranger tried to snatch her bag, no menacing figure lingered too close to the railing. The crossing was uneventful, almost disappointingly so. It allowed the paranoia to fester, unchecked by immediate confirmation. Had she overreacted back in Seattle? Was the mud smudge, the scratch on the doorplate, just her traumatized mind inventing threats where none existed? Could the email have been random spam, its wording a bizarre coincidence? Doubt gnawed at the edges of her resolve. Maybe Kestrel wasn't actively pursuing her. Maybe they were content with her silence, confident their threats and the weight of the NDA were enough.

But the feeling – the persistent, prickling certainty of being observed – wouldn't leave. It had been her constant companion since escaping AO Hollow, a sixth sense honed by weeks spent under the unseen gaze of the Stick-shí'nač. She trusted that feeling more than she trusted Kestrel's apparent inaction. Assume the worst. Prepare for it. It was the only survival strategy that made sense now.

Disembarking onto the island felt like stepping into a quieter, greener world, but not necessarily a safer one. The small ferry terminal bustled briefly, then emptied as cars drove off and foot passengers dispersed. Elise deliberately lingered, pretending to check a non-existent map, scanning the departing vehicles, the faces of those waiting. No one seemed overtly interested in her. No dark SUVs matching the description of the Kestrel vehicle waited nearby.

Still, the unease persisted. She needed a place to lie low, gather herself, and perform the necessary digital self-immolation before attempting the contact with Nora's intermediary on the Peninsula proper. Vashon, with its rural roads, dense woods, and relative anonymity compared to the mainland, seemed like a reasonable place for a brief pause.

She walked away from the ferry dock, following the main road inland for a mile or so, backpack feeling heavy, conspicuous. She needed to get off the beaten path. Spotting a sign for a state park trail leading down towards the shoreline, she ducked into the woods, the familiar scent of damp earth and cedar instantly calming and alarming her simultaneously. The forest felt like home, like refuge, after her experiences, yet every forest now also felt like potential Stick-shí'nač territory, imbued with watchful intelligence. She forced the thought away. Different woods, different rules. Kestrel was the predator here.

The trail wound downwards through second-growth fir and maple, eventually opening onto a rocky beach strewn with driftwood. The Sound stretched out before her, grey and choppy, the Seattle skyline a hazy, distant silhouette barely visible through the rain-heavy air. It felt remote, secluded. She walked along the beach for a while, the rhythmic crunch of her boots on pebbles a soothing counterpoint to the frantic pounding of her heart. She needed to find a place to spend the night, somewhere cheap, anonymous, paid for with cash. A quick search on the burner phone she risked turning on briefly (after removing the battery and SIM card again immediately) revealed a couple of older, slightly run-down motels further inland, catering perhaps to off-season tourists or transient workers. Perfect.

She hiked back up the trail and followed quiet, winding country roads, keeping an eye out for any vehicles that seemed out of place, any cars that passed more than once. The paranoia felt exhausting, a constant hum of anxiety beneath the surface. Was that beat-up pickup slowing down to look at her, or just navigating a pothole? Did that minivan turn around after passing her, or was it just heading back the way it came? She couldn't be sure. She felt exposed, vulnerable, every step a gamble.

Late in the afternoon, she found one of the motels identified on her burner phone search – the 'Anchor Inn,' a single-story structure with faded blue paint and a flickering neon vacancy sign, tucked away off a less-traveled road. It looked reassuringly neglected. She paid cash for one night, using a variation of her middle name and deliberately smudging the registration card signature. The clerk, an elderly man seemingly more interested in the static-filled baseball game on the small television behind the counter, barely glanced at her, just took the crumpled bills and handed over a key attached to a worn plastic fob.

Room 7 smelled faintly of stale cigarette smoke, damp carpet, and pine-scented cleaner – the universal scent of transient anonymity. It had a lumpy double bed, a scarred wooden desk, and a window that looked out onto the motel's gravel parking lot and the dripping woods beyond. It was bleak, but it felt blessedly private, a temporary burrow.

First, she checked the room meticulously. Pulled back the cheap art prints from the walls, checked behind the headboard, unscrewed the phone mouthpiece, ran her fingers under the desk and chair. She wasn't an expert, wouldn't likely find sophisticated Kestrel listening devices, but the ritual felt necessary. Finding nothing obvious, she wedged the room's flimsy chair under the doorknob, drew the thin, patterned curtains, and finally allowed herself to sag onto the edge of the bed, the tension of the day leaving her trembling.

She couldn't rest yet. Now came the hard part. She retrieved her burner laptop – another cash purchase, wiped clean before she even brought it here – and the array of public library Wi-Fi passwords she had collected. Connecting was risky, even with VPNs and encrypted browsers, but necessary. For the next three hours, she worked with grim, focused intensity. Deleting old email accounts, scrubbing social media remnants she'd missed, clearing browser histories, initiating secure wipes on cloud storage services she hadn't used in years but might still hold forgotten fragments of her digital life. Each click felt like snipping another thread connecting her to her past, another step into the shadows.

Then came the physical purge. She took out the small stack of documents she'd brought – old bank statements, utility bills, anything with her name and address. Methodically, she tore them into tiny, unreadable pieces, mixed them together into an incoherent confetti, then soaked the pile in the stained bathroom sink until it became a grey, pulpy mass. She flushed it down the toilet in small batches, hoping it wouldn't clog the ancient plumbing. She snapped old credit cards, broke expired SIM cards from previous burner phones, crushed USB drives containing non-essential academic data. It felt like destroying evidence, erasing herself piece by piece.

Finally, exhausted, hands aching, she repacked the go-bag, ensuring the hidden container with the memory card and logbook page was secure, undetectable. That was the only part of the past she couldn't, wouldn't, erase. It was the reason for this flight, the core of the Hollow Truth.

She allowed herself a brief, lukewarm shower, scrubbing away the grime of the city and the tension of the day, then collapsed onto the lumpy bed, fully clothed, pulling the thin bedspread over her. Sleep felt impossible, her mind buzzing with paranoia and the enormity of her situation. She lay staring into the darkness, listening to the rain drumming on the roof, the occasional swish of tires on the wet road outside. Every sound felt magnified, potentially threatening.

She must have drifted off eventually, succumbing to sheer physical and mental exhaustion. The sound that jerked her awake wasn't loud, but it was wrong. A soft crunch of tires on the gravel outside her window, moving slowly, deliberately. Not pulling into a parking spot, but idling, pausing.

Elise froze, instantly wide awake, every nerve ending firing. She slid silently off the bed, heart hammering, and crept towards the edge of the window curtain, peering through a tiny gap.

A vehicle sat idling in the rain-streaked darkness, maybe thirty feet away. It was a dark-colored sedan, nondescript, its make and model obscured by the gloom and the rain. Its headlights were off, but the faint glow of its dashboard lights illuminated the silhouette of a single occupant in the driver's seat. They weren't getting out. They weren't checking in. They were just... sitting there. Watching her room?

Coincidence? Someone lost? Someone waiting for an early start? Possible. But after the suspected surveillance in Seattle, the feeling of being followed, it felt chillingly deliberate.

Then, the sedan's engine revved slightly, and it began to move, not driving away, but slowly circling the small parking lot, its path taking it directly past her window again before it pulled back towards the motel entrance and paused near the road, still idling, partially hidden by the angle of the building.

They knew she was here. Or strongly suspected. They were confirming, observing, assessing. The net was tightening faster than she had anticipated. Staying here until morning was no longer an option. She had to leave, now, under the cover of darkness and rain, before they decided to move from observation to intervention.

Panic surged again, cold and sharp. She grabbed her backpack, checked the chair wedged under the door – flimsy security, but better than nothing. She needed a way out that wasn't the front door, wasn't visible from the parking lot. The window. It looked like an old, sash-style window, possibly painted shut, definitely not designed for egress.

She moved quickly, quietly, towards it. Tugged at the latch. Stuck fast. She tried forcing the lower sash upwards. It didn't budge, sealed tight by layers of old paint and damp-swollen wood. Desperation clawed at her. She scanned the room – the cheap lamp, the thin wooden chair. Nothing heavy enough to break the glass cleanly or quietly.

Then her eyes landed on the heavy ceramic base of the bedside lamp. Grabbing it, hefting its surprising weight, she took a deep breath. Noise was unavoidable now, but speed was essential. She moved back to the window, braced herself, and swung the lamp base hard against the lower pane of glass.

CRASH! The sound echoed shockingly loud in the small room, followed by the tinkle of falling shards onto the wet ground outside. She didn't wait to see if the noise attracted attention from the idling car. Using the lamp base again, she quickly knocked out the remaining jagged edges of glass from the lower sash frame, creating a rough opening just large enough to squeeze through.

Heart pounding, backpack scraping against the splintered wood, she wriggled through the opening, dropping awkwardly onto the muddy patch of grass beneath the window. She landed with a grunt, stumbling but staying upright. Instantly, she heard the sound of the sedan's engine revving louder, headlights snapping on, cutting bright swathes through the rain and darkness, swinging towards her side of the building.

They had heard. They were reacting.

No time to think. Elise scrambled away from the window, keeping low, using the shadows along the motel wall for cover. She needed to get to the woods behind the building, disappear into the darkness and the trees before the car could cut off her escape or its occupants emerged.

She sprinted across the small, soggy lawn towards the dark tree line fifty yards away. Behind her, she heard a car door slam, a muffled shout. Glancing back, she saw two figures emerging from the sedan, dark shapes moving quickly, flashlights cutting through the rain. They hadn't seen her exact location yet, momentarily confused by the broken window, but they were spreading out, searching.

Just as she reached the edge of the woods, plunging into the welcome, concealing blackness beneath the dripping branches, she heard one of them shout again, closer now. "There! Heading west!" A flashlight beam swept through the trees, narrowly missing her as she dove behind the thick trunk of a cedar.

She didn't stop. Pushing deeper into the woods, ignoring the branches that tore at her jacket, the roots that tripped her feet, she ran blindly, fueled by pure terror. The sounds of pursuit seemed to follow – crashing through undergrowth, shouted commands – but the darkness, the rain, and the dense forest were her allies now. She ran until her lungs burned, until her legs felt like lead, until the sounds of pursuit finally faded behind her, swallowed by the vast, wet, indifferent wilderness.

She finally collapsed at the base of another large fir, gasping for breath, soaked to the skin, trembling uncontrollably. The narrow escape had been terrifyingly close. They hadn't just been watching; they had been waiting, ready to move in. Her decision to flee hadn't been paranoid; it had been essential, possibly life-saving.

Lying there in the cold, wet darkness, listening to the rain drumming on the canopy high above, Elise knew her brief respite was over. Kestrel wasn't just monitoring her; they were actively hunting her. The subtle warnings had escalated to direct confrontation. They knew she was on the move, knew she was heading towards the Peninsula. The race was on. She had to reach Nora's contact point, had to get deeper underground or off-grid, before Kestrel's net closed completely. The watchers were no longer content to watch. The hunt had truly begun.

Chapter 4: Crossing the Sound

The adrenaline dump left Elise shaking uncontrollably, huddled at the base of the massive fir tree, soaked to the bone, teeth chattering violently against the raw chill of the late autumn night. Rain sluiced down through the dense canopy far above, dripping persistently onto the forest floor, onto her inadequate rain jacket, plastering strands of damp hair to her forehead and neck. The darkness was absolute, broken only by the faintest ambient glow filtering down from the overcast sky, barely enough to distinguish the hulking shapes of nearby trees. The sounds of pursuit had faded entirely, replaced by the steady drumming of rain and the frantic thumping of her own heart, gradually slowing from its panicked race.

She had escaped. For now. The realization brought little comfort, only a profound sense of exhaustion and escalating dread. They knew she was on Vashon. They knew she had fled the motel. They would be searching, expanding their perimeter, perhaps alerting local law enforcement with some plausible cover story – a missing person, potentially endangered, needing assistance. Her anonymity was shattered. Her time was running out faster than she'd thought.

Fighting down the tremors wracking her body, Elise forced herself to think, to plan. Staying put was suicide. Kestrel would likely bring in dogs, thermal imagers once daylight broke, resources far beyond what two men in a sedan could muster. She had to keep moving, put distance between herself and the motel, find a way off the island before they could lock it down completely.

Which way? Her internal compass felt scrambled by fear and disorientation. She fumbled in her pack for her physical compass – the reliable, old-school Silva that Boone had trusted, the one that hadn't (she hoped) been affected by the strange anomalies of AO Hollow. Shielding it from the rain beneath her jacket, she flicked on her headlamp to its dimmest red setting, just enough to read the dial. The needle swung, hesitated, then settled, pointing a reasonably steady North. Relief washed over her, disproportionate but vital. Basic physics still worked here, outside the valley's influence.

She needed to head south. The main ferry terminal she'd arrived at was back towards the north end of the island. Logic dictated Kestrel would focus their initial efforts there. Vashon had another, smaller ferry terminal at its southern tip, connecting across the Sound towards Tacoma or the Kitsap Peninsula near Southworth. It was further, meant crossing the bulk of the island on foot through unfamiliar terrain in the dark, but it felt like the less obvious, potentially safer route.

Decision made, she pushed herself stiffly to her feet, muscles protesting, joints aching with cold and strain. Every instinct screamed for rest, for warmth, for shelter. But survival demanded movement. Checking the compass again, orienting herself southwards, she began picking her way through the dense, dripping forest, moving as quietly as her exhausted body allowed.

Travel was torturous. The ground was a slick, uneven carpet of fallen needles, decaying leaves, hidden roots, and moss-covered rocks. Visibility was near zero beyond the weak pool of red light cast by her headlamp, forcing her to rely on feel as much as sight, one hand held out to ward off low-hanging branches, feet probing tentatively before committing weight. The rain continued relentlessly, soaking through her jacket, chilling her to the core. Devil's club, unseen in the darkness, snagged her pants, its fine thorns embedding themselves painfully in her skin. She stumbled frequently, catching herself against tree trunks, stifling cries of pain or frustration that might carry in the quiet woods.

She tried to parallel the main north-south road that bisected the island, staying perhaps half a mile deep in the woods, close enough to maintain a general sense of direction but far enough to avoid accidental discovery or Kestrel patrols. The sounds of occasional passing cars on the distant road served as both a navigational aid and a source of anxiety – was that just a local resident, or Kestrel agents methodically sweeping the area?

Her mind, frayed by lack of sleep and constant fear, became her enemy. Every rustle in the undergrowth sounded like stealthy pursuit. The wind sighing through the high branches morphed into whispers just beyond comprehension. The hulking shapes of ancient cedars seemed to transform into watchful giants in her peripheral vision, triggering visceral flashbacks to the Stick-shí'nač. She had to consciously fight down the panic, reminding herself: Different woods. Different threat. Kestrel is human. Predictable, perhaps, in their methods, even if their resources felt overwhelming. Focus on the immediate. One step, then the next.

Hours crawled by. She paused occasionally to sip water from her canteen, chew mechanically on a dense, tasteless energy bar that felt like sawdust in her mouth. The brief stops only emphasized her exhaustion, the deep ache in her muscles, the pervasive cold seeping into her bones. She pushed onward, driven by the image of the dark sedan, the flashlights cutting through the woods, the knowledge that capture meant, at best, interrogation and coercion, at worst, permanent silence.

Sometime before dawn, the rain finally began to ease, tapering off into a damp mist that hung heavy amongst the trees. The darkness lessened slightly, shifting from impenetrable black to shades of deep grey. Through breaks in the canopy, Elise could see the eastern sky beginning to pale. Daylight would bring both relief from the disorienting darkness and increased risk of detection. She needed to find the southern ferry terminal soon.

She risked moving closer to the road now, navigating by the sound of increasingly frequent early morning traffic. Staying hidden just within the tree line, she followed a winding secondary road that, according to her map memorized back at the library, led towards the Tahlequah ferry dock at Vashon's southern tip.

The final mile felt endless. Her body screamed for rest. Every muscle fibre protested. Her feet were numb inside her soaked boots. But the thought of Kestrel potentially closing off the island spurred her onward. Just get to the ferry. Get across the water. Put another barrier between herself and pursuit.

Finally, through the thinning trees, she saw it – the low buildings of the ferry terminal, the waiting lanes for cars, the wooden pilings of the dock stretching out into the grey water of the Sound. A small cluster of cars waited for the first morning run. A few walk-on passengers huddled near the ticketing booth, sipping coffee, faces obscured by hoods or hats.

Elise hesitated at the edge of the woods, observing the scene for several long minutes. Was it safe? Were any of the waiting cars unmarked Kestrel vehicles? Was one of the bundled figures waiting for the ferry an agent, scanning faces? She scanned the area intently, searching for anything out of place, any sign of unnatural interest. Nothing jumped out. The scene looked depressingly normal – early commuters, islanders heading to mainland jobs.

Taking a calculated risk, she stepped out of the woods, trying to look casual, just another person heading for the ferry, pulling her own hood lower, keeping her face angled downwards. She joined the short line at the walk-on ticket booth, paid cash again, received the small paper ticket, her hand trembling slightly as she tucked it into her pocket.

Waiting for the ferry to arrive felt like standing naked on a stage. She huddled near a piling, trying to appear inconspicuous, turning her back to the parking lot, focusing on the grey water, the distant shoreline of the Kitsap Peninsula barely visible through the morning mist. Every car that pulled into the waiting lanes sent a fresh jolt of anxiety through her. Every person who glanced her way felt like a potential threat. She kept her head down, avoided eye contact, radiating an air of weary anonymity she hoped was convincing.

The ferry finally arrived, a familiar white and green vessel churning through the choppy water, nudging gently against the dock pilings. The ramp lowered with a hydraulic whine. Cars began to rumble aboard. Elise joined the small group of walk-on passengers shuffling up the ramp, staying near the middle of the group, using the bodies around her as a temporary shield.

Once onboard, she didn't linger on the exposed vehicle deck. She climbed the stairs quickly to the upper passenger cabin, finding a seat in a corner booth, facing away from the main aisle, near a window overlooking the water but partially obscured by condensation. The cabin was sparsely populated – a few tired commuters reading newspapers or scrolling through phones, a mother trying to corral two restless toddlers. The air smelled of stale coffee and damp wool.

As the ferry horn blew its deep, resonant departure signal – another sound that triggered an involuntary flinch, echoing the deeper calls from the cavern – and the vessel began pulling away from the dock, Elise allowed herself a tiny, fragile moment of relief. She was off Vashon. She had slipped through the net, at least for now.

The crossing to Point Defiance near Tacoma took only about fifteen minutes, but it felt like an eternity. Elise remained hunched in her corner seat, pretending to doze, but her senses were on high alert. She watched the other passengers covertly, noting who seemed restless, who paid too much attention to the ferry's movement or the surrounding boats. Nothing seemed overtly suspicious, but the paranoia lingered. Kestrel could have assets anywhere, blending seamlessly into the mundane.

Disembarking at Point Defiance was another exercise in controlled anxiety. She moved with the small crowd of walk-ons, keeping her head down, scanning the terminal area, the parking lots. Again, nothing immediately alarming. No dark sedans waiting obviously. No figures in identical practical outerwear converging on the passengers.

But the risk wasn't over. From Tacoma, she needed to get north, up the Kitsap Peninsula, towards the small town whose library held the designated birdwatching guide and the potential connection to Nora's network. That meant more public transport, more potential exposure.

She found a local bus route heading north, paid her fare, and sank into a seat near the back, the familiar motion of the bus a jarring return to the world she had fled just hours before. The Kitsap Peninsula slid past the rain-streaked windows – suburban sprawl giving way to wooded hills, small towns clustered along the highway, glimpses of grey water through the trees. It looked so ordinary, so peaceful. Yet Elise knew that beneath this surface normality, Kestrel's network likely operated, silent and watchful. And deeper still, beneath the earth itself, lay the ancient passages, the hidden sanctuary, the domain of the Stick-shí'nač. Two secret worlds, overlaying the mundane one, both holding lethal danger for her.

She had to change buses twice, navigating the unfamiliar routes using the paper map and schedule she'd studied, the process adding hours to her journey. Each transfer point, each waiting period at a bus stop, felt fraught with risk. She kept moving, kept scanning, kept her interactions minimal. By early afternoon, exhaustion was a physical weight pressing down on her, making rational thought difficult, amplifying the fear.

Finally, the bus pulled into the small, unassuming town designated in her plan with Nora's intermediary. It was quintessential Pacific Northwest – a single main street with clapboard storefronts, a faded mural depicting leaping salmon on the wall of the post office, the smell of woodsmoke and rain hanging in the air. It looked quiet, sleepy, a world away from Kestrel operatives and subterranean horrors.

The library was a modest brick building near the center of town, nestled between a hardware store and a bakery emitting the comforting scent of fresh bread. Elise paused across the street, observing it for several minutes. A few cars parked outside. People coming and going at a relaxed pace – mothers with toddlers, teenagers browsing the internet, older residents returning books. It looked… normal. Safe.

Still, she hesitated. Walking into that library felt like stepping onto another stage, potentially triggering an alarm she couldn't foresee. Was this contact point compromised? Had Kestrel anticipated this, staked it out? Or was her paranoia just running rampant?

There was only one way to find out. Taking another deep breath, pulling her hood slightly lower, she crossed the quiet street and pushed open the heavy glass door of the library. The warmth inside, the smell of old paper and floor wax, the hushed atmosphere – it was blessedly, achingly normal.

She walked directly towards the reference section, avoiding the main circulation desk, trying to look like just another visitor seeking information. Locating the natural history shelves, she scanned the titles. *Birds of Washington State. Pacific Northwest Wildflowers. Olympic Peninsula Hiking Trails*. And there it was. *A Field Guide to Western Birds*, Peterson, fourth edition. The designated book.

Her heart hammered against her ribs. Hands trembling slightly, she pulled the familiar, slightly worn volume from the shelf. She carried it to a secluded reading carrel in a quiet corner, sat down with her back to the wall, affording her a view of the room while remaining partially obscured.

She opened the book, pretending to browse the detailed illustrations of woodpeckers and warblers. Then, flipping towards the back, towards the index section as planned, she searched for the specific entry: *Varied Thrush*.

Between the pages detailing the thrush's habitat and song, tucked loosely, was a small, folded piece of paper. Not Kestrel. This was it.

With shaking fingers, Elise unfolded the note. It wasn't handwriting she recognized. The message was brief, almost cryptic, adhering to the low-information protocol they'd discussed.

Creek flows south from Brothers' shoulder. Old cabin site, third bend past twin falls. Wait dusk.

No signature. Just geographic Coded instructions. The location was remote, deep in the National Forest foothills south of The Brothers peaks, requiring another leg of travel, likely hiking in. An old cabin site – abandoned, hopefully untraceable. Wait dusk. It implied the contact would come to her, reducing her exposure.

Relief washed over her, so intense it left her weak. The connection worked. Nora's network was active, responding. She wasn't entirely alone.

Carefully, she refolded the note, tucked it deep into her pocket. She replaced the bird guide precisely on the shelf, took one last cautious scan of the library – still quiet, still seemingly normal – and walked out, forcing herself not to hurry, not to draw attention.

Back on the street, the drizzle had stopped, though the sky remained a uniform grey. She had her destination, her next objective. Now she just needed to get there without being intercepted. Find a bus heading south towards the park boundary, then hike in, find the cabin site, wait. It felt manageable, a concrete plan after days of reactive flight.

But as she walked towards the bus stop at the edge of town, a flicker of movement across the street caught her eye. A man, leaning against the wall of the hardware store, seemingly reading a newspaper, partially obscured by a parked delivery van. He was nondescript – middle-aged, wearing a faded flannel shirt, jeans, work boots. A local logger or tradesman, perhaps. But something about his posture, the way he held the newspaper slightly too high, the almost imperceptible stillness as he watched her pass… it felt wrong. It felt like surveillance.

Elise didn't react, didn't change her pace. She continued towards the bus stop, pretending not to have noticed. But the cold dread returned, chilling the fragile warmth of relief. Had they followed her even here? Was the library contact already compromised? Or was he just a local man reading his paper, her paranoia painting threats onto innocent bystanders?

She couldn't know. All she could do was keep moving, stay vigilant, and pray that the path towards the old cabin offered sanctuary, not another Kestrel trap. The brief respite was over. The crossing was complete, but the hunt continued, the shadows deepening even as she moved closer to potential help.

Chapter 5: The Whispering Woods

The bus ride south from the small Peninsula town felt agonizingly slow, each mile crawled over representing both progress towards the rendezvous point and prolonged exposure. Elise sat near the back again, window seat, pretending to gaze out at the passing landscape of logged hillsides giving way to denser, older forests as they approached the boundary of Olympic National Park. In reality, her focus was internal, replaying the encounter at the library, scrutinizing the memory of the man with the newspaper.

Was he Kestrel? His appearance hadn't screamed 'agent'. He looked like countless other men she'd seen in these rural timber towns – weathered face, practical clothes, an air of quiet resignation. Yet, the stillness, the intensity she thought she'd glimpsed behind the shield of the newspaper… it felt professional, practiced. Had he followed her from the ferry? Had Kestrel anticipated her move towards this specific library, this contact method? The possibility sent ice water through her veins. If their low-tech communication channel was compromised, then Nora's entire network might be at risk. And her own chances of finding safe haven plummeted towards zero.

She forced herself to consider alternatives. Maybe he was just a local. Maybe her heightened senses, frayed by lack of sleep and constant fear, were misinterpreting innocent details. Maybe the brief glance she'd caught was just coincidence. She had to operate on the assumption that the contact was still viable, the rendezvous point secure. To do otherwise meant succumbing to paralysis, giving up. Vigilance, yes. But crippling paranoia wouldn't help her survive.

The bus eventually dropped her at a deserted crossroads miles from any town, marked only by a faded wooden sign indicating trailheads deeper within the National Forest. This was as close as public transport could get her to the area described in the note –

Creek flows south from Brothers' shoulder. From here, it was hiking. Miles of it, uphill, into increasingly remote wilderness.

The air felt different here, cleaner, sharper, carrying the familiar scent of damp earth, fir needles, and decaying leaves. The immense silence of the deep woods began to press in as soon as the bus rumbled away, leaving her utterly alone at the edge of the vast, brooding forest. It felt both intimidating and strangely comforting after the oppressive vigilance required in populated areas. Here, the watchers were less likely to be human, though the memory of the Stick-shí'nač ensured the solitude never felt truly empty.

She checked her compass, oriented herself towards the twin peaks of The Brothers looming faintly through the mist to the northeast, and consulted her topographical map. Based on the contours and the creek mentioned in the note, the old cabin site was likely five or six miles in, involving a significant elevation gain and at least one ridge crossing. With only a few hours of daylight remaining, she would be hiking well into the darkness again to reach the rendezvous point by dusk, as instructed.

Shouldering her pack, which felt lighter now without the purged documents but heavier with the weight of responsibility, Elise started walking, following a barely discernible path leading away from the road, likely an old logging spur or game trail. The forest floor was spongy underfoot, the air thick with the smell of decomposition and vibrant life intertwined. Towering Douglas firs and western red cedars formed a dense canopy overhead, filtering the already weak daylight into a dim, green-tinged gloom. Sword ferns grew in lush thickets, their fronds heavy with moisture.

The initial miles were a relentless uphill slog. The faint trail switchbacked steeply, forcing Elise to pause frequently, leaning against massive tree trunks, gasping for breath, her leg muscles burning with fatigue. Sweat beaded on her forehead despite the cool air. The silence was broken only by her own labored breathing, the drip of water from saturated branches, and the occasional indignant chatter of a squirrel disturbed by her passage.

She pushed onward, driven by the need to reach the cabin site before full dark, before the contact might give up waiting. The physical exertion was brutal, layering onto the deep bone-weariness accumulated over days of flight and sleeplessness. But in a strange way, the physical struggle felt cleaner, more honest, than the psychological warfare waged by Kestrel. Here, the challenges were tangible – steep slopes, tangled roots, aching muscles. They could be overcome, one step at a time.

As the light began to fail, the forest took on a different character. Shadows deepened, merging together, blurring the edges of trees and undergrowth. Familiar shapes became indistinct, potentially menacing. The wind picked up slightly, sighing through the high branches, creating phantom whispers and rustles that made Elise jump. The feeling of being watched returned, subtler than in the valley, less focused perhaps, but undeniably present. Was it just the forest itself, the weight of ancient trees and unseen wildlife? Or was it something more? Had the guardians' influence extended this far? Or was it simply her own trauma projecting fears onto the landscape? She couldn't be sure.

She had to rely on her headlamp again, the weak red beam barely penetrating the gathering gloom. Navigation became more difficult, the faint trail harder to follow. Several times she lost it completely, forcing her to backtrack, cast around in frustrating circles until she found the subtle indentation in the forest floor or the pattern of slightly less dense undergrowth that indicated the path.

It was during one of these moments, pausing to check her compass and map under the dim red light, straining to hear any sound over the wind, that she heard it. Not a footstep, not a growl, not the telltale signs of Kestrel pursuit. It was a voice. A woman's voice, singing softly, drifting faintly on the wind from somewhere ahead, further up the trail.

Elise froze, every muscle tensing. Singing? Out here? Miles from anywhere, deep in the forest after dark? It made no sense. Was it a hallucination brought on by exhaustion and stress? Or was it real? If real, who would be singing out here? A lost hiker? A homesteader living impossibly off-grid? Or... something else? The local Salish folklore was full of stories about spirits of the woods, some benign, some dangerous, often heralded by strange sounds or music.

She strained her ears, trying to pinpoint the direction, the quality of the sound. It was melodic, hauntingly beautiful, sung in a language Elise didn't recognize – perhaps Lushootseed, Nora's ancestral tongue? – but imbued with a deep, melancholic power that resonated strangely within her chest, calming her racing heart even as it amplified her unease. The singing seemed to weave through the sounds of the wind and dripping trees, ephemeral, almost dreamlike.

Cautiously, moving with infinite slowness now, Elise advanced towards the source of the sound, switching off her headlamp entirely, relying on the faint residual light and her own senses. The singing grew slightly louder, clearer, seeming to emanate from just beyond the next rise.

Reaching the crest of the small ridge, she peered down through the dense ferns. Below, nestled in a small, sheltered hollow beside a gurgling creek – the creek from the note? – was the faint outline of a structure. A small, dilapidated log cabin, barely visible in the deep twilight, its roof sagging, chimney long collapsed. And sitting on a moss-covered log just outside the cabin's dark entrance, silhouetted against the gloom, was a figure. An old woman, wrapped in a heavy woven blanket, rocking slightly back and forth as she sang her haunting melody to the whispering woods.

Elise's breath caught. This had to be the place. The old cabin site. But who was this woman? Was she the contact? She seemed too old, too frail perhaps, to be part of Nora's active network. Was she a hermit? A spirit?

Then the woman stopped singing. She slowly turned her head, her gaze seeming to pierce the darkness, fixing directly on Elise's hiding place amongst the ferns. Elise froze, convinced she'd been discovered, bracing for a reaction – alarm, anger, fear.

But the woman merely smiled, a gentle, knowing expression crinkling the corners of her deeply lined eyes. "Took you long enough, Child of Two Worlds," the woman said, her voice soft, carrying easily through the quiet air, surprisingly strong for her apparent age. "The path was difficult, yes?"

Elise stared, stunned into silence. Child of Two Worlds? How did she know? Who was she?

"Do not be afraid," the woman continued, her smile deepening. "Nora sent word you were coming. Said you carried heavy burdens, needed sanctuary. Said you walked between the world of stone and steel, and the world of deep roots and ancient guardians." She patted the log beside her. "Come. Sit by the dying embers. You look cold."

Hesitantly, Elise emerged from the ferns, moving cautiously down the slope towards the cabin clearing. The woman watched her approach, her gaze calm, appraising, yet filled with a profound, disconcerting wisdom. She was clearly Native, likely Tallsalt or from a neighboring tribe, her features strong beneath a web of wrinkles, her long grey hair neatly braided. She radiated an aura of quiet power, a deep connection to this place that felt ancient and unshakable.

"Who… who are you?" Elise asked, her voice barely a whisper as she reached the log, keeping a respectful distance.

"Some call me Auntie Whis Elem," the woman replied, her eyes twinkling faintly. Whis Elem – 'Singing Grandmother' in Lushootseed, Elise vaguely recalled Nora mentioning common honorifics. "I am… a keeper of old ways. A listener to the forest's whispers. Nora is my niece's daughter. She knew you would need a place where the wind does not carry voices easily back to those who hunt you."

Elise sank onto the log, relief washing over her, so potent it felt like weakness. She had found it. Sanctuary. Help. Nora's network was real, deeper, more hidden than she could have imagined. This old woman, living alone in a ruined cabin miles from anywhere... she was part of it. A guardian of a different sort.

"Thank you," Elise murmured, the words inadequate. "I... I was followed. From Seattle. I think they know I'm on the Peninsula."

Whis Elem nodded slowly, unsurprised. "The Men in Dark Jackets. Yes. Their presence is a sickness on the edges of the woods. They search, they pry, they do not respect the boundaries." Her gaze grew distant. "They seek to control things best left undisturbed. Like others before them." She glanced towards the ruined cabin. "This place remembers."

"The miners?" Elise asked, thinking of the logbook.

"And others," Whis Elem confirmed. "Surveyors. Hunters who pushed too far. Those who came seeking power or profit from the deep places. The guardians... they remember intrusions. They hold grudges long." She looked sharply at Elise. "You carry knowledge of them. Heavy knowledge. Dangerous knowledge." It wasn't a question.

Elise hesitated, then nodded. "I was there. In AO Hollow. In the... sanctuary."

Whis Elem's eyes widened almost imperceptibly, a flicker of profound awe crossing her features. "You saw the Silent Grove? Stood before the First People?" She leaned forward slightly, her gaze intense. "And you returned? With your spirit intact?"

"Barely," Elise admitted, the trauma raw in her voice. "Others... didn't." She recounted briefly, haltingly, the fate of Jules, Graves,

Boone, Levi, omitting the gruesome details but conveying the loss, the sacrifice.

Whis Elem listened patiently, her expression shifting from awe to deep sorrow. When Elise finished, the old woman reached out a surprisingly strong, wrinkled hand and placed it gently on Elise's arm. "Their spirits walk the high ridges now," she said softly. "Their sacrifice… it was not in vain, perhaps. It brought you here. It kept the deeper secret safe, for now."

Safe? Elise thought of the memory card hidden in her pack, the potential global ramifications if its contents were revealed. Was anything truly safe?

"Those who hunt you… Kestrel, you call them?" Whis Elem continued, withdrawing her hand. "They will not easily find this place. The paths are confused here. The woods whisper misdirection to those with ill intent. But they will keep searching. You cannot stay long."

"I know," Elise acknowledged. "I need… I need to decide what to do. With what I know. What I carry." She touched the hidden pocket containing the proof.

"Ah," Whis Elem nodded sagely. "The Hollow Truth. A heavy burden indeed." She rose stiffly from the log, gesturing towards the dark doorway of the ruined cabin. "Come inside. Rest. Warm yourself by the hearth – the embers still hold heat. We will share food. Then, we will talk. About burdens. About choices. About the paths that remain open, and those that are forever closed."

Elise followed the old woman into the small, dark cabin. It was rustic, primitive, yet surprisingly clean and orderly within. A small stone hearth glowed faintly in one corner, radiating welcome warmth. Dried herbs hung from the low rafters, filling the air with a complex, earthy fragrance. Woven blankets lay neatly folded on a simple sleeping platform. It felt like stepping back in time, into a pocket of existence untouched by the frantic pace and sterile anxieties of the modern world.

As Whis Elem began ladling a fragrant, steaming broth from a pot suspended over the embers, Elise felt a profound sense of dislocation, but also, for the first time since fleeing Seattle, a fragile flicker of genuine safety. She was hidden, sheltered by ancient woods and ancestral wisdom. But the respite felt temporary, borrowed. Kestrel was still out there. The burden of the Hollow Truth remained. And the whispering woods outside held not just sanctuary, but the lingering echoes of the guardians, a reminder that the boundaries between worlds were thin here, easily crossed, with consequences potentially devastating for all involved. The path forward remained shrouded in mist, both literal and metaphorical.

Chapter 6: Burdens and Bindings

The warmth emanating from the small stone hearth was a physical balm, seeping into Elise's chilled bones, thawing the icy knot of fear that had clenched deep within her gut for days. The interior of Whis Elem's cabin, though rustic and shadowed beyond the immediate firelight, felt profoundly secure, insulated from the howling wind and dripping darkness outside by thick log walls chinked with moss and time, and perhaps by something less tangible – the palpable aura of peace and ancient knowledge that seemed to surround the old woman herself.

Elise sat on a low, three-legged stool near the hearth, gratefully accepting a steaming mug of broth from Whis Elem. It was fragrant, savory, tasting of wild mushrooms, smoky herbs, and perhaps root vegetables Elise couldn't identify. It warmed her from the inside out, simple sustenance feeling like a feast after days of cold rations and gnawing hunger. She sipped it slowly, savoring the heat, the flavor, the sheer normalcy of sharing food in a sheltered place.

Whis Elem moved with a quiet, deliberate grace, adding small twigs to the embers, stirring the pot, her movements economical, practiced. She didn't press Elise with questions, allowing the silence to settle comfortably between them, broken only by the crackle of the fire, the sigh of the wind outside the sturdy door, and the rhythmic slurp of Elise enjoying the broth. It felt like a conscious offering of respite, a recognition of Elise's need for decompression after the relentless pursuit and terror.

After Elise had finished the broth and Whis Elem had refilled her mug with a strong, dark tea brewed from pine needles and other forest ingredients, the old woman finally spoke again, her voice soft but resonant in the firelit intimacy of the cabin.

"The burden you carry, Child of Two Worlds," she began, settling back onto her own stool, pulling her woven blanket tighter around her shoulders, "it is more than just the knowledge of the First People, the Stick-shí'nač. More than the grief for your lost companions. You carry the weight of your world's ignorance, its greed, its potential for destruction."

Elise looked up, surprised by the directness, the insight. "How… how do you know?"

Whis Elem smiled faintly, her eyes reflecting the firelight. "The woods whisper many things to those who listen. And Nora's message… it spoke of Kestrel, of lies, of danger not just from the guardians, but from your own kind." She paused, her gaze sharp. "You carry proof, don't you? Something tangible. Something the Men in Dark Jackets fear."

Elise hesitated. Admitting the existence of the memory card, the logbook page, felt like another risk, even here, in this seeming sanctuary. But denying it felt pointless, dishonest, especially to this woman who seemed to possess an almost uncanny intuition. She nodded slowly. "Fragments," she admitted quietly. "Photos from… a nest. A page from an old logbook, miners who were trapped, like us. Evidence that Kestrel knew, that others knew, decades ago. Evidence they tried to bury."

"Ah," Whis Elem nodded sagely. "Physical burdens, anchoring the spiritual ones. Such things have power. They demand action. They bind the carrier to the story."

"Bind me?" Elise echoed, feeling a chill despite the fire's warmth.

"Yes," Whis Elem confirmed. "You cannot simply walk away now, pretend you did not see, did not learn. The knowledge chooses its keepers. The story demands to be told, eventually. The question is how. And when. And to whom." She leaned forward slightly, her gaze intense. "Tell me, Child of Two Worlds, what does your heart tell you? Your world… does it deserve this truth? Can it handle it?"

It was the same question Nora had implicitly posed, the ethical tightrope Elise found herself walking. Could humanity handle the reality of the Stick-shí'nač? The existence of a sentient, powerful, non-human species living secretly alongside them? Elise thought of the likely reactions – panic, fearmongering, military mobilization, scientific exploitation, ecological disruption as hordes descended on the Olympics seeking proof or profit. The 'Goliath' autopsy proved Kestrel, at least, saw them as subjects, threats, potential assets, not as sovereign beings deserving respect or autonomy. Would the rest of the world react any differently?

"I don't know," Elise confessed honestly, the weight of the dilemma settling heavily upon her again. "My training… my instinct as a scientist… it says truth must be revealed. Knowledge shared. Secrets are dangerous." She thought of Kestrel's manipulations, the deaths caused by their secrecy. "But… seeing the sanctuary… seeing them… they have a right to exist. Unmolested. Protected. Revealing them could be… a death sentence for their entire world."

"A paradox," Whis Elem acknowledged, stirring the embers with a stick. "To protect one truth, you must bury another. To save one world, you risk destroying it with the knowledge meant to liberate it." She looked up, her eyes holding centuries of accumulated wisdom regarding the often-destructive nature of human curiosity and ambition. "Our ancestors understood this balance. They knew of the guardians, respected their power, their territory. They took only what was needed from the edges, offered respect, avoided the deep places. They knew that some doors are best left unopened, some mysteries best left unsolved. Your world… it has forgotten how to leave things alone."

"But Kestrel won't leave them alone," Elise argued, frustration and anger rising. "They know. They have files, samples from 'Goliath'. They might try again. Capture, containment… 'asset recovery'. Graves' mission wasn't just exploration; it was reconnaissance for

Phase Two. They need to be stopped. Their conspiracy needs to be exposed."

"And you believe your fragments of proof will achieve this?" Whis Elem asked gently. "Against an organization that commands helicopters, erases histories, perhaps even starts fires to cover its tracks? They will discredit you. Call you traumatized, delusional. Bury your proof beneath mountains of plausible denial and classified documents."

Elise felt a wave of despair. Whis Elem was right. Her meager evidence, presented by a lone, traumatized biologist with a signed NDA hanging over her head, would likely be dismissed, suppressed. Kestrel's resources were too vast, their control over the narrative too entrenched. Direct confrontation seemed futile, suicidal.

"So what then?" Elise asked, her voice barely a whisper. "Do I just... stay silent? Let Kestrel continue? Let Boone's sacrifice, Levi's death, mean nothing?" The thought felt like a betrayal.

Whis Elem was silent for a long moment, gazing into the flickering flames. "Meaning," she said finally, "is not always found in grand gestures, in exposing secrets to a world unready for them. Sometimes meaning lies in quieter actions. In bearing witness. In preserving knowledge responsibly. In seeking understanding, not conquest."

She looked at Elise again, her gaze penetrating. "You survived the sanctuary. You encountered the First People, face to face, and they let you live. They led you out, perhaps. Why? Did you feel... a connection? A communication beyond words?"

Elise thought back to the cavern, the intense gaze of the elder, the adolescent's hesitant curiosity, the resonant hums that vibrated through her bones. "Yes," she admitted slowly. "It felt... intelligent. Aware. Not just hostile. There was a moment... before the gunshot... where it felt like... understanding was possible."

"Ah," Whis Elem nodded, a flicker of something hopeful in her eyes. "Then perhaps that is your path. Not exposure to the outside world, not yet. But understanding. Learning their ways, their language – the language of the forest, the language of symbols, perhaps even the language of the resonance your miner's logbook spoke of. Seeking not to exploit, but to comprehend. Perhaps even… to mediate."

"Mediate?" Elise stared at her. "Between humanity and… them?" The idea was staggering, terrifying, impossibly ambitious.

"Why not?" Whis Elem countered gently. "You are a Child of Two Worlds now. You have seen what lies beneath the surface. You carry the burden of that knowledge. Perhaps that burden comes with a responsibility. Not just to protect the secret, but to bridge the gap. To find a way for both worlds to coexist, before one destroys the other." She smiled faintly. "A far more difficult path than simply leaking files to your news-papers, yes?"

Elise felt overwhelmed. Mediate? Learn their language? Bridge the worlds? It sounded like a task for mythic heroes, not a traumatized biologist running for her life. Yet… the idea resonated. It offered a purpose beyond mere survival or futile revenge against Kestrel. It reframed her burden as a potential calling. It offered a way to honor the Stick-shí'nač's sentience, their right to exist, while still potentially finding a way to thwart Kestrel's destructive agenda. If she could understand the guardians, perhaps she could anticipate Kestrel's moves, find ways to protect the sanctuary from within, subtly, without direct confrontation.

"How?" Elise asked, the single word encompassing a universe of doubt and questions. "How could I possibly learn? Communicate? They nearly killed us. They *did* kill…" She couldn't finish the sentence.

"Grief is a strong river," Whis Elem acknowledged softly. "It carves deep canyons in the heart. And fear… fear builds high walls. But the First People… they are more than just rage, more than just territoriality. They showed restraint. They showed curiosity. They possess intelligence, complex emotions, as you saw. They mourn their own losses – the one called Goliath, perhaps others taken by your kind over the long years. Perhaps... perhaps they recognized something in you. Your lack of aggression, maybe. Your respect, shown even in fear. Your offering."

She gestured around the small cabin. "This place... it is a listening post. Not with machines, but with spirit. I have felt their presence nearby, sometimes. Felt their sorrows, their anger, their watchfulness over the deep woods. They communicate in ways your science does not yet understand – through resonance, through shifts in the forest's energy, through dreams sometimes, for those open to listening."

She looked intently at Elise. "You survived their sanctuary. That binds you to them, in ways you cannot yet grasp. They may perceive you differently now. Not merely as intruder, but as... witness. Someone who has seen their heart-place and carries its echo."

The idea was both terrifying and strangely compelling. Bound to them? Could the persistent feeling of being watched, the echoes she felt even back in Seattle, be more than just PTSD? Could it be a lingering connection, a resonance established in the deep places?

"If... if I wanted to try," Elise began hesitantly, the concept still feeling impossibly large, "to understand... to listen... how would I even begin? Where would I go?"

"Not back to the sanctuary," Whis Elem said firmly. "Not yet. That would be foolish, provocative. You must learn the edges first. Learn the language of this forest," she gestured towards the dark woods outside, "its signs, its rhythms, its spirits. Learn from Nora, from our people, the protocols of respect, the ways of approaching sacred ground without causing offense. Learn to quiet your own world's noise within you, so you can hear the deeper whispers."

She suggested Elise stay hidden near her cabin for a time, resting, recovering, absorbing the atmosphere of the deep woods, letting the immediate fear recede, allowing the subtler senses to awaken. Whis Elem could teach her some of the plant lore, the tracking signs, the ways of moving silently, respectfully. She could share more of the old stories, providing context, potential interpretations for the Stick-shí'nač behavior.

"And the proof you carry?" Whis Elem added, nodding towards Elise's pack. "Keep it hidden. Safe. Its time may come, but that time is not now. Now is the time for listening. For learning. For healing the rift within yourself, between the two worlds you now inhabit."

It wasn't a plan for immediate action, for dramatic confrontation or exposure. It was a path towards something deeper, slower, more uncertain, but perhaps ultimately more meaningful. A path focused on understanding rather than conflict, on connection rather than conquest. It felt… right, in a way that fighting Kestrel directly or simply running forever did not. It felt like honoring the complexity of the situation, the sentience of the beings involved, the sacrifices made.

Elise looked around the small, firelit cabin, at the wise, calm face of the old woman offering her sanctuary and a different kind of guidance. She felt the immense weight of the burden, the bindings of knowledge and grief. But for the first time since stumbling out of the Crevice, she felt a flicker not just of hope, but of purpose. A difficult, dangerous, perhaps impossible purpose. But a purpose nonetheless.

"Okay," Elise said softly, meeting Whis Elem's gaze, a decision settling within her. "Okay. Teach me how to listen."

The journey into the Hollow Ground had ended in disaster and escape. But perhaps, Elise thought, the journey towards understanding the Hollow Truth was just beginning, here, in this quiet cabin, under the tutelage of a singing grandmother, learning the whispers of the ancient woods. The path forward was shrouded in mystery, but it was a path. And for now, that felt like enough.

Chapter 7: The Language of Silence

Elise woke slowly, reluctantly, dragged from a depth of sleep so profound it felt like surfacing from underwater. For a disorienting moment, the ceiling above her wasn't the familiar water-stained plaster of her Seattle apartment, nor the taut nylon of a tent, but rough-hewn logs, dark with age and smoke, interwoven with dried moss. The air didn't smell of city fumes or damp Gore-Tex, but of woodsmoke, dried herbs, earth, and something indefinably ancient. Panic surged briefly – where was she? – before memory rushed back in: the flight, the library, the trek through the darkening woods, the haunting song, the cabin, Whis Elem. Sanctuary.

She pushed herself up from the surprisingly comfortable sleeping platform, a simple wooden frame piled high with thick woven blankets and fragrant fir boughs. Sunlight, thin but persistent, streamed through a single small, glass-paned window set deep into the log wall, illuminating swirling dust motes in the cabin's compact interior. Every muscle in her body screamed in protest, a deep, aching soreness accumulated from days of relentless flight, climbing, and carrying Levi. But beneath the pain, there was a stillness she hadn't felt since before the expedition began. The constant thrum of anxiety, the hyper-vigilance that had become her default state, had eased slightly during the night, replaced by a profound, bone-deep weariness and the fragile comfort of four solid walls and a glowing hearth.

Whis Elem was already awake, tending the fire, adding small pieces of wood to the embers which pulsed with warmth, casting flickering light on her serene, wrinkled face. She moved with the quiet economy of age and long practice, seemingly unaware of Elise stirring. The cabin was small, perhaps only twelve feet square, but felt functional, lived-in. Bunches of dried herbs hung from the rafters, alongside strips of smoked fish and what looked like dried berries. Shelves carved crudely into the log walls held earthenware pots, woven baskets, and small, neatly stacked bundles tied with twine. A sturdy wooden table and two stools occupied the center of the room. It was a space stripped down to essentials, yet radiating a sense of enduring presence, of a life lived in deep communion with the surrounding wilderness.

"Tea?" Whis Elem asked without turning, her voice soft in the morning quiet.

"Please," Elise replied, her own voice raspy. She swung her legs stiffly over the side of the platform, testing her weight. The soreness was intense, but manageable. She felt bruised, battered, but fundamentally intact.

Whis Elem handed her a steaming mug of the same fragrant, piney brew from the night before. Elise cradled the warmth, letting it seep into her cold hands. Outside, the wind had died down, and the only sounds were the crackle of the fire, the gentle gurgle of the nearby creek, and the distant call of a Steller's Jay. No sirens, no traffic, no low hum of suspicious electronics. Just the breathing rhythm of the forest.

The first few days passed in a slow, restorative rhythm dictated by the rising and setting of the sun and the simple necessities of survival. Elise helped Whis Elem gather firewood from the surrounding forest, learning to identify standing deadwood that would burn clean, stacking it neatly near the cabin door. She fetched water from the clear, icy creek, her hands aching with cold as she filled the heavy earthenware jugs. She learned to tend the small, almost invisible garden patch hidden amongst ferns and salmonberry bushes behind the cabin, where Whis Elem cultivated hardy greens, medicinal roots, and pungent herbs Elise didn't recognize.

The work was physical, grounding. It forced Elise out of the frantic spinning of her own thoughts, anchored her in the present moment – the heft of an axe splitting kindling, the cold shock of creek water, the earthy smell of damp soil worked between her fingers. Her body, though still protesting, began to recover its strength, the constant physical exertion smoothing out the ragged edges of adrenaline and exhaustion.

But the mental landscape remained treacherous. Flashbacks ambushed her without warning. The sight of rust on an old hinge might trigger the memory of the carabiner found near David Chen's remains. The shadow of a hawk passing overhead could momentarily morph into the terrifying silhouette of the creature on the ridge. The simple act of closing her eyes at night often invited the full horror reel – Graves plucked from the cliff face, Boone's final charge, Levi's rattling breath. Sleep remained fractured, haunted.

And the silence... the silence was different here than in the Hollow. It wasn't the oppressive, unnatural void, but a living quiet, filled with subtle layers of sound – the whisper of wind, the chatter of squirrels, the distant tapping of a woodpecker, the rustle of unseen life in the undergrowth. Yet, beneath it all, Elise often felt that same profound stillness she'd sensed near the sanctuary, a deep, underlying quiet that spoke of immense age and power. Whis Elem seemed to inhabit this silence comfortably, moving through it like a fish through water, but Elise found it unsettling, amplifying her own inner turmoil, making the absence of the lost men feel even more acute.

Her scientific mind, long dormant or suppressed by trauma, began to stir again, but found itself grappling with a new paradigm. Whis Elem's teaching wasn't didactic; she didn't lecture or explain in scientific terms. She guided through observation, through quiet suggestion, through shared experience.

On their walks gathering firewood or herbs, Whis Elem would pause, pointing not with her finger, but with her chin or a subtle shift of her gaze. "Hear the jay?" she might murmur. "Sharp call. Angry. Something disturbs its territory downslope." Or, kneeling beside a patch of moss, "This one... grows only where the morning sun does not touch rock that holds deep cold. Tells you the way the frost lingers." She spoke of the forest not as an ecosystem to be analyzed, but as a community of beings, each with its own voice, its own purpose, its own mood.

Elise tried to translate this into her familiar framework. Bird vocalizations indicating predator presence or territorial disputes – standard behavioral ecology. Microclimate indicators based on cryptogam distribution – basic botany. But Whis Elem's understanding seemed deeper, more holistic, less analytical. She spoke of feeling the forest's "breath," sensing a "wrongness" in the air before a storm, discerning the passage of unseen things by the way the silence *felt* different.

"You look too hard with your eyes, Child of Two Worlds," Whis Elem told her one afternoon, as Elise squinted at a faint track in the mud, trying to determine if it was deer or perhaps something heavier. "Your science teaches you to dissect, to measure, to categorize. That is one way of knowing. Useful for building your metal birds and talking boxes." She smiled faintly. "But it misses the connections. It misses the spirit that flows through all things. To truly understand this place, you must learn to listen not just with your ears, but with your skin, your bones, your heart."

Elise found this frustratingly vague. How did one listen with one's bones? How did subjective feeling translate into reliable knowledge? Her training demanded objectivity, replicable data, verifiable evidence. Yet, the evidence she now carried – the memory card, the logbook page, her own traumatic memories – spoke of realities utterly outside that framework. The creatures, the sanctuary, the resonance, the dead electronics... none of it fit neatly into scientific boxes. Perhaps Whis Elem's intuitive, holistic approach held a different kind of validity, a necessary complement to empirical observation when dealing with forces that defied conventional understanding.

She tried. Sitting quietly by the creek, she closed her eyes, forcing herself to push past the internal noise of fear and analysis, trying to simply *feel* the environment – the cool dampness rising from the water, the vibration of the current through the rocks beneath her feet, the subtle shifts in air pressure as breezes moved through the trees. It felt alien, difficult, like learning a language with no alphabet, no grammar rules. Sometimes, fleetingly, she thought she grasped something – a sudden sense of stillness before a deer stepped silently into view, a prickling unease just before a raven cried a harsh warning overhead. But mostly, she felt only the familiar hum of her own anxious thoughts.

Whis Elem also taught her about respect, about boundaries. Certain areas deep within the woods surrounding the cabin were approached only with caution, or avoided altogether. "That ridge," she might say, pointing towards a dark, brooding crest visible through the trees, "holds old sorrow. A place of difficult passage for spirits. Best not to disturb it." Or, near a small, hidden waterfall cascading into a moss-lined pool, "This is a place for cleansing, for offering thanks. Approach quietly. Leave a small gift – a smooth stone, a bright feather."

Elise, the skeptical scientist, found herself following these protocols, leaving a small, interesting pebble near the waterfall, murmuring a quiet, awkward word of thanks for the water, feeling foolish yet strangely compelled. It felt like superstition, yet it also felt… right, in this place where the rules seemed different. It was about acknowledging forces beyond human comprehension, showing humility in the face of the vast, ancient power of the wilderness – a humility starkly lacking in Kestrel's approach, and perhaps even in her own initial scientific objectives for the expedition.

One cool, misty morning, while gathering edible ferns near a stream further down the hollow from the cabin, Elise felt it again – the distinct sensation of being watched. She froze, every muscle tensing, her hand instinctively reaching for the bear spray she still carried clipped to her belt. Slowly, she scanned the surrounding woods, the dense thickets of salmonberry, the shadowed bases of giant cedars. Nothing moved. No sound disturbed the dripping quiet except the murmur of the stream.

Yet the feeling persisted. Not the cold, calculating surveillance she'd felt from Kestrel. Not the heavy, menacing presence she'd associated with the Stick-shí'nač near the sanctuary. This felt... lighter. More curious. Almost... shy? Like a deer observing from cover, or a bird pausing on a branch.

She stayed motionless for a full minute, breathing shallowly, straining her senses. Was it just an animal? A cougar, perhaps, assessing potential prey? Or her imagination playing tricks again? Then, a flash of movement caught her eye, high in the branches of a fir tree across the stream. Not a bird, not a squirrel. Larger. Darker. Gone in an instant, melting back into the shadows of the dense needles.

Her heart pounded. Had she imagined it? It was too brief, too indistinct to be certain. She scanned the branches intently, but saw nothing more. The feeling of being watched lingered for another moment, then gradually faded, leaving only the damp silence and her own racing pulse.

When she returned to the cabin, mentioning the feeling casually to Whis Elem, the old woman simply nodded, her eyes holding that familiar knowing glint. "The woods have many eyes," she said cryptically. "Not all belong to the guardians. Not all are hostile. Some... are simply curious about newcomers." She offered no further explanation, leaving Elise to ponder the ambiguity, wondering if she meant animals, spirits, or perhaps even the younger Stick-shí'nač whose curiosity had briefly overcome its fear in the sanctuary.

The days turned into a week, then two. Elise felt her physical strength returning, the sharp edges of her immediate trauma beginning to dull slightly, replaced by a deeper, more pervasive ache of grief and unresolved questions. She grew more comfortable in the woods, her senses sharpening, learning to read the subtle signs Whis Elem pointed out, learning to move with greater quiet and awareness. She still felt like an outsider, a student struggling with a difficult new language, but progress was being made.

She rarely thought about the hidden proof in her pack now. The urgency to expose Kestrel felt distant, overshadowed by the immediate need to understand her surroundings, to master the lessons Whis Elem offered. The focus shifted from external conflict to internal landscape, to learning how to *be* in this place, how to listen.

Occasionally, reminders of the outside world intruded. One afternoon, the unmistakable sound of a low-flying aircraft, likely a helicopter based on the rotor beat, echoed through the hollow for several minutes before fading away to the south. It was distant, not directly overhead, but its presence was jarring, a stark reminder that Kestrel's reach extended far, their surveillance potentially ongoing, even if they hadn't pinpointed her exact location. Whis Elem had frowned, listening intently until the sound vanished, muttering something about "iron birds disturbing the spirits." The incident reinforced their isolation but also the fragility of their sanctuary.

Another time, exploring near the base of the ridge Whis Elem had warned her about, Elise found something half-buried in the moss – a heavily rusted metal canister, perforated with age, bearing the faint, almost illegible stencil of a chemical hazard symbol and faded military-style lettering. It looked like something from decades past, perhaps related to Project Backwoods, discarded or lost during those secret operations. She felt a jolt of cold confirmation – Kestrel wasn't the first arm of the outside world to bring its dangerous tools into these guarded woods. She left the canister undisturbed, feeling its presence like a toxic blight on the land, another secret the forest held.

She spent the evenings by the fire, sometimes talking quietly with Whis Elem, absorbing the old woman's stories – tales not just of the Stick-shí'nač, but of Raven and Coyote, of transformations and spirit quests, of the intricate web of life and power that defined the

Salish worldview. Other times, she sat in silence, trying to practice the 'listening' Whis Elem encouraged, attempting to quiet the relentless chatter of her analytical mind and simply *feel* the pulse of the forest night, the deep earth beneath her feet, the vast starry sky obscured by the canopy.

She began to notice patterns she hadn't before. The way the energy in the hollow seemed to shift with the phases of the moon. The subtle changes in animal behavior that preceded shifts in the weather. The almost imperceptible hum that sometimes seemed to emanate from the ground itself, particularly during the deep quiet of moonless nights – the 'resonance' the miners had written about? She tried to describe it scientifically – low-frequency sound, infrasound, localized seismic activity? But the feeling went beyond measurable phenomena. It felt like the heartbeat of the mountain itself, ancient and powerful.

One evening, as they sat by the fire, Elise finally voiced a question that had been burning within her. "Whis Elem," she began hesitantly, "the Stick-shí'nač… the guardians… you speak of them with respect, even reverence. But they killed my friends. They tried to kill us. They build nests with human bones. How… how do you reconcile that? The sacredness and the savagery?"

Whis Elem gazed into the flames for a long time before answering, her face deeply shadowed. "Nature itself is both beautiful and brutal, is it not?" she said softly. "The river provides life-giving water, yet it can drown you in its flood. The fire provides warmth, yet it can consume everything in its path. Power demands respect precisely because it can be dangerous when crossed."

She poked the embers with a stick. "The First People… they are like a deep forest fire, perhaps. Necessary, sometimes, for clearing out decay, for protecting the health of the whole. They uphold ancient laws, maintain boundaries essential for the balance of this place, a balance your world constantly seeks to disrupt. Their methods… seem savage to you, yes. Collecting bones?" She shrugged slightly. "Perhaps it is their way of remembering, honoring even, the lives intertwined with this land, animal and human. Or perhaps it is a warning. A tangible reminder of the consequences of trespass."

She looked at Elise, her eyes holding no easy answers, only complex understanding. "They are not human. Their morality, their ways, are not ours. To judge them solely by human standards is… arrogant. Like judging the wolf for killing the deer, or the earthquake for shaking the ground. They *are* the power of this place made manifest. Fierce, ancient, demanding respect. Sometimes, tragically, that respect is learned through loss."

Her words didn't erase the horror of the nest, the brutality of the deaths. But they offered a different lens, a perspective rooted in ecological balance and indigenous understanding rather than purely human-centric morality. It didn't excuse the violence, but it contextualized it within a larger, more ancient framework.

Elise fell silent, pondering the immense gap between her world's view of 'Bigfoot' – a monster, a myth, a potential scientific specimen – and Whis Elem's understanding of the Stick-shí'nač – ancient guardians, forces of nature, complex beings deserving of respect even in their fearsome power. Bridging that gap felt like the work of lifetimes.

As she sat there, listening to the fire crackle, feeling the deep quiet of the surrounding woods settle around the small cabin, she realized Whis Elem was right. The immediate path forward wasn't confrontation or exposure. It was listening. Learning. Trying to understand the language of silence, the whispers of the ancient woods, the complex truth of the beings who guarded the Hollow Ground. It was a slow, uncertain, perhaps perilous education, but it felt like the only way to truly honor the burdens and bindings she now carried.

Chapter 8: Resonance and Risk

Weeks bled into a month, measured not by calendar pages but by the slow turning of autumn leaves from vibrant green to fiery hues of gold and crimson, by the lengthening shadows stretching across the forest floor earlier each afternoon, and by the deepening chill in the pre-dawn air. Elise found a rhythm in the quiet solitude of Whis Elem's hollow, a routine grounded in the essential tasks of survival – chopping wood until her palms blistered then calloused, hauling water until the ache in her shoulders became a familiar companion, tending the small garden, foraging for late-season berries and mushrooms under the old woman's expert guidance.

Her body, starved and battered during the escape, slowly healed, regaining strength and resilience. The gauntness in her face softened slightly, replaced by a leaner toughness honed by physical labor. The tremors in her hands lessened, though they never vanished entirely, sometimes returning unexpectedly when a sudden noise or shadow triggered a cascade of traumatic memory.

More significantly, something subtle began to shift within her perception. The constant effort to quiet her analytical mind, to follow Whis Elem's guidance and simply *listen* with all her senses, started to yield fleeting results. She began noticing things she would have previously overlooked or dismissed. The way different species of ferns held moisture differently after a rain, indicating subtle variations in soil depth or drainage. The almost imperceptible shift in the scent of the air that heralded an approaching weather front, hours before the sky showed any visible change. The unique cadence in the alarm call of a Douglas squirrel that distinguished between an aerial predator like a hawk and a ground threat like a weasel.

One misty morning, while checking snares Whis Elem had set for snowshoe hares along a game trail – a necessary addition to their diet as winter approached – Elise froze, head tilted. Not because of a sound, but because of a sudden, intense *stillness*. The usual background chatter of chickadees and winter wrens had abruptly ceased. The air felt heavy, expectant. Her skin prickled, the hairs on her arms rising despite the cool dampness. She remembered the unnatural silence of the cedar grove in AO Hollow, the oppressive void in the heart of the sanctuary. This wasn't that absolute, but it was a significant dampening, a holding of breath by the surrounding woods.

She crouched low, scanning the dense undergrowth, her hand automatically going to the bear spray canister still clipped to her belt. After a long moment, a flicker of movement resolved itself into the sleek, tawny form of a cougar, slinking silently across the trail fifty yards ahead, utterly oblivious to her presence, focused intently on something further down the path. It paused, sniffed the air, then melted back into the shadows, vanishing as quickly as it had appeared. Slowly, cautiously, the normal forest sounds resumed, the chickadees returning with tentative, inquiring calls.

When she recounted the experience later to Whis Elem, describing the preternatural quiet that preceded the cougar's appearance, the old woman merely nodded. "The forest speaks," she said simply. "It warns. It acknowledges presence. You are learning to hear its quieter words, Child of Two Worlds."

This subtle sensory awakening extended to the 'resonance' as well. Elise still couldn't define it scientifically, but she became more attuned to its fluctuations. Sometimes, particularly during the deep stillness of night or moments of intense quiet concentration, she could almost feel it – a low-frequency vibration seeming to emanate from the earth itself, a subsonic thrum that resonated within her bones, creating a feeling of pressure behind her eyes. It seemed stronger during certain weather patterns, or perhaps linked to geological stresses deep beneath the mountains. Whis Elem spoke of it as the mountain's "heartbeat," or sometimes, more ominously, as the "guardians' dreaming," suggesting it might be connected to the Stick-shí'nač's own state of being, their collective consciousness somehow interacting with the deep earth energies.

Elise documented these sensations carefully in her notebook, sketching graphs correlating perceived intensity with time of day, weather, even her own emotional state, searching for patterns, clinging to the scientific method even as the phenomenon itself defied easy explanation.

Despite these small steps towards understanding her new environment, the ghosts of the expedition remained constant companions. Grief ambushed her unexpectedly. Finding a particularly large, clear animal track near the creek – likely elk – brought Boone's face vividly to mind, his grim expertise, his haunted eyes. She remembered him kneeling by the creek near their first camp, pointing out the impossible eighteen-inch footprints, his voice tight with conviction. "You still thinkin' 'bear,' Doc?" His sacrifice in the fissure felt raw, immediate, a debt she could never repay. She found herself talking to him sometimes, whispering questions into the uncaring woods, seeking the guidance he could no longer provide.

Levi's presence haunted her attempts at first aid. Treating a deep scratch on her own arm from a devil's club thorn, cleaning it with antiseptic wipes from her depleted kit, she saw his face, pale and determined, tending to her blister back at the first camp, then later, feverish and resolute, forcing himself upright to make his final, terrible sacrifice. The weight of his choice, his belief that he needed to atone, felt crushing. Had she made the right decision, accepting his sacrifice? Or should they have stayed with him, faced the end together? The question offered no easy answer, only the dull ache of unresolved guilt.

Even Graves intruded on her thoughts, less with grief and more with a complex tangle of anger, betrayal, and reluctant pity. She remembered his icy composure cracking after the clear sighting on the ridge, the flicker of fear in his eyes as he realized the true nature of the forces Kestrel had unleashed. He had been following orders, yes, driven by ambition or perhaps even a misguided belief in the 'strategic importance' he'd cited. But he had also been a victim, ultimately, plucked from the rock face, his meticulously planned mission ending in brutal, unforeseen reality. His hidden files, buried now in the cave, felt like his only epitaph, a testament to the deadly secrets he had guarded.

Whis Elem offered quiet wisdom during these moments of surfacing grief. She didn't offer platitudes or easy comfort, but shared stories from her own long life, tales of loss endured by her people – losses to sickness, to harsh winters, to conflicts with encroaching settlers, even, obliquely, to the guardians themselves when boundaries were crossed unwisely. Loss, she conveyed, was woven into the fabric of life, especially life lived close to the bone, close to the wild power of nature. Honoring the dead, she suggested, wasn't about dwelling on the pain, but about carrying their memory forward, learning from their sacrifices, striving to live with greater wisdom and respect.

"Their spirits are part of the mountain now," she told Elise one evening, gazing into the fire. "Their energy feeds the cycle. Boone, the tracker who finally understood the tracks led deeper than he knew. Levi, the healer who chose sacrifice. Even Graves, the soldier lost fighting a war he didn't comprehend. Their stories are woven into this place now. Listen, and you might still hear their echoes, learn from their journeys."

Listening. It always came back to listening.

But the outside world, and its threats, refused to remain entirely at bay. One clear, cold afternoon, while venturing slightly further afield than usual, following a stream searching for late-season watercress, Elise stumbled upon something that immediately set her nerves on edge. Tucked into a dense thicket of rhododendrons, almost completely concealed, was a small, metallic object hanging from a low branch. It was sleek, grey, about the size of her fist, with a small, dark lens aperture on one side. A motion-activated wildlife camera? Perhaps. But it looked newer, more sophisticated than standard research equipment. And its placement felt wrong – too low for typical deer or elk monitoring, angled slightly upwards, overlooking the game trail she had just followed. It felt... tactical. Like surveillance.

She backed away slowly, carefully, erasing her tracks as best she could, her heart pounding. Had Kestrel found this area? Were they deploying remote sensors, sweeping the forests systematically, searching for her, for Nora, for any sign of Stick-shí'nač activity outside the quarantined valley? Or was it something else entirely – unrelated research, Park Service monitoring? She couldn't be sure, but the discovery shattered the fragile sense of security she had begun to feel in Whis Elem's hollow. The watchers were potentially closer than she thought.

She reported the finding immediately to Whis Elem upon returning to the cabin. The old woman listened intently, her brow furrowed. "An electronic eye," she murmured, distaste evident in her voice. "They try to capture the world in their little glass boxes. They do not understand that seeing is not the same as knowing." She grew thoughtful. "This is not good. It means they search widely. Or, perhaps," her eyes grew troubled, "they were led here."

"Led here? By what?" Elise asked, alarmed.

"Sometimes," Whis Elem said reluctantly, "when the balance is disturbed, when great fear or violence echoes through the woods, other... less predictable things are drawn to the disturbance. Things that feed on chaos. Things the guardians themselves usually keep in check." She didn't elaborate, but the implication of other, potentially darker, forces stirring in the deep woods added another layer of fear to Elise's already burdened mind.

A few days later, confirmation of external activity arrived more directly. Whis Elem returned from a long walk towards the lower end of the hollow, her face unusually grim. She carried a small, smooth river stone, unremarkable except for a single, dark line etched sharply across its surface – a line broken deliberately in two places.

"A message," Whis Elem stated, holding out the stone for Elise to see. "From my niece's cousin, down near the Hoh River crossing. Left by the Singing Falls, as agreed."

"What does it say?" Elise asked anxiously, recognizing it as part of the low-tech communication network.

"Broken line," Whis Elem interpreted, tracing the etching with her finger. "Interference. Disruption. He says… Kestrel – the Men in Dark Jackets – have increased their presence along the park boundaries. Roadblocks on some of the old logging spurs. Unmarked helicopters patrolling more frequently, further west than before. And," her voice lowered, "two hikers went missing last week, near Lake Quinault. Officially, 'lost in sudden storm'. Unofficially… the tracks found nearby did not match bear or cougar. And they were heading *away* from the restricted AO Hollow zone."

Elise felt a chill spread through her. Kestrel expanding their perimeter, locking down access. And the creatures… active outside the valley? Agitated by the fire, by Kestrel's presence, by the intrusion into their sanctuary? Or was Kestrel themselves responsible for the new disappearances, silencing potential witnesses under the guise of wilderness accidents? The possibilities were equally terrifying.

"Are they looking for us specifically?" Elise asked.

"Perhaps," Whis Elem conceded. "Or perhaps they cast a wide net, suppressing any anomaly, any hint of the truth getting out. And perhaps," she added, her eyes dark with worry, "the guardians themselves are… unsettled. Expanding their patrols. Reacting to the disturbance we brought into their world."

The news shattered the relative peace of their refuge. The listening, the learning, the slow healing – it felt like a luxury they could no longer afford. Kestrel was actively tightening the cordon. The Stick-shí'nač might be ranging further afield, potentially becoming a wider threat, or drawing Kestrel's attention towards new areas. And Elise and Nora were caught in the middle, possessing knowledge that made them targets for both human agencies and potentially the guardians themselves if they misinterpreted their presence or intentions.

"We have to leave, don't we?" Elise said quietly, voicing the conclusion that felt inevitable. "Staying here... we're just waiting for them to find us. Or for the guardians to become aware of this hollow."

Whis Elem nodded sadly. "Yes. The sanctuary I could offer was always temporary. The woods whisper your name too loudly now, carried on the wind, picked up by the machines. You must move. Decide your path."

The choice, deferred for weeks, now pressed upon Elise with urgent, unavoidable force. What now? Try to disappear completely, live off-grid forever, hoping Kestrel eventually gave up the hunt? Impossible, likely. Attempt to reach the outside world, expose the truth, using the proof she carried, risking global chaos and the creatures' destruction? Terrifyingly dangerous, ethically fraught. Or... the third path Whis Elem had hinted at? The path of understanding, mediation, somehow trying to bridge the gap, protect the sanctuary from within, while simultaneously thwarting Kestrel? It still felt impossibly idealistic, bordering on suicidal.

Yet, sitting there in the quiet cabin, the weight of Boone's and Levi's sacrifices heavy upon her, the image of the adolescent creature's tentative curiosity vivid in her mind, the third path felt like the only one that truly honored the complexity of what she had witnessed. It was the path that acknowledged the creatures' sentience, sought a balance, resisted the simple narratives of 'monster' or 'specimen'. It was the path of the Child of Two Worlds.

"Alright," Elise said, meeting Whis Elem's wise, steady gaze, a new, albeit fearful, resolve hardening within her. "I can't just run. I can't just hide. And I can't unleash this truth onto the world unprepared. There has to be another way." She took a deep breath. "I need to go back. Not into the sanctuary – not yet. But closer. I need to find a way to observe them, understand them, without intruding, without provoking. And I need to find out exactly what Kestrel is planning next, find a way to stop their 'Sanitization Protocol' before it's too late."

It sounded insane, walking back towards the danger zone. But it felt like the only meaningful course of action left.

Whis Elem regarded her for a long moment, then nodded slowly. "A dangerous path," she murmured. "Walking the knife edge between worlds. The guardians will sense you. Kestrel will hunt you. Success is… uncertain."

"I know," Elise acknowledged. "But doing nothing feels worse."

"Then you will need more than just listening skills," Whis Elem stated. "You will need allies. You will need guidance deeper than I alone can provide. You must seek out Nora. She carries her own burdens, her own knowledge from the Tallsalt elders about navigating these forces. Together… perhaps you stand a chance."

The plan began to form, desperate, fragile, but a plan nonetheless. Leave the relative safety of the hollow. Travel cautiously towards Nora's community, using the network to arrange a secure meeting. Combine Elise's scientific knowledge and recovered Kestrel intel with Nora's cultural wisdom and practical survival skills. Find a way to monitor Kestrel activity, anticipate their moves. And somehow, simultaneously, find a way to study the Stick-shí'nač from a distance, seeking understanding, hoping for non-hostile interaction, potentially finding leverage against Kestrel or a way to warn the creatures of the impending threat.

It was a tightrope walk over an abyss. But as Elise prepared her pack again, carefully checking the hidden container with its explosive secrets, she felt a flicker of the determination she'd felt leaving Seattle. The period of listening was over. The time for cautious, informed action, however perilous, had arrived. The whispering woods had offered sanctuary, but now they called her back towards the heart of the conflict, towards the dangerous intersection of human conspiracy and ancient power. The true journey into the Hollow Ground was about to begin in earnest.

Chapter 9: Kestrel's Hidden Scars

Leaving Whis Elem's secluded hollow felt like stepping out of a pocket of suspended time back into the urgent, dangerous present. The old woman stood at the edge of the clearing, wrapped in her blanket, her face serene but her eyes filled with concern, watching Elise disappear back into the dense forest. Her parting words echoed in Elise's mind: *"Walk softly, Child of Two Worlds. Listen deeply. And trust the balance, even when it feels most precarious."* Sound advice, Elise thought grimly, but trusting anything felt like a luxury in a world where shadowy organizations deployed lethal force and ancient guardians might interpret any misstep as aggression.

The journey towards Nora's community was fraught with calculated risk. Following Whis Elem's guidance and the coded directions relayed through the network (a marked stone left by another stream, a specific bird call imitated at a certain trail junction), Elise traveled circuitously, avoiding main trails and roads, sticking to the deep woods, moving primarily during the low-light hours of dawn and dusk to minimize potential observation from Kestrel patrols or aerial surveillance.

Her senses, honed during her weeks with Whis Elem, felt sharper now. She moved more quietly, scanned the forest more effectively, paid closer attention to the subtle cues – the sudden silence of birds, the snap of a twig that sounded unnatural, the faint, lingering scent of something metallic or chemical that might indicate recent human passage. Several times, she caught the distant thrum of a helicopter, forcing her to take immediate cover beneath dense foliage, heart pounding, until the sound faded. Once, while scouting a ridge line for a safer route, she spotted them through her binoculars – two figures clad in dark gear moving stealthily through the trees far below, methodically sweeping the area. Kestrel ground teams, still active, still searching. The sight sent a chill down her spine, reinforcing the need for constant vigilance.

The rendezvous with Nora was arranged for a location deep within traditional Tallsalt hunting grounds, an area supposedly shielded by both rugged terrain and cultural protections that discouraged casual intrusion. After three days of tense, exhausting travel, Elise finally reached the designated spot – a small, moss-draped clearing beside a waterfall cascading into a deep, green pool, a place Whis Elem had described as holding significance for Nora's family line.

Nora was already there, sitting quietly on a smooth, grey boulder, seemingly meditating amidst the roar of the falling water. She looked leaner, perhaps, her face more deeply etched with the lines of strain and grief, but her eyes, when they met Elise's, held the same steady, resilient light. Seeing her again, the only other person who truly understood the depth of the horror and wonder they had shared, brought a wave of immense relief, tinged with the shared sorrow for those they had lost.

They didn't waste time on lengthy greetings or emotional outpourings. The urgency was too great. Sitting together beside the thundering waterfall, the noise providing a natural shield against potential listening devices, Elise quickly recounted her escape from Vashon, the Kestrel surveillance, her time with Whis Elem, the message about increased Kestrel activity and the new disappearances near Lake Quinault.

Nora listened intently, her expression growing grimmer with each detail. "Yes," she confirmed when Elise finished. "The hunters who vanished near the lake… my cousins helped with the unofficial search, after the Park Service gave up. They found tracks. Large ones. Like before. But," she hesitated, her brow furrowing, "they said the pattern felt… different. More erratic. Angrier, maybe. Less clean than the signs we saw near the sanctuary."

"Angrier?" Elise questioned. "Could the fire, Kestrel's presence… could it be affecting their behavior? Driving them out, making them less predictable?"

"Perhaps," Nora conceded. "Or perhaps... Kestrel's actions are disturbing more than just the Stick-shí'nač." She echoed Whis Elem's ominous hint about other forces potentially stirred by the disruption. "The Men in Dark Jackets... they move without respect. They drill into the earth, set fires, spill chemicals. They leave scars, both visible and invisible. Such actions can awaken things best left sleeping."

Elise shared the contents of the Kestrel files she'd recovered from Graves' pack – the Goliath autopsy summary, the Project Backwoods references, the Sanitization Protocol, the ruthlessness towards witnesses. Nora absorbed the information with a quiet intensity, the confirmation of Kestrel's long history of intrusion and violence seemingly aligning with older, darker Tallsalt stories her elders had only hinted at, tales of powerful outsiders meddling with forces they didn't understand, always leading to tragedy.

"Project Chimera," Nora murmured, testing the name. "A fitting title. A beast made of ill-fitting parts, stitched together by arrogance and lies. This Kestrel... they seek to capture or destroy what they cannot comprehend. They are like children playing with thunderstones."

"They need to be stopped, Nora," Elise stated, her voice urgent. "Before they implement the rest of that protocol. Before they cause irreparable damage – to the sanctuary, to the creatures, maybe even trigger something worse."

"Stopping them directly... feels like catching smoke," Nora mused, echoing Elise's own sense of futility regarding direct confrontation. "They are too many, too well-equipped, too protected by layers of secrecy."

"But maybe," Elise pressed, leaning closer, "we can find their weakness. Their hidden scars, like you said. Places they operated secretly, where they might have made mistakes, left evidence behind. The miners' logbook mentioned tunnels, survey sites... Graves' files hinted at older operations. If we could find one of these places, maybe there's something there Kestrel missed during their cleanup. Something concrete we can use."

Nora considered this, her gaze thoughtful. "There are... places," she admitted slowly. "Old mines that scarred the land before the park was fully protected. Places where strange work was done during the cold war years, bunkers hidden in hillsides, whispered about by hunters who stumbled upon fenced-off areas and armed guards where none should be. Most are collapsed, flooded, forgotten. Dangerous to seek."

"We're running out of safe options," Elise countered. "If Kestrel is preparing another phase, we need leverage, information, anything that could expose them or disrupt their plans."

Nora fell silent for a long moment, seemingly weighing the risks, consulting her deep well of ancestral knowledge and intuition. Finally, she nodded. "There is one place," she said reluctantly. "North of here, near the Elwha River headwaters. An old copper mine, abandoned long ago, even before my grandfather's time. But later... during the time of great fear between your people and the Russians... lights were seen there at night. Strange vehicles on the old access roads, which were then mysteriously washed out by 'natural' landslides. Guards who discouraged hunters. Then... silence again. The mine entrance was sealed, dynamited shut. Locals said it was unstable. But some elders whispered it was sealed for other reasons. Because something had gotten out. Or because something dangerous remained within."

A hidden Cold War site? Possibly repurposed by Kestrel or a precursor agency like Project Backwoods? It fit the timeline, the secrecy, the potential for hidden labs or containment facilities hinted at by the Goliath autopsy. It felt like a long shot, but the most promising lead they had.

"Can we get there?" Elise asked. "Is it accessible?"

"The main entrance is sealed," Nora reiterated. "But... there might be other ways. Ventilation shafts mentioned in old mining maps. Drainage tunnels. Natural cave connections, perhaps, known only to... others." She left the implication hanging. Accessing it would likely mean traversing areas potentially frequented or guarded by the Stick-shí'nač themselves.

Despite the immense risks, the potential reward – finding concrete evidence of Kestrel's long-term operations, perhaps even biological samples or logs detailing their unethical research – felt worth the gamble. They agreed. Their next objective: locate the abandoned Elwha mine site, find a way inside, and search for Kestrel's hidden scars.

The journey north took another two days of arduous travel through dense, trackless wilderness. Nora navigated with uncanny skill, avoiding Kestrel patrol routes based on the intelligence from her network, leading them through deep forests, across rushing rivers on precarious logjams, and up steep, mist-shrouded ridges. They moved cautiously, conserving energy, acutely aware that they were entering territory potentially closer to the Stick-shí'nač's known range, though still west of the primary AO Hollow sanctuary. Signs of large game were plentiful – elk tracks, deer scat, bear claw marks on trees – but they saw or heard nothing that definitively indicated the guardians themselves. The woods remained watchful, silent, holding their secrets close.

Finally, late on the second day, descending into a steep-sided valley carved by a tributary of the Elwha River, Nora pointed towards a heavily overgrown scar on the opposite slope – the faint indentation of an old mining road, barely discernible beneath decades of returning forest. Following this ghost of a road, they arrived at the site.

It was eerily quiet. The main mine entrance, as Nora had said, was completely collapsed, sealed by a massive, deliberate rockslide that looked far too uniform to be entirely natural. Rusted remnants of mining equipment – ore cart wheels, collapsed wooden structures, sections of pipeline – lay scattered amongst the encroaching trees, monuments to a forgotten industrial past. There were no fences now, no obvious signs of recent activity. Just the silence of abandonment, underscored by the rush of the nearby river.

"Vent shafts," Nora murmured, scanning the steep slope above the collapsed entrance. "Mining maps showed several, higher up. For air circulation."

They spent the next hour carefully scouring the hillside, pushing through dense thickets of devil's club and thorny salmonberry. Finally, hidden beneath a thick carpet of moss and ferns, Boone would have been proud, Elise thought, they found one. A circular opening, perhaps three feet in diameter, lined with crumbling brickwork, descending vertically into darkness. A rusted metal grate lay nearby, torn from its mounting. The air emanating from the shaft felt cold, stagnant, carrying the faint, metallic tang of old machinery and deep earth.

"This is it," Nora confirmed, peering down into the blackness. "Deep. No ladder remains."

Elise shone her headlamp beam down the shaft. It seemed to drop vertically for at least fifty feet before disappearing from view. Too far to jump, impossible to climb back out without ropes. But tied securely around a nearby sturdy tree root, almost invisible unless specifically searched for, was a relatively new-looking length of dark, synthetic rope, expertly knotted, dangling down into the shaft. It wasn't ancient mining rope; it looked modern, high-strength climbing or tactical rope.

"Kestrel?" Elise whispered, exchanging an alarmed look with Nora. Had Kestrel been here recently? Accessed the mine this way? Was it a trap?

Nora examined the rope, the knotwork, the anchor point. "The knot is… Tallsalt style," she said slowly, surprise in her voice.

"Used for securing fishing nets, or sometimes for descent into canyons. Not Kestrel." She looked around the silent woods again, then back at the rope. "Someone from my people... left this? Recently? Why?"

The mystery deepened. Was another faction involved? Someone from Nora's own community, acting secretly? Or perhaps someone trying to help them, anticipating their arrival? The rope felt like both an invitation and a warning.

Deciding the risk of Kestrel finding them outweighed the uncertainty of the rope's origin, they made a pact. They would use the rope to descend. If it felt unstable, they would abort. If they reached the bottom, they would search for evidence quickly, cautiously, ready to retreat at the first sign of danger or Kestrel presence.

Securing their packs tightly, checking their meager gear one last time, Elise went first, testing the rope's anchor, then slowly rappelling down into the cold darkness of the ventilation shaft, the rough brickwork scraping against her back. Nora followed close behind, moving with surprising agility.

The descent was nerve-wracking, the rope disconcertingly thin-feeling, the darkness absolute below the reach of their headlamps. After what felt like an eternity, Elise's feet touched solid ground – the uneven, debris-strewn floor of a mine tunnel. Nora landed silently beside her a moment later.

They were inside. The air was thick with the smell of rust, damp rock, and something else – a faint, unpleasant chemical odor, acrid and unfamiliar. Their headlamp beams cut through the oppressive darkness, revealing a narrow tunnel shored up with rotting timbers, railway tracks disappearing into the gloom in both directions. Side passages branched off, some collapsed, others dark and forbidding. Water dripped incessantly, echoing strangely.

"Which way?" Elise whispered, feeling exposed, vulnerable.

Nora pointed down the main tunnel, towards the direction the chemical smell seemed strongest. "That way feels… wrong," she murmured. "A place of sickness. Where Kestrel's scars might lie deepest."

Moving cautiously along the main tunnel, stepping over fallen timbers and pools of stagnant, iron-red water, they began their search. They passed collapsed side tunnels, abandoned ore carts frozen on rusted tracks, heaps of discarded rock and tailings. The chemical smell grew stronger, making Elise's eyes water.

After maybe a hundred yards, the tunnel opened into a larger chamber, clearly artificially widened, similar to the miners' chamber near the sanctuary but larger, more reinforced with steel beams, now heavily corroded. And here, the evidence was undeniable.

Against one wall stood rows of empty metal cages, large enough to hold something bigger than a human, their bars bent and broken in places, doors hanging open. Chains lay coiled on the floor, thick, heavy-duty restraints ending in ominous padded cuffs. In the center of the chamber sat a large metal table, bolted to the floor, stained with dark, indeterminate substances. Nearby lay discarded syringes, shattered glass vials, and ominous-looking metal instruments that looked disturbingly like surgical or sampling tools designed for non-human subjects.

And leaning against the far wall, partially covered by a fallen sheet of rusted metal, was a single, heartbreakingly small object: a crudely carved wooden doll, resembling a small Stick-shí'nač figure, its form worn smooth as if clutched by a small hand for a long time.

"Goliath," Elise breathed, the connection hitting her with sickening force. The autopsy report – *subject died attempting to protect juvenile*. Had they captured the young one too? Held it here? Experimented on it? The wooden doll suggested a prolonged captivity, a desperate attempt by the parent or the child itself to maintain a connection to its culture, its identity, in this sterile hell.

Nora let out a soft cry, stepping back, her hand flying to her mouth, tears welling in her eyes. "Abomination," she whispered, her voice trembling with rage and sorrow. "This place... this is where they tortured them. Defiled them."

This chamber was Kestrel's hidden scar, laid bare. Not just a listening post, but a capture and experimentation site. The chemical smell likely residual tranquilizers, cleaning agents, preservatives. This was where the trauma inflicted upon the Stick-shí'nač lineage began, or at least significantly escalated. This was the source of the deep distrust, the potential rage, the reason the guardians might react with such ferocity to human intrusion. Kestrel hadn't just stumbled into a conflict; they had actively instigated it, poked the ancient power with sharp, cruel sticks, decades ago.

As Elise began documenting the horrific scene with her camera, forcing herself to capture the damning evidence – the cages, the instruments, the pathetic doll – Nora pointed towards a heavy steel door set into the far wall, partially hidden behind the stained table. Unlike the rest of the decaying site, the door looked relatively intact, though heavily rusted. It bore a faded biohazard symbol and Cyrillic lettering beneath peeling English warnings.

"Cold War," Nora murmured. "This place... older than Kestrel alone, perhaps. Built by others who feared the unknown."

Could there be records inside? Samples? More files? Or just deeper horrors?

Driven by a grim need to know the full extent of the desecration, Elise approached the door. A heavy wheel mechanism, rusted tight, seemed to be the primary lock. Working together, straining against decades of corrosion, they managed, finally, to turn the wheel with a screech of protesting metal. The heavy door groaned inwards, opening onto pitch blackness and a blast of frigid air that carried the scent of decay and something else... something sharp, sterile, deeply wrong.

They shone their lights inside. It wasn't another tunnel, but a room. A laboratory. Stainless steel counters lined the walls, holding shattered glassware, overturned microscopes, banks of dead electronic equipment coated in frost. Frost covered everything, clinging to the walls, the floor, the ceiling, suggesting a catastrophic failure of a refrigeration or containment system long ago.

And in the center of the room, strapped onto a tilted metal gurney beneath flickering, dying emergency lights that cast long, distorted shadows, lay a shape shrouded in a frost-covered, yellowed sheet. It was large, disturbingly humanoid in outline.

With dread coiling in her stomach, Elise slowly approached the gurney. Reaching out a trembling hand, she hesitated, then pulled back the stiff, frozen corner of the sheet.

She recoiled instantly, clapping a hand over her mouth, stifling a scream. Lying there, desiccated, partially dissected, yet horribly preserved by the extreme cold, was the body. Not Goliath; this one was smaller, perhaps female, its features frozen in a rictus of agony and fear. Wires trailed from its skull, connected to a bank of dead machinery. Vials containing dark, frozen liquid lay scattered around the gurney.

This was it. Kestrel's dark secret. Decades-old proof of their unethical, horrific experiments. A hidden lab, a preserved victim, evidence Kestrel had clearly failed to sanitize completely when they abandoned this site. They had found the scar, deeper and more horrifying than they could have imagined. But discovering it also meant they were now standing in one of the most dangerous places imaginable, a place Kestrel would undoubtedly kill to keep hidden forever. And the frigid air seemed to whisper that they were not alone in the frozen silence.

Chapter 10: The Frozen Heart

The blast of frigid air escaping the opened laboratory door carried more than just the scent of decay and chemicals; it carried the palpable weight of decades of suffering, a violation so profound it seemed to have permanently chilled the very stone around them. Elise stumbled back from the gurney, the horrific image of the frost-covered, dissected figure burned into her retinas. It wasn't Goliath, the massive male described in the autopsy report she'd found in Graves' files. This victim was smaller, slighter, its frozen agony a silent testament to Kestrel's (or its predecessors') long and brutal history with the Stick-shí'nač.

Nora stood frozen near the doorway, her face ashen, her eyes wide with a mixture of horror and sacrilegious dread. This wasn't just a lab; it was a tomb, a place where the sacred essence of one of the First People had been desecrated, violated by cold science and colder cruelty. Her hand tightened on the handle of her axe, not for defense, but perhaps as an anchor against the wave of revulsion and sorrow threatening to overwhelm her.

The silence in the frozen lab was absolute, broken only by the ragged sound of Elise's breathing and the faint, persistent drip of condensation forming and refreezing on the frost-coated equipment. The emergency lights, miraculously still drawing power from some long-dying internal battery, flickered erratically, casting the scene in strobing, grotesque shadows, making the desiccated figure on the gurney seem to twitch with phantom life.

Elise forced herself to look again, pushing past the initial wave of revulsion, the scientist in her battling the traumatized human. This was critical evidence, horrifying but potentially pivotal. She had to document it, understand it. Taking slow, deliberate steps back towards the gurney, she raised her camera, its small electronic components protesting slightly in the extreme cold. Her hands trembled, making it difficult to focus.

The body, likely female based on pelvic structure visible beneath the tattered remnants of the sheet, showed clear signs of extensive invasive procedures. Incisions, crudely stitched in some places, left open in others, revealed glimpses of internal anatomy pinned back for examination. Electrodes were still attached to the skull, trailing wires towards a bank of complex, dead machinery – neurological monitoring equipment? Attempts to study brain activity? Or worse, attempts at control? Vials lay scattered nearby, some containing frozen, dark liquid – blood samples? Tissue cultures? Unknown chemical agents? Others were shattered, their contents long evaporated or frozen into crystalline residue on the floor.

The level of violation was staggering. This wasn't just an autopsy; it was prolonged experimentation on a captive subject. How long had this individual suffered here? Days? Weeks? Months? The sheer callousness of it, the reduction of a sentient being to mere data points and biological material, reinforced Elise's conviction that Kestrel, and the agencies that preceded it, saw the Stick-shí'nač not as a species to be understood, but as a resource to be exploited or a threat to be neutralized.

"When?" Nora whispered, her voice hoarse, finally moving further into the frigid room, her gaze fixed on the victim with profound sadness. "How long ago did they do this?"

Elise scanned the equipment, the logs scattered on a nearby counter, coated in frost but potentially holding clues. Carefully, using a gloved finger, she brushed frost from the cover of a thin binder lying near the bank of machinery. The title, barely legible beneath the ice crystals, read: *Project Chimera – Phase 1B – Subject 'Echo' – Neurological Response Trials – Dr. Aris Thorne / Dr. Ivan Volkov – Log Entries 1988-1989.*

Echo. They had named her. And the dates… late 1980s. Almost two decades after the miners' disaster chronicled in the logbook Elise carried, but still decades ago. This facility had been operational long after the initial 'Project Backwoods' cover-up. And

Dr. Aris Thorne's name appeared again, linked this time with a Russian-sounding name – Volkov. Cold War collaboration? Or defection? Kestrel's tendrils, Elise realized, likely stretched internationally, intertwined with the secret histories of global powers. 'Echo' might have been captured during that later period, perhaps during a different Kestrel operation aimed at securing live specimens based on initial findings from Goliath. Thorne's later memo urging cessation of active recovery protocols now seemed even more pointed – perhaps driven by guilt or horror over what had happened here, to Echo.

"Almost thirty-five years ago," Elise answered Nora quietly, indicating the dates. "They held her here. Studied her brain, it looks like." The words felt clinical, inadequate to describe the horror before them.

As Elise continued documenting the scene – the body, the equipment, the logs – Nora moved slowly around the perimeter of the lab, her eyes scanning the frost-covered walls, the floor, seemingly searching for something else. She paused near a bank of lockers, heavily rusted but still sealed. Using the edge of her axe, she carefully pried open one of the frozen doors.

Inside, hanging from a hook, was a single, pathetic garment – a child's worn sweater, hand-knitted, faded blue. Below it on the locker floor lay a small, leather-bound book. Nora reached in and gently retrieved the book. It wasn't a logbook. The cover was embossed with a simple cross. A Bible.

Nora opened it carefully. Tucked inside the front cover was a faded black-and-white photograph: a smiling man in miner's gear, arm around a woman holding a baby, standing proudly in front of a rough log cabin. A name was written beneath in careful script: *John Miller and Family, 1972*.

Miller. The miner from the 1973 logbook. The one who had supposedly cracked, slipped out into the natural caves seeking escape, presumed dead. But this Bible, this photo... found here, in a Kestrel lab operational years later?

"He didn't die in the caves," Nora breathed, realization dawning, her voice filled with disbelief and horror. "He found this place. Or... they found him."

Had Miller survived his desperate flight through the caves, only to stumble upon this hidden Kestrel facility? Had they captured him? Interrogated him? Silenced him to protect their secret? Or worse, had he become another subject? The presence of his personal Bible in this locker felt deeply ominous.

Elise felt another layer of the conspiracy peel back. Kestrel hadn't just covered up the existence of the creatures; they had likely covered up the fate of human witnesses and victims as well, erasing inconvenient truths from multiple angles. Miller's official fate – lost in the caves – was likely another fabrication.

As this new horror settled upon them, a sudden noise from the tunnel outside the lab jolted them back to immediate peril. A sharp scraping sound, followed by a low, guttural cough. Not the deep rumble of the elder, but the higher-pitched, more hesitant sound Elise associated with... the adolescent.

They froze, exchanging panicked glances. Had it followed them? Had it known about this place? Was it drawn by their presence, their lights, the disturbance of opening the sealed door?

"Douse the lights," Elise hissed, quickly switching off her headlamp. Nora did the same. Plunged into near-absolute darkness, relieved only by the faint, flickering emergency lights near the gurney casting long, dancing shadows, they pressed themselves against the cold, frosted wall near the lab entrance, weapons ready, straining their ears.

The scraping sound came again, closer now, just outside the heavy steel door. Then, silence. A long, tense moment stretched. Was it listening? Assessing?

Slowly, cautiously, the massive steel door began to creak inwards, pushed from the outside. A sliver of darkness appeared, widening inch by agonizing inch. Elise held her breath, pistol raised, finger hovering near the trigger, memories of Levi's fatal shot flashing through her mind. Don't shoot unless... unless what? What constituted aggression from a being they barely understood?

A large, dark head peered around the edge of the door. Deep-set eyes, reflecting the faint emergency lights, scanned the frozen laboratory. It was the adolescent. It looked hesitant, cautious, its earlier curiosity replaced by something else – wariness, perhaps even sadness? Its gaze swept over the frosted equipment, the scattered vials, then lingered on the shrouded figure on the gurney.

It let out a soft whimper, a low, mournful sound utterly different from its previous calls or the elders' aggressive roars. It sounded like... grief. Recognition. Did it know Echo? Was this a relative? A memory from its own childhood, perhaps, if it had been the juvenile Goliath died protecting?

The creature took a tentative step into the lab, its massive feet crunching softly on the frost-covered floor. It ignored Elise and Nora completely, its attention fixed entirely on the gurney. It approached slowly, cautiously, extending a long-fingered hand as if to touch the frozen sheet covering Echo's body.

Elise remained frozen, unsure whether to react, to reveal their presence. This felt like intruding on a private moment of grief, a sacred encounter across decades of loss.

But before the adolescent could touch the gurney, another sound echoed from the tunnel outside – a deeper growl this time. The adult male? Or the elder? The adolescent flinched, instantly withdrawing its hand, casting a fearful glance back towards the doorway. It whimpered again, a soft, distressed sound, then turned and slipped back out of the lab as silently as it had entered, vanishing into the darkness. The heavy steel door slowly swung partially shut behind it, moved perhaps by air currents or its departing passage.

Silence returned, heavy, profound. Elise and Nora exchanged bewildered, terrified glances. What had just happened? Had the adolescent defied its elders to come here? Was it grieving? Why had it retreated? Were the others nearby?

The encounter, brief and ambiguous as it was, reinforced the complexity of the Stick-shí'nač. They weren't monolithic monsters. They possessed individual awareness, curiosity, memory, grief. The adolescent's reaction to Echo's body suggested deep emotional capacity, a connection to their past, perhaps even an understanding of the violation that had occurred here. It made Kestrel's actions, their clinical detachment and brutal experiments, seem even more monstrous by comparison.

But the immediate danger remained. The other creatures were nearby. They knew Elise and Nora were inside the lab now. The adolescent's brief visit might have been driven by personal grief, but it had also confirmed their location.

"We have to get out," Elise whispered urgently, the need to escape this frozen tomb suddenly overwhelming. "Now. Before the others come."

"Which way?" Nora asked, glancing towards the dark tunnel entrance, then scanning the lab walls. "Back the way we came? Or… is there another exit? Miller… Davies… the logbook mentioned shafts, natural caves…"

Elise quickly scanned the lab again with her reactivated headlamp. The main tunnel they'd entered through felt like certain death now. Were there other passages leading from this chamber? Her beam swept across the frost-covered walls, the banks of dead equipment.

Near the back corner, partially hidden behind a large, overturned piece of machinery crusted with ice, she saw it – a darker patch on the wall, suggesting an opening, maybe a ventilation duct access or another exploratory tunnel connected to the original mining operation.

"There," she breathed, pointing. "Maybe."

Moving quickly, cautiously, they navigated around the central gurney, averting their eyes from Echo's tragic form. They reached the back corner, confirming it was indeed another passage, narrower than the main tunnel, choked with frost and debris, its destination unknown. It might lead nowhere. It might lead deeper into unexplored caves. It might lead them straight into another Stick-shí'nač encounter. But it was the only option besides returning towards the waiting guardians.

As Nora used her axe to carefully chip away the thickest ice blocking the entrance, Elise took one last look back at the frozen lab, at the preserved horror on the gurney, at the discarded Bible hinting at another lost soul. She had found Kestrel's hidden scar, proof of their decades-long monstrosity. But the discovery offered no triumph, only a deeper understanding of the cycle of violence and grief that bound humans and guardians together in this secret war beneath the Hollow Ground. Getting this new, horrifying proof out felt more critical than ever, yet survival seemed more precarious with every passing moment. The frozen heart of Kestrel's darkness had been breached, but escaping its chilling grasp alive felt increasingly unlikely.

Chapter 11: Echoes in the Stone

The darkness that swallowed them beyond the narrow opening felt fundamentally different from the merely unlit tunnels they had traversed before. This was the profound, absolute blackness of deep earth, untouched by even the faintest memory of sunlight, a darkness that felt ancient and heavy, pressing in from all sides. The frigid air, thick with the scent of wet stone, mineral dust, and the lingering, stomach-churning metallic tang from the abandoned laboratory, seemed to deaden sound almost immediately, muffling their ragged breaths, Levi's distant moans (had they imagined them, carried through the rock?), and the frantic hammering of Elise's own heart against her ribs.

Squeezing through the opening behind Nora felt like being born into a nightmare. The passage was tight, claustrophobic, forcing Elise to turn sideways, scraping her pack and shoulders against rough, unseen rock formations. Loose scree shifted treacherously underfoot. For a terrifying moment, she imagined the passage closing in, the mountain itself squeezing the life out of them, burying them alive alongside the lab's frozen secrets. She pushed forward desperately, following the faint halo of Nora's headlamp beam just ahead, focusing only on the next handhold, the next patch of relatively stable ground.

Once through the initial constriction, the passage remained narrow but opened up just enough for them to stand hunched over, moving in a shuffling single file. It wasn't a drilled mining tunnel like the main access shaft; this felt like a natural fissure, perhaps slightly widened by water erosion over millennia, or maybe crudely enlarged in places by the desperate miners seeking escape decades ago. The walls were jagged, irregular, slick with moisture that reflected their weak headlamp beams in disorienting patterns. Water dripped incessantly from unseen cracks above, each drop echoing unnervingly in the confined space.

They moved in near silence for what felt like a long time, conserving breath, straining their ears for any sound – pursuit from behind, unknown threats ahead. The only noises were their own cautious movements, the drip of water, and the occasional dislodged pebble skittering away into the darkness. The immediate horror of the laboratory, of Echo's frozen form, receded slightly, replaced by the pressing, primal fear of the deep underground, of being lost in the labyrinthine bowels of the earth.

"Did you… see its face?" Elise finally whispered, the sound barely carrying even the few feet to Nora just ahead. She had to break the silence, needed the anchor of connection, needed to process the encounter with the adolescent creature. "In the lab? The younger one?"

Nora paused, turning her head slightly, her profile illuminated briefly by the reflected glow of her lamp. "I saw… sorrow," she replied, her voice low, heavy. "Old sorrow. Not just its own. Echoes."

Elise shivered, understanding perfectly. The adolescent's reaction hadn't been simple fear or surprise; it had been imbued with a profound, heart-wrenching grief, a recognition of the desecration, perhaps even a personal connection to the victim. "It knew her? Or knew *of* her?"

"Perhaps," Nora murmured. "The First People… their memories are long. They pass down stories, warnings, griefs, generation to generation, not just in words, but in spirit, in the resonance of places like that lab. He felt the pain lingering there. He mourned."

The thought was staggering. If the creatures possessed that level of emotional depth, that capacity for memory and empathy across decades… then Kestrel's actions, the cold clinical brutality of the experiments on Echo, the hunt for Goliath, felt even more monstrous. They hadn't just been attacking animals; they had been attacking a people, inflicting wounds that resonated through generations.

"But why retreat?" Elise pressed, needing to understand the baffling sequence of events. "Why show grief one moment, then flee when it heard the others coming?"

Nora navigated a particularly slick patch of rock before answering. "Fear, perhaps. The elders… their rage was great after the gunshot. The young one may have acted against their will, drawn by curiosity or the pull of that sorrowful place. Defying the elders, especially in anger, carries risk in any family, any clan." She paused, her voice dropping lower. "Or perhaps… it was a warning. To us. Showing us the grief, the history, letting us see the truth of what was done, then retreating before the cleansing rage arrived fully."

A warning disguised as grief? It fit the pattern of the creatures' unnervingly sophisticated psychological tactics. Show them the horrors committed by their own kind, emphasize their vulnerability, then withdraw, letting the implications sink in. Elise felt a new wave of dread. If the adolescent's appearance was a calculated warning, what came next?

They continued their descent, the passage twisting, turning, sometimes splitting briefly around large rock pillars before rejoining. The air grew colder, the dripping water more persistent. Several times they had to crouch low to pass under heavy stone lintels, remnants perhaps of the miners' attempts to shore up sections of the natural cave. In one wider section, Elise's light picked out rusted metal fragments embedded in the wall – broken drill bits, a discarded shovel head – confirming the 1973 expedition had indeed penetrated this deep, likely following Miller in his desperate flight.

They found another sign soon after. Lying half-submerged in a pool of stagnant, mineral-stained water was a battered metal canteen, military style, identical to the ones depicted in old photos of geological survey teams from that era. No name, no initials. Just another silent testament to a forgotten presence, a life lost in this crushing darkness. Had Miller carried this? Or Davies? Or McClary, the first miner to disappear according to the logbook?

The passage began to slope downwards more steeply. The sound of dripping water intensified, coalescing into the distinct sound of flowing water ahead. A subterranean stream? Hope surged briefly – fresh water, a potential guide outwards?

Rounding a sharp bend, they saw it. The passage opened into a slightly larger cavern, maybe twenty feet across, but the floor ahead plunged downwards into black, rushing water. A subterranean river, flowing swiftly through the cavern, disappearing into another dark tunnel on the far side. The water wasn't deep, perhaps only waist-high judging by the debris caught on rocks near the edge, but the current looked powerful, turbulent, and impossibly cold.

The passage they were in ended abruptly at a narrow, crumbling ledge overlooking the dark river. There was no bridge, no obvious way across. Looking down, Elise saw no sign of footholds beneath the churning surface. To proceed meant wading into that freezing, fast-moving water, fighting the current, hoping the floor didn't suddenly drop away, hoping to reach the opposite bank and the continuation of the passage before hypothermia set in or the current swept them away into unknown depths.

"Miller's arrow pointed this way," Elise said grimly, shining her light across the dark water towards the opening on the far side. "He must have crossed this. Or tried to."

Nora peered into the churning blackness, her expression deeply troubled. "This water… it runs deep," she murmured. "Feels wrong. Cold that steals the spirit, not just the warmth." She pointed towards the far bank. "The passage continues, yes. But crossing…" She shook her head slowly. "Even strong swimmers would struggle in that current, in the dark. And with Levi…"

She didn't need to finish. Getting Levi across seemed utterly impossible. Even Elise and Nora, exhausted as they were, would be taking an immense risk plunging into that icy torrent.

"Is there another way?" Elise asked, scanning the cavern walls desperately. "Higher up? A ledge?"

They swept their beams upwards. The cavern ceiling arched high above, lost in darkness. The walls were sheer, smooth, water-polished, offering no obvious handholds or alternative routes. This river crossing seemed to be the only path forward indicated by Miller's desperate sign. Had he made it? Or had this been his final resting place?

As they contemplated the daunting obstacle, Elise became aware of it again – the low, subsonic hum. The Resonance. It felt stronger here, closer to the rushing water, vibrating up through the soles of her boots, creating a faint pressure in her ears. It seemed to pulse in rhythm with the flow of the river, a deep, subterranean heartbeat.

"Do you feel that?" she asked Nora quietly.

Nora nodded, her eyes closed for a moment, listening intently not just with her ears, but with her whole being, as Whis Elem had described. "Yes," she breathed. "Stronger here. The water carries it. Amplifies it, perhaps. This river… it flows from a deep place. A place of power. Maybe," her eyes opened, holding a mixture of fear and speculation, "maybe the place the guardians draw their strength from? Or the place the resonance originates?"

The thought was both fascinating and terrifying. Could the strange phenomena – the dead electronics, the spinning compass, the potential psychological effects the miners described – be linked to this subterranean river system, flowing from some powerful geological or energetic source deep within the mountains? And were the Stick-shí'nač intrinsically connected to it, their abilities somehow derived from or amplified by proximity to this resonant power? It opened up entirely new avenues of speculation, suggesting the creatures' relationship with their environment was far deeper, far more complex, than simple ecology.

But the immediate problem remained: crossing the river. As they stood debating the impossible logistics, a new sound reached them, faint but distinct, echoing from the passage *behind* them, the way they had come. A scrape. A heavy footfall, clumsy on the loose rock.

They froze, exchanging terrified glances. Pursuit. The creature — likely the adult male, or perhaps even the wounded elder — hadn't given up. It had followed them through the fissure, tracked them through the winding passages, and was now closing in, trapping them here, between the deadly river and its own relentless approach.

"No time," Boone would have said. They had to move. Now. But how?

Suddenly, Nora gripped Elise's arm, her eyes wide, staring intently not at the river, but at the cavern wall to their right, near where the passage ended at the ledge. "Elise, look! Your light, higher!"

Elise swung her beam upwards along the smooth, damp rock face. At first, she saw nothing but sheer stone. Then, following Nora's gaze, she saw it. About fifteen feet above the ledge, almost invisible against the dark rock, was a narrow horizontal crack, a darker line suggesting a bedding plane or a different rock stratum. And wedged into this crack, spaced several feet apart, were several dark, metallic objects. Pitons. Old, rusted mining pitons, driven deep into the rock decades ago.

"The miners," Elise breathed, realization dawning. "They didn't cross the river here! They traversed *above* it!"

It made sense. Faced with the dangerous current, the experienced miners would have sought an alternative. They must have found this higher crack system, hammered in pitons, likely strung ropes (long since rotted away), and created a precarious hand-traverse route across the cavern, high above the deadly water, presumably reaching another ledge or passage on the far side.

Could they use it? The pitons were ancient, rusted. Would they still hold weight? The traverse itself would be terrifyingly exposed, requiring strength and nerve they barely possessed, especially without ropes. But it was the only alternative to the river or facing the creature closing in behind them.

"The sound behind us... it's closer," Nora urged, her voice tight with urgency. "We must try. Quickly!"

There was no time for hesitation. Stowing her headlamp securely, relying now only on Nora's beam from below, Elise reached for the first piton, grabbing the cold, rusted metal loop. She tested it cautiously, pulling sideways, then downwards. It seemed surprisingly solid, anchored deep in the granite. Taking a deep breath, whispering apologies to Boone and Levi for leaving them behind and for what she was about to attempt, she pulled herself up, finding a precarious foothold on a tiny nubbin of rock, and began the traverse.

It was like clinging to the side of a slick, vertical wall in near darkness, high above a churning abyss. Her fingers, raw and aching, strained to hold the cold metal pitons. Her boots scraped desperately for purchase on tiny irregularities in the rock face. The roar of the river below filled her ears, amplifying the sense of vertigo. She moved agonizingly slowly, inch by painstaking inch, reaching for the next piton, testing it, transferring her weight, acutely aware that a single slip, a single corroded piton giving way, meant a fatal plunge into the icy darkness.

Behind her, Nora began her own ascent, moving with a climber's innate balance and efficiency, despite her age and exhaustion. Her quiet words of encouragement, "Steady now... good hold there... breathe, Child, breathe..." were a lifeline in the terrifying exposure.

They were perhaps halfway across the cavern, maybe thirty feet along the traverse, when a deafening roar echoed from the passage they had just exited. Elise risked a glance downwards. Illuminated briefly by Nora's swinging headlamp beam, a massive, dark shape stood on the ledge below, peering into the river, then tilting its head upwards, its eyes locking onto their exposed figures clinging to the wall.

The adult male. It had found them.

It roared again, a sound of frustration and fury, seeing its prey escaping via an unexpected route. It couldn't reach them directly on the narrow traverse. But it didn't need to.

It lowered its head and charged, not towards the wall, but straight into the churning river. The icy water seemed to barely impede its immense strength. It forged through the current, heading directly for the opposite bank, for the passage entrance they were aiming for. It intended to cut them off, trap them when they tried to descend on the far side.

"Faster, Elise!" Nora urged, her voice sharp with alarm. "It will reach the other side before us!"

Fear lent Elise a desperate, reckless strength. Ignoring the screaming protests of her muscles, the terror clawing at her throat, she scrambled along the remaining pitons, moving faster now, taking more risks, her boots slipping on the wet rock, her fingers numb on the freezing metal. The dark opening on the far side seemed impossibly distant. Below, the creature surged through the turbulent water, its massive shoulders powering against the current, getting closer and closer to the opposite ledge.

Just as Elise reached the final piton, clinging desperately above the dark passage entrance on the far side, the creature hauled itself out of the river onto the opposite ledge, shaking spray from its thick fur, turning its burning gaze upwards towards her. It was waiting. Blocking their descent. Trapping them high on the cavern wall.

There was nowhere left to run. The desperate escape route had led them directly into a final, seemingly inescapable confrontation, high above a deadly subterranean river, face to face with the enraged guardian whose pursuit had been relentless, patient, and ultimately, successful. The echoes in the stone had led them not to safety, but to the very edge of the abyss.

Chapter 12: The Heart of the Mountain

Trapped. High above the churning black river, clinging precariously to the final rusted piton, Elise stared down into the furious eyes of the adult male Stick-shí'nač standing on the ledge below. Its massive chest heaved, water streaming from its dark, matted fur. A low growl rumbled in its throat, a promise of imminent violence. It had cut them off, anticipated their desperate traverse, and now held them pinned against the cold, unforgiving rock face. Nora clung to the piton just behind Elise, her breathing ragged, her usual calm composure finally cracking under the strain and the immediacy of the threat. There was no escape route upwards; the fissure ended here. Descending meant dropping directly into the creature's waiting grasp. They were utterly, terrifyingly cornered.

"Well, shit," Elise heard herself whisper, the absurdity of the situation hitting her alongside the wave of terror. All the running, the hiding, the desperate climbs and crawls, the sacrifices made – all for it to end here, clinging to a corroded piece of metal sixty feet above a subterranean river, facing down a creature of myth and nightmare.

The creature didn't charge immediately. It seemed to be assessing them, perhaps savoring the moment, its deep-set eyes moving from Elise to Nora, then scanning the empty traverse line back the way they had come. Did it realize they were the last? Did it sense their exhaustion, their despair? Its intelligence felt palpable, calculating, making the confrontation even more terrifying than a simple predatory attack.

"What do we do?" Elise breathed, glancing back at Nora, her voice barely audible over the roar of the river below.

Nora shook her head slowly, her face grim. "There is... nowhere to go," she murmured, stating the obvious. She shifted her grip slightly, readying the axe that still hung from her belt — a pitiful weapon against such power, but a symbol of defiance, perhaps.

Down below, the creature shifted its immense weight, took a step closer to the base of the rock face directly beneath them. It tilted its head back, exposing the thick column of its neck, and let out a series of sharp, guttural barks — not a roar of rage this time, but clearly a signal, echoing down the dark passage from which it had emerged. Was it calling the others? The elder? Reinforcements? The thought sent a fresh wave of panic through Elise. Facing one was impossible; facing more was unthinkable annihilation.

Think, Elise, think! Her scientific mind, battered by trauma and fear, struggled to assert itself. Analyze the situation. Observe the behavior. Find a weakness. Exploit an opportunity. The creature was immensely strong, clearly intelligent, possessed intimate knowledge of this subterranean environment. But what were its limitations? Its motivations? It hadn't killed Levi immediately; it had carried him off. It hadn't attacked them directly in the lab, allowing the adolescent its moment of grief. Its violence seemed triggered primarily by perceived threats (the gunshot), direct challenges (Boone's attack), or attempts to escape its perceived territory or control (Graves' climb, their traverse).

Could they de-escalate again? Unlikely, after the events in the sanctuary. Could they fight? Suicidal. Could they... distract it? Divert its attention long enough to attempt... what? Descending past it seemed impossible.

Her eyes scanned the cavern frantically, searching for any advantage, any anomaly. The rushing river below. The smooth, sheer walls. The darkness of the passages leading away. The rusted pitons they clung to... And then she saw it. Not a weakness, but a potential tool. A desperate, incredibly risky idea sparked in her oxygen-starved brain.

Hanging from one of the pitons midway along the traverse, snagged perhaps during their panicked scramble across, was a loose coil of the thin, dark rope they had found dangling down the ventilation shaft – the rope Nora had identified as Tallsalt knotwork. Elise hadn't even noticed it until now. It wasn't thick enough or long enough to rappel down safely, but perhaps... perhaps it could be used differently.

"Nora," Elise whispered urgently, nodding towards the dangling rope. "Can you reach that?"

Nora followed her gaze, understanding dawning instantly. "Maybe," she breathed, assessing the distance, the precarious reach required. "If I swing out slightly..."

"No time!" Elise hissed, hearing movement, heavy shuffling sounds echoing from the passage behind the creature below. The others were coming. "Just... try!"

While the creature below seemed momentarily distracted, perhaps listening for its approaching kin, Nora, with astonishing agility born of desperation, leaned out precariously from her piton, stretching, her fingers just brushing the dangling rope. She hooked it, pulled it towards her, securing the loose end quickly around her wrist with a practiced knot.

"Got it!" she confirmed, her voice tight with strain.

"Okay," Elise said, her mind racing, formulating the desperate plan. "The pitons... they're old, rusted. Strong enough to hold our weight, barely. But maybe not strong enough to hold... *its* weight, if enough force is applied." She looked down at the creature, then back at the piton she currently clung to, the one closest to the ledge. "We need to anchor this rope securely to this last piton, then somehow… get the other end down there, loop it around its ankle or leg when it moves closer?"

It sounded insane. Trying to lasso a nine-foot-tall subterranean giant from sixty feet above?

Nora didn't question the madness. She simply began working, her deft fingers securing one end of the thin rope firmly to the rusted metal loop of the final piton, reinforcing the knot several times.

Below, the creature barked again, impatiently. Heavy footsteps echoed closer from the passage behind it. Time was up.

"Okay," Elise took a shaky breath. "The loop. Can you make a wide loop on the free end? Big enough…?"

Nora worked quickly, forming a large, loose loop, maybe six feet across, in the remaining length of the rope. "Ready," she whispered.

Now came the impossible part. Elise looked down. The creature stood almost directly beneath them now, head tilted back, watching them, growling low in its chest, waiting for its companions to emerge. If she dropped the loop now, it would likely land around its head or shoulders, easily shrugged off or grabbed. She needed it lower, around its powerful legs, its anchor point, hoping its forward momentum combined with the leverage from above might be enough to pull the ancient piton free from the rock.

"I need… to make it move," Elise muttered, more to herself than Nora. "Make it lunge… just a little."

She looked down into those dark, intelligent eyes. She thought of the adolescent's curiosity, the elder's focused rage, the power, the history, the pain inflicted by her own kind. An idea, utterly reckless, terrifying, sparked. She met the creature's gaze directly. And then, drawing on the memory from the sanctuary, forcing the sound past the lump of terror in her throat, she hummed. Low, resonant, mimicking the sound the elder had made, the sound the adolescent had echoed. HMMMMMMMMMMMM.

The reaction was instantaneous. The creature recoiled slightly, startled by the sound coming from her, its growl cutting off abruptly. Its head cocked, confusion warring with hostility in its deep-set eyes. It took an involuntary half-step backwards, momentarily off balance.

"NOW!" Elise screamed.

Nora, anticipating the moment, didn't hesitate. With a flick of her wrist honed by years of casting fishing nets, she dropped the looped end of the rope downwards. It fell through the dim air, uncoiling, guided by gravity and Nora's expert aim.

The loop landed perfectly, settling around the creature's thick, hairy ankles just as it regained its footing, preparing to lunge forward again, enraged by the mimicry. It roared, startled by the sudden entanglement, stomping its massive foot, trying to shake the rope free.

"PULL!" Elise yelled, throwing her entire weight, along with Nora's, backwards against the final piton, yanking the rope taut.

For a heart-stopping second, nothing happened. The creature strained against the rope, immense muscles bulging. The piton groaned in the rock, flakes of rust showering down. Elise felt the metal begin to give, to shift slightly in its ancient seating.

Just then, two more massive figures emerged from the passage behind the first creature, likely the elder and another adult, drawn by the commotion. Seeing their companion snared, they roared in fury and confusion.

The snared creature, perhaps panicked by the arrival of the others or enraged by the constraint, gave a final, tremendous heave, lunging forward towards the rock wall, intending to climb, to reach them.

That was the critical moment. Its forward momentum, combined with the sudden, sharp backward pull from Elise and Nora, put an intolerable strain on the ancient piton. With a horrifying screech of protesting metal and fracturing rock, the piton ripped free from the wall.

Elise and Nora cried out, swinging violently sideways, held only by Nora's grip on the next piton back along the traverse. The rope, now anchored only to empty air, snapped taut around the creature's ankles.

The creature, caught mid-lunge, its balance already compromised, roared in surprise and agony as the sudden loss of resistance from the piton sent it stumbling forward uncontrollably. Its massive feet slipped on the slick ledge. For a terrifying instant, it flailed, its long arms windmilling, trying to regain purchase. But its own immense weight and momentum were too much.

With a final, echoing bellow that seemed to shake the entire cavern, the adult male Stick-shí'nač tumbled backwards off the ledge, plunging into the churning black water of the subterranean river below. The splash was colossal, echoing like depth charge. The creature surfaced briefly, roaring, thrashing against the powerful current, tangled in the now-useless rope. But the river was too strong, too cold. It was swept swiftly downstream, disappearing into the darkness of the tunnel on the far side, its roars fading into the rush of the water.

Silence descended again, broken only by the roar of the river and the ragged gasps of Elise and Nora, clinging desperately to the remaining pitons. They stared downwards, then at each other, disbelief warring with shock. Their insane gamble had worked. They had used the creature's own strength, the decay of human intrusion, and a desperate understanding of leverage against it. They had eliminated the immediate threat.

But their relief was short-lived. On the ledge below, the two remaining creatures – the elder and the other adult – stood staring first at the river where their companion had vanished, then slowly, deliberately, up towards Elise and Nora. Their faces were unreadable in the dim light, but the silence radiating from them felt heavier, colder, more menacing than the earlier rage. They didn't roar. They didn't charge. They simply watched.

Then, the elder slowly raised its massive head and let out a single, long, mournful howl. It wasn't a sound of anger or aggression. It was a sound of profound loss, of deep, echoing grief, a lament that seemed to resonate with the very heartbeat of the mountain, acknowledging the death of one of its own. The sound tore through Elise, bypassing fear, striking directly at the shared vulnerability of mortality, of loss.

After the howl faded, the elder turned its gaze back to Elise and Nora, pinning them with an intensity that felt ancient and absolute. It held their gaze for a long, silent moment. Then, without another sound, it turned, and with the other adult following closely, melted back into the darkness of the passage they had emerged from, disappearing completely.

They were alone again. Clinging to the rock face, trembling with reaction, staring into the empty passage below. The creatures hadn't attacked again. They had mourned their fallen companion, then… withdrawn. Why? Was it respect for their desperate, successful tactic? Was it a strategic retreat, recognizing the traverse was now impassable without the final piton? Or was it something else? Had the howl been not just grief, but a signal? A marking? A deferral of vengeance?

Elise didn't know. All she knew was that they were still alive, miraculously. The immediate threat had passed, but the cost was another death – not one of theirs this time, but one of the guardians. Had they just escalated the conflict irrevocably? Or had their desperate act somehow, paradoxically, earned them a different kind of passage?

Slowly, carefully, muscles screaming, nerves frayed beyond measure, Elise and Nora began the painstaking process of descending the last few feet from the remaining pitons onto the now-empty ledge beside the river. Reaching solid ground felt like landing after a fall from a great height. They collapsed onto the cold stone, side-by-side, too exhausted, too shocked to speak, listening to the roar of the river that had become both their adversary and their unlikely savior, carrying away the body of their pursuer into the unknown depths of the earth. They had reached the heart of the mountain, faced the guardians, and survived through desperate ingenuity and tragic necessity. But the way forward remained shrouded in darkness, and the echoes of the elder's mournful howl promised that their journey through the Hollow Ground was far from over.

Chapter 13: The River Runs Deep

The silence that followed the elder's mournful howl was heavier, colder, than any physical weight. It pressed down on Elise and Nora, clinging to the damp rock ledge beside the churning subterranean river, magnifying the roar of the water until it felt like the only sound left in the universe. They huddled together, shoulders touching, drawing a fragile warmth from proximity, shivering uncontrollably in the aftermath of terror and exertion.

Elise stared into the blackness of the passage where the Stick-shí'nač elder and its companion had retreated. They hadn't attacked again. After the devastating loss of their kin, after cornering the humans who had caused it, they had simply… left. It made no logical sense according to any predatory or territorial behavior Elise understood. An apex predator, enraged and grieving, faced with cornered, weakened prey responsible for its loss – the outcome should have been swift, brutal annihilation. Yet, they had withdrawn.

"Why?" Elise whispered again, the question echoing the hollow space inside her chest. "Why didn't they finish us?"

Nora shook her head slowly, her gaze also fixed on the empty passage. She pulled her thin blanket tighter, though it offered little protection against the penetrating cold radiating from the wet rock and the river's icy breath. "Perhaps… perhaps the death was enough," she murmured, her voice thick with exhaustion and awe. "An eye for an eye, a life for a life. Boone… and the one who fell into the river. Balance restored, in their way?"

It was a chilling thought – that these ancient beings might operate under a code of retribution so stark, so immediate. Did Boone's unseen death in the fissure count in their calculus? Had their desperate act of self-defense, resulting in the creature's plunge into the river, inadvertently balanced the scales? Elise couldn't accept it, couldn't reduce Boone's sacrifice or the creature's death to some primitive equation. Yet, the alternative explanations – strategic retreat, simple disinterest now that the immediate threat (Boone) was gone, or some deeper motive beyond human ken – felt equally inadequate. The guardians remained an enigma, their actions defying easy categorization, terrifying in their unpredictability.

"Or maybe," Elise offered another possibility, her mind grasping for strategic rather than spiritual explanations, "they know we can't get out this way either. The piton's gone. We can't go back across the traverse. Maybe they sealed the other entrance behind us, and this passage…" she glanced towards the dark opening beside them, "…is another dead end. Maybe they're content to let the mountain finish us. Starvation. Hypothermia."

Nora considered this grimly. "Possible. This deep… the earth itself can be the hunter." She pushed herself stiffly upright, wincing as sore muscles protested. "But we cannot stay here. This ledge offers no shelter. And the river… its voice speaks of deeper cold ahead."

Elise forced herself to move as well, her body screaming with fatigue. Every joint ached, her hands were raw and bleeding from the traverse, her clothes were soaked and freezing. But Nora was right. Staying here meant surrendering to the elements, to despair. Their only path, however uncertain, lay forward, into the passage the creatures had used.

They took a moment to assess their meager resources. Half a canteen of water each, perhaps two crushed energy bars between them. Their first aid kit was depleted of painkillers and heavy bandages used on Levi. Their headlamp batteries were fading fast, casting increasingly weak, yellowish beams. Their physical reserves were almost gone. Hope felt like a distant memory. All that remained was stubborn, instinctual survival.

"Okay," Elise said, taking a shaky breath. "Let's see where this leads. Stay alert. Move slow."

Nora nodded, retrieving her axe, its weight seeming to offer her some small comfort or resolve. Elise checked the action on her pistol – only a few rounds left – before holstering it, knowing it was likely useless but unable to discard the habit of readiness.

They turned towards the dark opening. Unlike the fissure they had descended or the tight passage from the miners' chamber, this tunnel felt different. Larger, more uniform in shape, the walls smoother, almost polished in places, suggesting frequent passage by immense bodies over vast stretches of time. The air within felt slightly less frigid than the river cavern, carrying the familiar musty scent of the creatures, but also a cleaner, drier undertone, hinting perhaps at ventilation or connection to other systems.

They moved forward cautiously, headlamp beams cutting weakly through the profound darkness. The tunnel floor was mostly level, packed earth mixed with fine gravel, bearing the faint, smoothed impressions of enormous, unshod feet. It sloped gently downwards, following the likely course of the subterranean river flowing somewhere nearby, its roar now a muffled presence felt more through the rock than heard directly.

After a hundred yards or so, the tunnel began to curve gently to the right. And here, new features emerged on the walls, confirming this was more than just a natural passage; it was part of the Stick-shí'nač's established domain. Faint carvings, similar to the complex, interwoven patterns Elise had seen in the sanctuary and along the Hollow Trail, appeared sporadically, etched deep into the stone. They weren't warnings like the X's or the crude figure in the Grove of Symbols; these felt more like markers, perhaps indicating direction, clan boundaries, or sites of significance. Some depicted stylized animal forms – giant elk with exaggerated antlers, powerful-looking bears or cave bears, serpentine shapes that might represent the river itself. Others were purely abstract, labyrinthine designs that seemed to draw the eye inwards, hinting at a complex symbolic language Elise couldn't begin to decipher.

Integrated with the carvings were physical objects, placed deliberately in niches or on natural ledges along the tunnel walls. Carefully stacked piles of unusually shaped river stones. Arrangements of large animal vertebrae – elk, perhaps even mammoth or mastodon from a previous geological era? – forming strange, almost architectural patterns. And in one wider alcove, leaning against the wall, was a single, immense spear, easily fifteen feet long, its shaft fashioned from a smooth, dark wood Elise didn't recognize, its tip a wickedly sharp shard of obsidian hafted expertly with sinew and pitch. A weapon. Confirmation of tool use far beyond simple digging sticks. The scale of it, designed for a hand and strength far exceeding human capability, was chilling.

"They pass this way often," Nora murmured, running a hand gently over a smooth section of wall, worn down by the passage of countless bodies over countless years. "This is... a main thoroughfare for them. Leading deeper."

"Deeper towards what?" Elise wondered aloud, feeling increasingly like an ant crawling through the hidden corridors of giants. "More sanctuaries? Nesting grounds? Or just... further into the earth?"

The tunnel continued its gentle descent. The roar of the river grew slightly louder again, suggesting they were nearing its course once more. The air remained still, the silence broken only by their own footsteps and the distant water sounds. The feeling of being watched had lessened somewhat since the creatures' withdrawal, replaced by a sense of profound intrusion, of walking through someone else's home uninvited.

They encountered another obstacle soon after: a place where the tunnel ceiling had partially collapsed eons ago, creating a low, narrow crawlspace choked with debris. Immense slabs of rock lay tilted against each other, leaving only a gap perhaps two feet high. It looked impassable. But closer inspection revealed the debris within the crawlspace had been deliberately shifted, smaller rocks moved aside, creating a narrow, tight passage through the blockage, just large enough for something immensely strong and determined to wriggle through. Smoothed earth and drag marks indicated the Stick-shí'nač used this constricted passage regularly.

For Elise and Nora, already weakened and carrying packs, it presented a terrifying challenge. Stripping off their backpacks, pushing them ahead, they had to get down on their bellies, wriggling through the tight, claustrophobic space, sharp rocks scraping against their clothes and skin, the immense weight of the collapsed ceiling pressing down just inches above their heads. Dust filled their noses and mouths, the air thick and stagnant. Elise fought back waves of panic, imagining the crawlspace collapsing further, trapping them, burying them alive. It took ten agonizing minutes to push through the thirty-foot blockage, emerging on the other side coated in dust, hearts pounding, muscles trembling with exertion and relief.

Beyond the crawlspace, the tunnel widened again, opening into another vast cavern. This one, however, was different from the river cavern or the hidden sanctuary. It was filled with water. A huge, subterranean lake stretched out before them, its surface perfectly still, black as obsidian, reflecting the weak beams of their headlamps like a void staring back. The cavern ceiling was invisible, lost in impenetrable darkness far above. The only sounds were the echo of their own breathing and the impossibly faint drip... drip... drip of water from unseen stalactites, each drop landing with a soft plink that resonated eerily across the vast, silent lake.

The tunnel they were in ended at the water's edge, a narrow beach of fine, dark sand. There was no obvious path around the lake; the cavern walls seemed to plunge directly into the black water on all sides. Across the immense expanse of water, perhaps several hundred yards away, Elise could just make out the faint suggestion of another opening, another passage leading onwards, barely discernible in the distant gloom.

"Now what?" Elise breathed, staring out across the unnerving stillness of the underground lake. "Swim?" The thought of plunging into that cold, bottomless blackness, unsure of the distance, unsure what might lurk beneath the surface, was horrifying.

Nora knelt at the water's edge, dipping her hand in cautiously. She drew it back quickly. "Cold," she confirmed. "Deep cold. Like the river. And... still. Too still." She scanned the surface, her expression troubled. "This water... it feels old. Undisturbed. Places like this... sometimes hold things other than fish."

Elise followed her gaze, peering into the black depths near the shore. The water was surprisingly clear, though dark. She could see the sandy bottom sloping away rapidly. And lying partially submerged near the edge, half-hidden by shadows, were more bones. Not the scattered leavings of nests, but large, articulated skeletons, seemingly undisturbed for centuries. She recognized the massive rib cage of an elk, the skull of a large bear... and something else. Something bigger. Immense, curved tusks, partially buried in the sand, connected to a colossal skull fragment. Mammoth? Mastodon? Creatures extinct for ten thousand years, preserved perfectly in this cold, anaerobic environment. This lake was a graveyard, a repository of ancient life and death.

And if creatures that large were preserved here... what else might be?

As if summoned by the thought, a faint ripple disturbed the perfect stillness of the lake surface, far out towards the center. Not caused by dripping water. Something larger, moving beneath. Elise froze, grabbing Nora's arm, pointing silently. They watched, breathless, as another ripple appeared, then another, tracing a slow, deliberate path across the black water, heading vaguely in their direction before submerging again, leaving the surface once more like polished obsidian.

"What was that?" Elise whispered, her voice tight with renewed fear.

"Something swims," Nora murmured, her hand gripping her axe handle. "Something large. And comfortable in the dark."

They backed away from the water's edge, retreating further into the tunnel entrance, scanning the lake surface, the surrounding darkness. The feeling of being watched returned, but this time it felt different – colder, less intelligent perhaps, more primally predatory. Was this lake inhabited by some unique, adapted cave fauna? Giant salamanders? Blind cave fish grown monstrous in the absence of predators? Or something stranger, something drawn to the resonance, thriving in the deep earth alongside the Stick-shí'nač?

The path forward was blocked again, this time by a seemingly impassable body of water potentially inhabited by unknown dangers. Escape seemed more impossible than ever. They were trapped between the known threat behind them (the potentially pursuing guardians) and the unknown threat lurking within the black lake before them.

Elise slumped against the tunnel wall, despair washing over her in a debilitating wave. Every route led to a dead end, an insurmountable obstacle, a new terror. They had survived so much, pushed through exhaustion, grief, fear... only to end up here, facing a bottomless lake in the heart of the earth, with unseen things stirring in its depths.

"Maybe... maybe Graves was right," she choked out, the words tasting like ash. "Maybe this is just a dead end. No way out."

Nora didn't respond immediately. She stood staring out at the black lake, her face etched with concentration, seemingly listening again, not just with her ears, but with her whole being, trying to read the energy of this deep, silent place. The faint resonance Elise had felt earlier seemed stronger here too, a low thrumming pulse that seemed to emanate from the water itself.

After a long moment, Nora turned to Elise, her eyes holding a strange mixture of fear and... something else. Determination? Understanding? "The miners," Nora said slowly. "Miller, Davies... they wrote of resonance. Of the stones whispering. Of being shown the way." She looked back towards the lake. "This place holds power, Elise. Deep power. The water carries it. Perhaps... perhaps the path isn't *around* the lake, or *through* it." She pointed towards the dark, still surface. "Perhaps the path *is* the lake."

Elise stared at her. "What are you saying? Swim? With that... thing... out there?"

"No," Nora shook her head. "Not swim." She pointed towards the far side of the small sandy beach where the tunnel ended. Partially hidden behind a cluster of stalagmites, almost invisible until pointed out, was something that didn't look entirely natural. A collection of large, unusually buoyant-looking logs, lashed together crudely with what looked like thick, fibrous vines, forming a rough, primitive raft. Beside it lay several long, pole-like branches, smoothed and slightly charred at one end.

It was unmistakable. A means of transport across the lake. Crude, ancient, but functional. Created and left here by... the Stick-shí'nač?

"They cross here," Nora breathed, awe in her voice. "This is their passage. Their boat." She approached the raft cautiously, examining the construction, the immense logs clearly carried here from the surface world somehow, the thick vine lashings. "They navigate the darkness. They know the currents. They understand the lake, perhaps even... the things within it."

The implications were staggering. The creatures didn't just use the tunnels; they navigated subterranean waterways. They built tools for transport. Their understanding and mastery of this deep, hidden world was far greater than Elise had imagined.

But why was the raft here? Left conveniently for them? Or simply awaiting its owners' return? And the creature in the lake… did the Stick-shí'nač coexist with it? Avoid it? Control it?

Using the raft felt like another immense gamble. It was their only way forward, seemingly. But taking it felt like stealing from the guardians, a further violation. And crossing that black, silent lake, potentially sharing it with the unseen swimmer, felt like paddling into the jaws of a different kind of monster.

Yet, as Elise looked at Nora's determined face, at the primitive raft waiting silently at the edge of the abyss, she knew they had no other choice. The path forward lay across the water, into deeper darkness, relying on the tools of the very beings they feared, hoping to navigate a passage meant for giants, praying the price of crossing wasn't higher than they could possibly imagine. The heart of the mountain held one more terrifying trial.

Chapter 14: The Black Mere

The silence of the vast cavern pressed in, heavy and expectant, broken only by the steady drip, drip, drip of water from the unseen ceiling high above and the faint, ragged counterpoint of their own breathing. Before them stretched the subterranean lake, a sheet of perfect black glass reflecting the feeble beams of their dying headlamps, seeming to swallow the light rather than return it. The air hung cold and still, thick with the scent of ancient stone and the faint, unsettling metallic tang of deep earth minerals. Across the water, impossibly distant, lay the suggestion of another passage, a dark promise of continuation into the unknown heart of the mountain.

Elise stared at the crude raft nestled amongst the stalagmites at the water's edge – immense logs, clearly dragged here from some surface world long ago, lashed together with thick, fibrous vines, a testament to the Stick-shí'nač's surprising ingenuity and mastery of this hidden realm. It was their only conceivable way forward. The alternative was backtracking towards the certain threat of the pursuing guardians, or remaining here to succumb to starvation and the cloying darkness.

Yet, the thought of launching onto that black, silent water, knowing something large and unknown had disturbed its surface moments before, felt like stepping willingly into an open grave. The lake felt wrong, ancient, imbued with a sentience colder and perhaps even older than the Stick-shí'nač themselves. Nora's unease was palpable beside her, a shared vibration of fear and reluctance.

"We have to try," Elise said finally, her voice barely a whisper, yet sounding unnaturally loud in the stillness. The words felt inadequate, forced, a statement of desperation rather than conviction. "It's the only path left."

Nora didn't reply verbally, but gave a slow, almost imperceptible nod. Her face, illuminated fleetingly by the sweep of Elise's weakening beam, was a mask of weary determination, overlaid with the deep, ingrained respect her people held for places of potent natural power. She approached the raft cautiously, running her hands over the rough logs, the taut vine lashings.

"Strong," she murmured, assessing the construction. "Built to last. Built to carry… great weight." She looked back at Elise, her eyes dark with unspoken meaning. "Taking it… feels like borrowing power we haven't earned. It might carry a cost."

"Staying here costs us everything," Elise countered grimly, though Nora's words resonated with her own deep unease. She pushed aside the ethical qualms, the fear of transgression. Survival demanded action, however risky, however potentially disrespectful to the unseen owners of this vessel.

Together, they began the arduous process of maneuvering the raft towards the water. It was incredibly heavy, the waterlogged timber resisting their combined, depleted strength. They strained, grunting with effort, muscles screaming, feet slipping on the damp sand and loose pebbles. The scraping sound of the logs moving across the beach echoed alarmingly in the vast cavern, seeming to broadcast their intentions into the listening darkness. Elise kept casting fearful glances towards the black, still surface of the lake, half-expecting the ripples to reappear, half-expecting something monstrous to rise from the depths in response to the disturbance. But the water remained placid, inscrutable, reflecting only their own wavering lights.

Finally, with a last, desperate heave, the raft slid partially into the frigid water, bumping gently against the submerged skeletons near the shore. It floated, surprisingly buoyant despite its immense size. They retrieved the long, smoothed poles left beside it – steering implements, likely – and gathered their meager packs, securing them as best they could to the center of the rough log platform.

"Ready?" Elise asked, her voice trembling slightly.

Nora took a deep breath, closed her eyes for a moment as if offering a silent plea or apology, then nodded. "Ready."

Wading into the shockingly cold water up to their knees, they pushed the raft further out until it floated freely, then scrambled aboard, collapsing onto the damp, uneven logs, shivering violently from the cold and reaction. The raft dipped alarmingly under their weight but remained stable. They were afloat, adrift on the black mere, the shore they had just left already receding into the oppressive darkness behind them.

Using the poles, they began propelling the raft slowly, awkwardly, away from the shore, aiming towards the faint suggestion of the passage on the far side. Poling was difficult; the lake floor seemed to drop away steeply, offering little purchase for the poles beyond the first few yards. Soon, they were relying on using the poles like crude paddles, digging into the heavy, still water, each stroke requiring immense effort from their exhausted arms. Progress was agonizingly slow.

The darkness was absolute beyond the small pools of light cast by their headlamps. The cavern walls were invisible, the ceiling lost in infinite blackness. They felt utterly adrift in a void, the only reality the small circle of the raft, the cold black water beneath, and the rhythmic splash and drip of their poling. The silence pressed in, broken only by their own exertions and the pervasive drip… drip… drip… from somewhere high above, echoing like a metronome marking their slow passage across the abyss.

It was here, in the center of the lake, surrounded by darkness and silence, that the Resonance returned with overwhelming intensity. It wasn't just a faint vibration felt through the soles of their boots anymore; it was a physical presence, a low-frequency thrum that seemed to emanate from the depths beneath them, vibrating through the water, through the logs of the raft, into their very bones. It created a disorienting pressure behind Elise's eyes, made her teeth ache, induced a faint nausea. The air itself seemed to hum, thick with an unseen energy.

"Nora… do you feel it?" Elise gasped, pausing her poling, feeling suddenly dizzy.

Nora nodded grimly, her knuckles white where she gripped her pole. "The mountain's heart," she breathed, her voice tight. "Or… the lake's song. Strong here. Very strong." She looked down at the black water warily. "This power… it can… change things. Change perceptions. Show you things that are not there. Or hide things that are."

Elise understood. The miners' logbook – *the stones whisper… showed him the way…* Miller and Davies hadn't just succumbed to despair; perhaps they had been overwhelmed, their minds fractured, by this pervasive, psychoactive resonance, amplified by the deep water. Was it affecting her now? Was the dizziness, the nausea, just exhaustion, or the beginning of something worse? She forced herself to focus, to breathe deeply, fighting against the disorienting thrum.

As if in response to the intensified resonance, or perhaps just coincidence, the lake's stillness was broken again. A slow, oily swirl appeared on the surface twenty yards to their left, the water bulging upwards slightly before subsiding, leaving behind concentric ripples spreading outwards across the black glass.

Elise's breath hitched. Nora stopped poling, her eyes fixed on the spot. They floated in silence, raft drifting slightly, every nerve ending screaming.

Then, directly beneath them, something immense shifted in the darkness. It wasn't a visual sighting, but a feeling, a displacement of water, a sudden pressure wave that made the heavy log raft bob sickeningly. Elise felt a cold sweat break out on her forehead. It was down there. Right beneath them. Huge. Ancient. Aware.

She shone her headlamp beam downwards into the water, but the light penetrated only a few feet, revealing nothing but impenetrable blackness. Whatever lurked below remained hidden, a creature perfectly adapted to this lightless, timeless abyss.

For several terrifying minutes, they remained frozen, waiting for an attack that didn't come. The presence beneath them seemed to fade, the pressure lessened. Had it lost interest? Or was it simply circling, observing, deciding?

"Keep poling," Nora whispered finally, her voice strained but steady. "Do not show fear. Do not provoke. We are… guests in its house. Uninvited. Show respect. Move steadily."

Finding reserves of strength fueled by sheer terror, they resumed their laborious paddling, trying to maintain a steady rhythm, trying not to betray their panic with erratic movements. Every splash echoed too loudly. Every creak of the vine lashings felt like a gunshot. They kept their headlamp beams pointed forward, towards the distant promise of the far shore, deliberately avoiding shining them directly into the water, following Nora's instinct to show deference, avoid challenge.

The crossing felt endless. Time lost all meaning. There was only the rhythmic paddling, the cold, the darkness, the oppressive silence broken by drips and splashes, the constant thrum of the Resonance, and the terrifying knowledge of the unseen presence sharing the black water with them.

Elise's mind drifted, exhaustion blurring the edges of reality. She saw images swim before her eyes – the Stick-shí'nač elder's mournful howl, Levi's face pale in the fissure's gloom, Boone charging into the darkness, the frozen agony of Echo on the gurney. Grief and fear washed over her in waves, threatening to pull her under, into the cold apathy of despair. She thought of the files hidden back in the cave, the miners' logbook. Was this their fate too? To become another mystery swallowed by the deep earth, another set of bones preserved in the cold silence?

"Almost there, Child." Nora's voice, quiet but firm, broke through her dark thoughts.

Elise blinked, forcing her focus back to the present. Nora was right. The darkness ahead seemed slightly less absolute. The faint outline of the far cavern wall was becoming discernible, and the opening of the passage they aimed for looked closer, larger. Hope, thin but tenacious, flickered again.

They paddled with renewed urgency, arms burning, shoulders screaming, driven by the proximity of solid ground. The last fifty yards felt like miles, the raft seeming to move sluggishly through water that felt unnaturally thick, resistant. Elise didn't dare look back, didn't dare scan the lake surface, focusing only on the approaching shore.

Finally, with a gentle bump, the front logs of the raft nudged against submerged rocks near the edge. They had made it.

Scrambling off the raft into the knee-deep, numbing water felt glorious, despite the cold. Reaching the narrow strip of sandy beach felt like reaching paradise. They stood for a moment, leaning against the cavern wall, gasping for breath, looking back at the raft floating silently just offshore, then out at the vast, black expanse of the lake. The surface remained still, offering no clue to the presence beneath. Had it simply tolerated their passage? Or had it been assessing them, deciding they weren't worth the effort, perhaps? The ambiguity was almost as terrifying as an overt attack.

"Leave the raft?" Elise asked, breathing heavily.

Nora considered it, looking from the raft back towards the passage they needed to enter. "Yes," she decided. "Leave it as we found it. A sign of… respect. Or perhaps, simply acknowledgment. We borrowed passage. Now we return their vessel." It felt right. Any other action – hiding it, damaging it – felt like inviting further retribution.

They gathered their packs, took one last look at the silent, black mere and the immense cavern housing it, then turned towards the new passage. This opening was similar in size to the one they had exited on the other side, a natural tunnel leading away from the lake shore, sloping slightly upwards. The air inside felt marginally fresher, though still cold and damp.

As they stepped into the darkness of the new tunnel, Elise glanced back one last time. Did she see a flicker of movement on the lake surface far out in the center? A ripple? Or just a trick of her fading headlamp beam, her exhausted eyes? She couldn't be sure.

They left the lake behind, plunging once more into the uncertainty of the subterranean labyrinth. They had survived the crossing, endured the Resonance, evaded the unseen swimmer. They had used the guardians' own tools to traverse their hidden waterway. But the cost had been immense, draining their last physical reserves. And the path ahead remained unknown, leading deeper still into the heart of the mountain, towards a destination they could only guess at, driven by the faintest glimmer of hope that somewhere, somehow, this oppressive darkness held a path back towards the light. The river ran deep, and its secrets, like those of the valley above, were far from fully revealed.

Chapter 15: Whispers of the Lost

The darkness that enveloped them in the passage beyond the subterranean lake felt different yet again. It was a dry, dusty blackness, less heavy than the crushing silence of the Hollow, less resonant than the air within the river cavern, yet somehow older, imbued with the stillness of ages undisturbed. The faint, musty scent of ancient decay mingled with the sharp tang of mineral dust, hinting at immense geological time scales. Their headlamp beams, reduced now to pitifully weak, flickering circles of yellowish light, barely penetrated the gloom, revealing a tunnel that seemed more natural cave system than deliberately constructed passage.

Elise stumbled forward, leaning heavily on Nora for support, her legs trembling violently, reaction setting in after the terrifying lake crossing. Every muscle fibre screamed with fatigue. The cold from the lake water had seeped deep into her bones, leaving her shivering despite the slight rise in ambient temperature within this drier tunnel. Hunger was a constant, hollow ache low in her belly. Beside her, Nora moved with a similar, deep weariness, her usual resilience strained to its absolute limit, though her steps remained marginally steadier, her senses still alert.

They pushed forward, driven by the primal need to put distance between themselves and the black mere, the unseen swimmer, the memory of the creature plunging into the depths. The floor here was uneven, littered with fallen rocks and coated in a fine, almost powdery dust that rose in choking clouds with each step. Water still dripped from the unseen ceiling high above, but less persistently than before, the echoes softer, less menacing in the drier air.

"We need… to rest," Elise gasped finally, after perhaps twenty minutes of stumbling progress, her vision blurring, knees threatening to buckle entirely. "Just… five minutes."

Nora didn't argue. She guided Elise towards the tunnel wall, helping her slide down onto the dusty floor, slumping against the cold stone. Nora sank down beside her, pulling her thin blanket around both their shoulders, a small gesture of shared warmth against the encroaching chill and exhaustion. They sat in silence for a few moments, the only sounds their own ragged breathing and the distant, almost forgotten drip of water.

"Do you think… they followed?" Elise whispered eventually, voicing the fear that lingered despite the creatures' withdrawal at the river cavern. "The elder… the others?"

Nora tilted her head, listening intently to the profound silence. "I do not feel… their immediate presence," she replied slowly. "The anger… the focused intent… it is gone. Faded. Like a storm that has passed over." She paused, her brow furrowed. "But this place… it remembers. Their passage is etched into the stone. We walk their ancient paths. They are never truly far away in spirit, even if their bodies have retreated."

The thought offered little comfort. Elise shone her weak beam around the immediate area. The tunnel walls here were different – less smooth, more fractured, showing layers of sedimentary rock tilted at odd angles. And embedded within the rock, visible where sections had flaked away, were fossils. Elise, her scientific training flickering back to life despite her exhaustion, recognized the delicate, swirling patterns of ammonites, the segmented shapes of trilobites – creatures extinct for hundreds of millions of years. They were impossibly deep, impossibly far back in geological time. This cave system wasn't just ancient; it was primordial.

"Look," Elise murmured, pointing her light towards a particularly clear ammonite fossil, easily two feet across, embedded in the wall near them. "This cave… it must predate the mountains themselves, formed in ancient seabeds, then uplifted…" Her voice trailed off, the implications staggering. The Stick-shí'nač hadn't just found refuge in recent lava tubes or glacial caves; they inhabited a network potentially formed during the Paleozoic era, a realm utterly disconnected from the surface world's ephemeral cycles of ice ages and erosion. How had they found it? How had they adapted to it?

As she scanned the walls, her beam caught something else, something that didn't belong. Not a fossil, not a natural rock formation. Tucked into a high crevice, almost at the limit of her headlamp's reach, was a small, dark object. It looked like... a boot. An old, leather boot, stiff and cracked with age, wedged tightly into the rock.

"Nora..." Elise pointed.

Nora followed the beam, her eyes narrowing. Carefully, using the end of one of the steering poles they had salvaged from the raft (more out of instinct than any real hope of using it again), Nora reached up and managed to dislodge the boot. It tumbled down, landing with a soft thud in the dust at their feet.

It was undeniably a human boot, heavy-duty, hobnailed sole, thick leather upper – the style common to miners and prospectors in the mid-twentieth century. It was empty, save for dust and the desiccated remnants of what might have been a wool sock. There was no sign of other remains nearby. Just the boot, inexplicably wedged high in the crevice.

"Miller?" Elise whispered, thinking of the miner who had supposedly fled into the natural caves. Or Davies, who followed him? Or McClary, the first to vanish?

Nora picked up the boot, turning it over in her hands. "Perhaps," she said quietly. "Or another, even earlier. Many have been lost seeking riches in these mountains over the years." She ran a finger over the worn leather. "To end up here... alone... his boot preserved while his bones scattered..." She shuddered slightly, placing the boot gently back on the ground, like marking a grave.

The discovery spurred them onward, a grim reminder that others had passed this way, seeking escape, likely finding only death in the endless darkness. They pushed forward, following the main passage as it continued its winding, unpredictable path. The air remained dry, dusty, the silence profound.

Their headlamps grew progressively dimmer. Nora's began to flicker ominously, threatening to fail entirely. Elise's own beam was reduced to a pale yellow circle barely illuminating the ground directly in front of them. They resorted to using them only intermittently, navigating stretches in near-total darkness, relying on touch, memory, and Nora's uncanny sense of direction. The darkness felt absolute, pressing against their eyes, making them stumble, amplifying the sense of disorientation. Fear became a tangible thing, a suffocating blanket threatening to smother their remaining resolve.

It was during one of these periods of near-blindness, feeling their way along the tunnel wall, that Elise's hand brushed against something that wasn't rock. It was smooth, cold, metallic. Fumbling for her headlamp switch, she flicked it on briefly, directing the weak beam at the wall.

A metal plate, bolted securely into the rock face. Rusted, grime-covered, but clearly artificial. And set into the plate was a small, recessed lever handle, also rusted tight. It looked like… an access panel? Or a control mechanism for something?

"Nora, look," Elise whispered, excitement momentarily overriding her fear.

Nora felt the plate, the lever. "Miners," she murmured. "Or… Kestrel's predecessors? What does it open?"

Together, they gripped the rusted lever. It resisted at first, frozen by decades of disuse and corrosion. They threw their combined weight against it, straining, grunting with effort. With a loud screech of protesting metal that echoed alarmingly down the tunnel, the lever finally moved, grinding downwards perhaps six inches.

For a moment, nothing happened. Then, with a low, hydraulic hiss that startled them both, a section of the rock wall beside the plate began to slide inwards, revealing a dark opening behind it. Not a natural cave, but a constructed doorway, leading into another hidden space.

They shone their dying lights through the opening. It led into a small chamber, similar in size to the miners' failed camp near the sanctuary, but clearly not part of the original 1970s exploration. This looked… different. More modern, in a decaying, Cold War sort of way. Banks of dead electronic equipment lined one wall – reel-to-reel tape machines, oscilloscopes with cracked screens, communication consoles with Cyrillic labels alongside English ones, reminiscent of the equipment near Echo's frozen body. Against the far wall was a metal desk, overturned, spilling drawers full of mildewed papers. And slumped in a rusted metal chair beside the desk, skeletal remains clad in the tattered remnants of what might have been a lab coat or uniform, was a human figure.

Another tomb. Another victim. But this one felt different. Less prospector, more… operative?

With extreme caution, they stepped inside the hidden chamber. The air here was stale, stagnant, carrying the faint, acrid scent of ozone and decay. The silence was absolute. Elise approached the skeletal figure in the chair. It sat slumped forward, skull resting on the overturned desk amidst the scattered papers. A jagged hole marred the side of the skull – a self-inflicted gunshot wound? Or execution? Lying near the skeleton's outstretched hand was a corroded handgun, seemingly confirming the former.

"Who was he?" Elise wondered aloud, carefully trying not to disturb the remains.

Nora pointed towards the scattered papers on the floor near the desk. Many were illegible, destroyed by damp and time. But one folder, made of thicker, water-resistant material, lay slightly apart, as if deliberately placed or dropped last. Elise carefully picked it up.

The cover bore no title, only a stamped, faded symbol: a stylized bird of prey – a Kestrel? – superimposed over a jagged mountain range, beneath which were Cyrillic letters Elise couldn't read, and the English designation: *Project Backwoods – Sub-station Gamma – Eyes Only*.

Project Backwoods. The joint Forest Service / Army operation Graves' files had mentioned, the one recommending restricted access and information suppression back in the 70s. This hidden chamber wasn't just a mining relic; it was part of *that* secret government project, likely abandoned around the same time as the main mining operation failed, possibly due to the same creature encounters. And this skeleton… likely one of their operatives, left behind, perhaps choosing suicide over capture or madness.

Heart pounding, Elise carefully opened the folder. Inside were several pages of microfiche, miraculously preserved within protective sleeves, and a slim sheaf of typed documents, brittle with age but still legible. She scanned the first document, dated 1976: MEMORANDUM FOR RECORD. SUBJECT: *Containment Breach – Sub-station Gamma. Following Incident 76-Alpha (loss of Peterson survey team, suspected Subject hostility), Gamma operative Davies, P. reported unauthorized access to natural cave network via Shaft Gamma-Prime. Subsequent seismic event sealed primary access. Davies presumed compromised or KIA. Recommend immediate termination of Project Backwoods active monitoring at Gamma site. Initiate Level 3 Information Suppression. Facility sterilization protocols pending.*

Davies. The miner who followed Miller. He hadn't just vanished into the caves; he had reached this secret government listening post, perhaps seeking help, perhaps perceived as a threat. The 'seismic event' that sealed the miners' fate – was it natural, or deliberately triggered by Backwoods operatives to contain the breach, sacrificing Davies and any remaining miners? The callousness was chillingly familiar.

She quickly scanned the microfiche viewer – miraculously, a small, hand-cranked portable viewer lay amongst the desk debris, its lens dusty but functional. The fiche contained grainy photographs, seismic readings, acoustic recordings logs… and personnel files. She found Davies' file – geologist, ex-military signals specialist. And Miller's – experienced miner, noted independent streak, flagged as potential security risk due to 'local folklore inquiries'. And McClary's – missing prior to the main incident, file marked 'Inconclusive – Possible Subject Interaction'.

Then she found another file, one that made her breath catch. *THORNE, Aris. Civilian Consultant – Xenobiology/Primate Ethology. Security Clearance: BW-SPECIAL ACCESS.* Dated 1975. Aris Thorne, the Kestrel pathologist from the Goliath and Echo reports… he had been involved even back then, during Project Backwoods, before Kestrel was likely even formally constituted. His involvement wasn't recent; it spanned decades. Had he been a key figure from the very beginning? Perhaps even influencing the shift from passive observation to Kestrel's later, more aggressive 'asset recovery' approach?

The final document in the folder was a directive, stamped TOP SECRET, dated 1977. *SUBJECT: Project Backwoods Transition to Project CHIMERA (Phase 1A). Assets and viable data from Sub-stations Alpha, Beta, Gamma to be transferred to Kestrel Foundation oversight. Remaining sites to be sanitized/sealed under Protocol Sierra. Mandate: Passive observation shifts to feasibility assessment for potential Subject Recovery/Neutralization. Extreme prejudice authorized* RE: *security breaches.*

There it was. The direct lineage. Project Backwoods, the government cover-up, transitioning directly into Kestrel's Project Chimera, shifting from mere observation and suppression to active planning for capture or killing, with lethal enforcement of secrecy baked in from the start. Graves hadn't just been following Kestrel orders; he had been executing a phase of a clandestine government-spawned operation decades in the making.

This wasn't just a hidden scar; it was the rotten root of the entire conspiracy. This forgotten chamber held the missing link, the proof connecting the government cover-up to Kestrel's later atrocities.

"Nora, we found it," Elise whispered, her voice trembling with the enormity of the discovery. "The proof. The connection. Backwoods, Kestrel… it's all here."

But as she looked up, relief warring with horror, she saw Nora wasn't looking at the files. She was staring past Elise, towards the back wall of the small chamber, her face pale, her eyes wide with alarm.

"Elise," Nora breathed, pointing a trembling finger. "The wall… it's not solid."

Elise spun around, directing her fading headlamp beam towards the back wall behind the desk. Nora was right. It wasn't uniform rock. Sections of it seemed… different. Smoother, almost glassy in texture, emitting the faintest, almost imperceptible blue-green luminescence, identical to the light from the hidden sanctuary. And woven into this strange, semi-luminescent rock were intricate patterns, the familiar spirals and interwoven lines of Stick-shí'nač carvings, but these seemed integrated into the very substance of the wall itself, glowing faintly from within. It looked less like a natural cave wall and more like… architecture. Ancient, non-human architecture, forming the back boundary of the human-built chamber.

And set into the center of this strange wall was what looked like a doorway. Not blasted or drilled, but perfectly formed, arched, sealed by a single, massive slab of the same faintly glowing, carved stone, fitting so precisely it was almost invisible until examined closely.

Had the Backwoods operative known this was here when he chose this chamber? Had he tried to open it? Or had he died facing away from it, never realizing what lay just beyond his final resting place?

As they stared at the impossible doorway, the Resonance returned. Stronger than ever before. Not just a hum felt in the bones, but an almost audible, deeply resonant chord that seemed to emanate directly from the glowing wall itself. It pulsed through the chamber, making the dust motes dance, making the loose papers on the floor tremble. It pressed against their minds, not painful, but immensely powerful, ancient, filled with... what? Inquiry? Warning? Invitation?

The air grew thick, charged with static electricity. The faint emergency lights in the lab outside flickered violently, then died completely, plunging that outer chamber into absolute blackness. Their own headlamps dimmed further, the beams becoming almost useless pinpricks against the growing luminescence of the strange wall.

"What is this place?" Elise whispered, awestruck and terrified. They hadn't just found a hidden government outpost; they had stumbled upon a boundary, a gateway constructed by the Stick-shí'nač themselves, leading... where? Deeper into their sanctuary? Into the very heart of the Resonance? Into something else entirely?

The whispering the miners had described seemed tangible now, a sibilant chorus just beneath the resonant hum, seeming to emanate from the glowing stone door. It wasn't language, not words, but pure sensation – age, power, deep earth, warnings, secrets.

Nora gripped Elise's arm, her knuckles white. "We should not be here," she breathed, her voice filled with primal fear. "This is too deep. Too sacred. This door... it was not meant for us to find."

But even as she spoke, the massive stone slab sealing the arched doorway began to vibrate, humming in tune with the intensifying Resonance. A thin line of brighter blue-green light appeared around its edges, growing brighter, outlining the portal. And then, with a sound like continents shifting deep within the earth, the stone slab began to slide silently inwards, revealing not darkness, but a passage filled with the same soft, ethereal, blue-green light that illuminated the hidden sanctuary.

An invitation? Or the opening of a tomb?

The choice was stark. Retreat back through the darkness, past the dead operative, past the frozen lab, towards the pursuing guardians? Or step forward, through the impossible doorway, into the heart of the mountain's mystery, into the source of the Resonance, into the unknown depths of the Stick-shí'nač world?

The whispers intensified, swirling around them, pulling at their minds. The Resonance pulsed, promising knowledge, power, madness, dissolution. The light beckoned, beautiful and terrifying. They had followed the whispers of the lost, found the hidden scars, and now stood at the threshold of the Hollow Truth itself, a truth guarded by glowing stone and the heartbeat of the ancient earth. Stepping through felt like shedding the last vestiges of their own world, embracing the impossible, and surrendering completely to the unfathomable depths of the Hollow Ground.

Chapter 16: The Heart of the Mountain

The silence stretched, taut and humming, amplifying the rhythmic pulse emanating from the glowing stone doorway. It wasn't just sound, Elise realized, fighting against the dizzying pressure behind her eyes; it was a physical force, vibrating through the floor, through the stale air of the dead operative's tomb, resonating deep within her own chest cavity. It felt ancient, impossibly powerful, like the slow, deep breathing of the mountain itself. Before them, the massive stone slab slid further inwards, retracting smoothly into the surrounding wall with impossible mechanics, revealing a passage bathed not in darkness, but in the same soft, ethereal blue-green luminescence they had witnessed in the hidden sanctuary.

Retreat was impossible. The way back led past the frozen horrors of the Kestrel lab, past the skeletal reminder of Project Backwoods' fatal end, and likely towards the waiting, enraged guardians. Staying here meant succumbing to the crushing resonance, the whispering madness the miner's logbook described, perhaps eventually joining the forgotten skeleton slumped at the desk. The only path was forward, through the impossible door, into the heart of the mystery.

"Nora?" Elise whispered, her voice trembling, needing affirmation, connection, before taking the irrevocable step.

Nora turned from the doorway, her face illuminated by the strange light spilling from within. Her eyes, usually filled with quiet strength or weary sorrow, now held a look Elise hadn't seen before – a profound, almost fearful awe, mixed with an undeniable pull, a sense of homecoming to a place only ever visited in the deepest layers of ancestral memory.

"It is… the Heart," Nora breathed, her voice barely audible above the pulsing hum. "The place where the First People touch the Deep Power. Where the mountain dreams." She met Elise's gaze, her expression conveying both immense risk and inescapable destiny. "We were led here. Or allowed here. To turn back now… might be the greater offense."

Her words resonated with Elise's own reluctant conclusion. They had been spared, guided, perhaps even tested. To refuse this final threshold felt like rejecting the possibility of understanding, condemning themselves to the darkness behind them. Taking a ragged breath, steeling herself against the unknown, Elise nodded. "Together, then."

Nora reached out, gripping Elise's forearm tightly for a moment, a gesture of solidarity that transcended words. Then, turning back towards the glowing portal, Nora stepped through first, disappearing into the soft luminescence. Elise hesitated for only a heartbeat, casting one last glance back at the dead operative slumped in the chair, a silent promise to carry his story, too, then followed Nora into the light.

The transition was immediate, profound. The oppressive cold and stale air of the human-violated chamber vanished, replaced by a warmth that felt clean, vital, almost alive. The blue-green light intensified, seeming to emanate not from a single source but from the very walls of the passage itself, which were no longer rough-hewn rock but impossibly smooth, almost glassy surfaces, swirling with intricate, faintly luminous patterns that seemed to shift and flow like captured nebulae. The Resonance deepened, surrounding them, permeating them, no longer just a physical vibration but an almost musical presence, complex chords of deep earth energy washing over Elise's senses. It felt less threatening here, less like pressure and more like… communication? A vast, ancient, non-verbal language she couldn't comprehend but felt instinctively held immense meaning.

The passage wasn't long. It sloped gently upwards for perhaps thirty feet, the glowing walls curving smoothly, before opening out into a space that defied all geological possibility, stealing Elise's breath with its sheer, impossible grandeur.

They stood on a wide, crystalline platform overlooking a cavern so vast it seemed to swallow the light from their failing headlamps, rendering them useless. The chamber stretched downwards into misty depths and upwards into a darkness so profound it felt infinite. But the space wasn't truly dark. The source of the sanctuary's ethereal glow was here, magnified a thousandfold.

Immense crystal formations, taller than coastal redwoods, jutted from the unseen floor far below and descended like frozen lightning bolts from the vanished ceiling, pulsing with their own internal blue-green light. Veins of the same luminous material snaked across the cavern walls, tracing complex, geometric patterns interspersed with the familiar Stick-shí'nač carvings, but rendered here in glowing light rather than etched stone. Waterfalls cascaded down sheer, obsidian-like cliffs in the distance, catching the light, shattering into millions of glittering droplets that created shimmering rainbows in the misty air. Strange, bioluminescent fungi clung in vast, intricate tapestries to ledges and rock faces, adding softer hues of violet and gold to the dominant blue-green palette.

And the Resonance… here, it was overwhelming, a symphony of subsonic vibrations and almost-audible harmonics that resonated not just in bone, but directly within the mind. It felt like standing inside a colossal, living instrument, played by the slow, deep rhythms of the planet itself. Elise felt dizzy, disoriented, yet simultaneously exhilarated, her scientific mind struggling to reconcile the impossible beauty and power of the place with the known laws of physics and geology. Geothermal energy? Piezoelectric effects from tectonic stress? Bioluminescence on an unimaginable scale? None of the explanations felt adequate. This place felt… intentional. Anciently engineered, perhaps, by forces geological or otherwise, and discovered, utilized, perhaps even worshipped, by the Stick-shí'nač.

"The Heart-Chamber," Nora whispered, her voice filled with reverence, tears streaming freely down her face now, tears of awe, not sorrow. "The legends... they spoke of it. A place where the world was sung into being. Where the spirits of the mountain sleep and dream."

They stood on the crystalline platform for a long time, simply absorbing the overwhelming sensory input. There was no sign of the creatures here. The space felt empty of immediate life, yet profoundly alive with energy, with ancient power. It felt less like a dwelling place and more like a cathedral, a nexus point of immense natural force.

As her eyes adjusted, Elise began to notice more details. The air was warm, humid, carrying the scent of ozone, wet rock, and strange, sweet vegetation unlike anything she'd encountered on the surface. Below their platform, winding pathways paved with smooth, dark stones crisscrossed the cavern floor, connecting different clusters of the giant, pulsing crystals. Strange plants grew near the base of these crystals, absorbing the light, their leaves displaying intricate fractal patterns, some emitting their own faint luminescence. It was a self-contained ecosystem, thriving in isolation for millennia, utterly alien.

And the carvings... etched into the glowing crystal pillars themselves were depictions far older, far more detailed, than those in the sanctuary or along the trail. They seemed to tell a vast, complex history. Elise saw images resembling the Stick-shí'nač, but subtly different – perhaps ancestral forms? – interacting with megafauna now long extinct on the surface. She saw depictions of catastrophic geological events – earthquakes, volcanic eruptions, floods – survived, it seemed, by retreating into these deep places. She saw complex astronomical charts, star patterns rendered with uncanny accuracy, suggesting a sophisticated understanding of celestial cycles.

And most disturbingly, she saw images depicting conflict. Stick-shí'nač figures battling not just giant beasts, but other entities – shadowy, less defined shapes drawn with jagged lines suggesting fear or hostility. And later, much later in the chronology it seemed, encounters with small, stick-like figures carrying sharp implements – early humans? The carvings depicted initial curiosity, then avoidance, then outright hostility and defense as the smaller figures encroached, cut down trees, drove away game. The historical record of their retreat from the surface world, their long conflict with humanity, was etched here in glowing crystal.

But it was one set of carvings, located on a massive pillar directly across the cavern from their platform, that drew Elise's attention most forcefully. These seemed more recent, though still ancient by human standards. They depicted Stick-shí'nač figures interacting with strange, metallic objects – crashed cylinders, smoking wreckage, unmistakably technological debris. And figures emerging from this debris – small, grey-skinned beings with large, dark eyes, rendered with a mixture of fear and curiosity. Later panels showed interaction, perhaps even cautious communication, between the Stick-shí'nač and these alien visitors, followed by conflict, betrayal, and the eventual departure or destruction of the newcomers, leaving behind only resonant warnings carved into the crystal.

Elise stared, her mind reeling. Extraterrestrial contact? Ancient astronauts? It seemed utterly insane, the stuff of fringe conspiracy theories. Yet the carvings were undeniably there, part of the creatures' own recorded history, predating Kestrel, predating Project Backwoods by millennia. Could this be the ultimate source of the mystery? Could the Stick-shí'nač's unique physiology, their potential psychic abilities, their connection to the Resonance, be somehow linked to this ancient, forgotten encounter? Did Kestrel know? Was *this* the 'asset' they were truly after – not just the creatures, but the remnants of alien technology, the source of the strange energy signatures?

The possibility reframed everything. Kestrel wasn't just covering up cryptids; they were potentially covering up evidence of non-human intelligence on an entirely different scale, a secret far more explosive than Bigfoot. The 'Goliath' and 'Echo' experiments took on a new, horrifying light – were they trying to understand or replicate abilities derived from this ancient contact? Was the Resonance itself a byproduct of leftover alien technology, or a natural energy source the visitors had merely tapped into?

"Nora," Elise whispered, pointing towards the carvings across the cavern. "What… what are those?"

Nora followed her gaze, squinting into the distance. Her expression tightened, a mixture of recognition and deep cultural taboo crossing her features. "The Sky Visitors," she murmured, her voice barely audible. "Forbidden stories. Whispered only by the oldest shamans. Tales of beings who came from the stars, long ago, before the great floods, before the mountains were fully formed. They shared knowledge, power… but also brought imbalance. Conflict. The guardians fought them, drove them away, or buried what remained of their passage. It is said their power still sleeps deep in the earth, dangerous, corrupting. We were taught never to seek it."

Forbidden stories. Buried technology. Ancient conflicts. It all fit together with a terrifying, unbelievable coherence.

As they absorbed the implications, the Resonance in the cavern seemed to shift subtly. The steady hum deepened, intensified, and the whispers Elise had felt before returned, clearer now, seeming to coalesce into fragmented thoughts, images, feelings within her own mind, not her own. Glimpses of immense time, slow geological processes, the patient growth of crystals, the quiet life of the deep forest, punctuated by flashes of terror, loss, rage – the capture of Goliath, the agony of Echo, the violation of the sanctuary by gunfire. It wasn't just ambient energy; it felt like the collective consciousness of the Stick-shí'nač, perhaps amplified by this chamber, bleeding through, a raw transmission of their long history, their deep connection to this place, their pain, their vigilance.

Elise gasped, stumbling back, pressing her hands to her temples, overwhelmed by the influx of alien sensation, alien memory. Nora steadied her, her own face pale, eyes wide. "Too strong," Nora breathed. "The Heart speaks too loudly here. It can break a mind not prepared."

They needed to leave the main chamber, find shelter from the overwhelming Resonance. Looking around, Elise spotted another passage leading away from their crystalline platform, this one smaller, darker, heading back into rock that didn't glow with the same intensity. It looked like an exit, or at least a refuge from the main power source.

"That way," Elise croaked, pointing.

Supporting each other, they staggered away from the breathtaking, terrifying vista of the Heart-Chamber, plunging back into a more conventional darkness. This new tunnel felt blessedly normal after the sensory overload – just rock, dampness, and blessed, relative silence, though the underlying Resonance still hummed faintly in the background.

They collapsed just inside the entrance of the new passage, utterly drained, physically and psychically. They had glimpsed the core of the mystery, discovered secrets far deeper and stranger than they could have imagined, touching upon ancient histories, alien encounters, and the profound power source that likely fueled the guardians' existence and abilities. They had found evidence that could potentially expose not just Kestrel, but perhaps redraw humanity's understanding of its place in the universe.

But the discovery brought them no closer to immediate safety. They were still trapped deep underground, exhausted, with dwindling resources. And now they carried knowledge far more dangerous than before. Kestrel's motives seemed terrifyingly clear – control or containment of not just a cryptid species, but potentially alien technology or energy sources. Their ruthlessness made perfect sense in that context. And the Stick-shí'nač…

understanding their history, their connection to this place, their past traumas inflicted by outsiders… it made their fierce territoriality, their violent defense of their sanctuary, tragically understandable.

Elise looked at Nora, saw her own exhaustion and fear mirrored there, but also a flicker of shared resolve. They had seen the Heart of the Mountain. They carried its echo, its burden. Somehow, they had to survive. Somehow, they had to find a way to use this overwhelming knowledge, not to destroy, but perhaps, as Whis Elem suggested, to bridge. The path remained impossibly steep, impossibly dangerous, but the glimpse into the luminous heart had ignited something within Elise – a fierce determination to see this through, to protect this fragile, impossible world from the consuming darkness of her own.

Chapter 17: Echoes in the Stone

The transition from the overwhelming energy of the Heart-Chamber back into near-absolute darkness was jarring, like stepping from a sun-drenched peak into a deep cellar. The passage they had stumbled into offered refuge from the intense Resonance, but its oppressive blackness, broken only by the pathetic, flickering yellow circles cast by their dying headlamps, felt suffocating in its own right. The air was cool, still, carrying the scent of dry dust and ancient stone, a welcome change from the humid, ozone-tinged atmosphere of the immense cavern, yet holding its own desolate emptiness.

Elise leaned heavily against the rough rock wall just inside the entrance, her body trembling violently, reaction setting in. The sheer sensory overload of the Heart-Chamber – the impossible scale, the pulsing blue-green light, the symphony of subsonic vibrations, the overwhelming psychic intrusion of shared memories and emotions – had pushed her beyond mere exhaustion into a state of profound psychic and physical depletion. Her mind felt scoured, raw, echoing with fragments of alien thought and millennia of geological time. She squeezed her eyes shut, trying to block out the lingering afterimages, the faint whispers that still seemed to cling to the edges of her hearing.

Nora slumped down beside her, her breathing harsh and ragged. Even her remarkable resilience seemed taxed to its absolute limit. She didn't speak, just rested her forehead against her drawn-up knees, pulling her blanket around her shoulders, a small, weary figure dwarfed by the immense darkness and the weight of their discoveries.

They remained there for uncounted minutes, simply trying to regain equilibrium, letting the relative quiet of the passage soothe their overstimulated senses. The deep, pervasive hum of the Heart-Chamber faded from immediate perception, receding back into the background, though Elise suspected its influence lingered, a subtle pressure beneath the silence.

"We... we saw it," Elise finally managed to whisper, the words feeling inadequate, almost profane, after the immensity of the experience. "The source. The... the Heart."

Nora lifted her head slowly, her eyes reflecting the weak lamplight, looking distant, profoundly shaken. "More than saw," she corrected softly, her voice rough. "We felt it. Listened to its song. Stood in its presence." She shuddered slightly. "It is a place of great power, Elise. Dangerous power. The guardians draw strength from it, yes. But it demands respect. It can... unmake those who are not strong enough, those who listen too closely without understanding." She looked pointedly at the rusted handgun still holstered at Elise's hip, then towards the darkness where the miners' chamber lay. "Like the miners, perhaps. Their minds fractured by the Resonance, by the whispers they mistook for guidance."

The thought sent another chill through Elise. Had Miller and Davies been driven mad by this power? Had their desperate flight through these caves been less an escape attempt and more a descent into delusion, led by the mountain's alien consciousness? And were she and Nora now susceptible, having been exposed so directly, so intensely? The vigilance required wasn't just against Kestrel or the Stick-shí'nač, but potentially against their own fracturing perceptions.

"We need to keep moving," Elise said, forcing herself to focus on the practical, the immediate. "Away from... that." Staying too close to the Heart-Chamber felt inherently dangerous. "And we need... water. Shelter. Somewhere to rest properly."

Nora nodded, pushing herself stiffly upright. "Yes. Forward. This passage... it feels like it leads upwards. Towards drier ground, perhaps."

Their progress was agonizingly slow. Elise's headlamp was now barely producing enough light to illuminate the ground directly at her feet, forcing her to rely heavily on Nora's slightly stronger, though also fading, beam. They shared the lead, the one behind using their light to help the one ahead pick a path through the treacherous, uneven floor littered with fallen rocks and deep drifts of fine, ancient dust. The tunnel wound onwards, sometimes widening slightly, sometimes narrowing into tight squeezes that scraped their packs and shoulders raw. It seemed entirely natural now, no more signs of Stick-shí'nač carvings or pathways, no more remnants of human intrusion. Just primordial darkness, dripping water, and the immense weight of the mountain above.

The silence was broken only by their own movements and the occasional, unnerving skittering sound from unseen crevices – cave crickets, perhaps, or bats disturbed by their passage. Elise found herself listening intently, straining for any hint of pursuit, any scrape or growl that might indicate the elder Stick-shí'nač or its companions had followed them from the river cavern. But there was nothing. Only the deep, profound silence of the inner earth. Had they truly been allowed to pass? Or was something else tracking them now, something adapted to this deeper darkness?

After what might have been an hour, or three – time felt fluid, meaningless in the disorienting dark – Nora's headlamp began to flicker violently, the beam dimming to a barely visible orange glow before sputtering out completely, plunging her into absolute blackness.

"Nora!" Elise cried out, swinging her own weak beam back towards her.

"I am here," Nora's voice came, steady despite the sudden blindness. "Battery... finally gone."

Now they had only one light source, feeble and failing. Panic threatened to overwhelm Elise. Being lost in this labyrinth was terrifying enough with minimal light; being lost in total darkness felt like a death sentence.

"Okay," Elise said, forcing her voice to remain calm. "Okay. Stay close. Hold onto my pack. We'll share my light, move slower."

They continued onwards, Nora's hand now gripping Elise's backpack strap, the two women moving as one awkward unit through the blackness, guided only by the pitifully weak circle of light cast by Elise's lamp. Every shadow seemed deeper, every unseen obstacle more menacing. The darkness felt alive, pressing in, threatening to swallow them.

It was shortly after Nora's light failed that they found the sign. Elise's weak beam happened to catch a faint marking on the tunnel wall, low down, almost at floor level. Not a carving, but scratches. Three parallel lines, gouged deeply into the rock, pointing roughly in the direction they were heading. They looked fresh. Too fresh.

Elise knelt, examining them closely. The edges were sharp, dust disturbed around them. These weren't ancient markings. These were recent. And the depth, the spacing... suggested immense strength, large claws or tools.

"Stick-shí'nač?" she whispered, her blood running cold. Had one passed this way recently? Or...

Then she saw it. Just below the three parallel lines, almost invisible in the dust, was a small, smeared brown stain. Dried blood. And caught within the smear, a tiny fragment of dark blue fabric, synthetic, like... like the jacket Boone had been wearing.

"Boone..." Elise breathed, touching the fabric fragment, her heart clenching with a painful mixture of grief and desperate hope. He had come this way. After the fight in the fissure near the miners' chamber... he hadn't died there. He had somehow escaped the elder, wounded perhaps, and fled deeper into these caves. These markings... were they his? A desperate signal? Or left by the elder pursuing him? The three lines… did they signify the three survivors he thought remained (himself, Elise, Nora)? Or something else entirely?

Nora knelt beside her, examining the marks, the bloodstain, the fabric. Her face was unreadable in the dim light. "He passed this way," she confirmed quietly. "Wounded, it seems. But moving." She looked deeper into the darkness ahead. "Alone? Or pursued?"

The discovery, ambiguous as it was, shifted the atmosphere. Boone might still be alive. Wounded, lost, hunted perhaps, but alive. The thought ignited a desperate spark within Elise. They couldn't just focus on their own escape now. They had to find him. Help him.

"We follow the marks?" Elise asked, looking at Nora.

Nora hesitated, her gaze troubled. "He bleeds," she stated simply. "In these deep places… blood attracts things. Not just the guardians. Older things. Things that hunger in the dark." Her reluctance was clear, rooted in ancient warnings.

"He saved us, Nora," Elise argued, her voice fierce with sudden loyalty. "He drew the elder away. We can't abandon him now. Not if there's a chance."

Nora looked at Elise, saw the desperate conviction in her eyes, perhaps recognized the debt owed. After a long pause, she nodded slowly. "We follow," she agreed. "But with great caution. We honour his sacrifice by surviving, not by joining him foolishly if the path becomes too perilous."

Renewed purpose, however dangerous, lent them strength. They pushed onward, following the faint indication of the scratches, scanning the walls constantly for more signs, their single headlamp beam sweeping back and forth, searching the oppressive darkness. The tunnel remained narrow, winding, occasionally opening into small, intersecting caverns filled with strange, calcite formations that glittered like alien jewels in the weak light.

They found two more sets of the parallel scratch marks over the next hour, confirming they were on Boone's trail. Each time, the marks seemed slightly less distinct, the accompanying bloodstains smaller, suggesting either his wound was clotting or his strength was failing, his movements becoming less certain. Worry gnawed at Elise. How badly was he hurt? How far ahead could he be?

The air began to change again. A definite current could be felt now, flowing towards them, carrying a scent that was startlingly familiar: fresh air. Damp earth, pine needles, the unmistakable smell of the surface world.

"Elise! Air!" Nora breathed, lifting her face towards the unseen source. "We are close! Close to an opening!"

Hope surged, powerful and intoxicating. An exit. A way out. They pushed forward faster now, stumbling over rocks, heedless of scrapes and bruises, drawn towards the promise of breathable air, of potential escape. The passage began to slope steeply upwards. Roots, thick and tenacious, began to appear, dangling down from cracks in the ceiling high above, confirming their proximity to the surface.

The scratch marks appeared one last time, near the base of a steep, final ascent choked with roots and loose earth. But here, they were accompanied by something else. A large, heavy object lay discarded amongst the roots, half-buried in the dirt. Elise's light fell upon it. Boone's shotgun. Empty. Casings scattered nearby.

Elise's heart sank. He had made it this far, but clearly, something had happened here. Had he run out of ammunition? Made a final stand? Been cornered? There were signs of a struggle – disturbed earth, broken roots, more smeared bloodstains, larger this time. And leading away from the struggle, heading upwards towards the surface opening, were two sets of tracks pressed into the damp earth. One set was Boone's heavy boot prints, shuffling, uneven, dragging. The other set… was immense. The unmistakable splayed, five-toed prints of a Stick-shí'nač.

But strangely, the tracks didn't indicate a violent dragging. They moved side-by-side, almost... supportively? Had the creature captured him? Or... helped him? The ambiguity was maddening, terrifying.

"What happened here?" Elise whispered, staring at the tracks.

Nora knelt, examining the sign with intense concentration. "Struggle," she confirmed. "Then... assistance? Or capture? Hard to say. The guardian's tracks are... measured. Not enraged." She looked up towards the opening, now visible as a definite patch of lesser darkness perhaps fifty feet above them at the top of the root-choked slope. "He reached the surface. With the guardian. Or *because* of it."

Driven by desperate hope and profound confusion, they scrambled up the final slope, using the thick roots as handholds, hauling themselves upwards. Just as Elise's headlamp beam flickered and died completely, plunging them into absolute blackness for a terrifying second, they broke through the opening.

They emerged, blinking, gasping, into... twilight. Not the deep gloom of the forest, but the soft, grey, mist-filtered twilight of a high mountain pass. They stood on a narrow, windswept saddle between two rocky peaks, the air shockingly cold and thin after the stagnant depths. Below them, shrouded in mist, lay valleys they didn't recognize, different drainages entirely from AO Hollow or Cougar Creek. They had emerged miles away, perhaps tens of miles, from where they had descended into the Crevice, spat out onto the roof of the world by the mountain's secret passages.

They were out. Free of the crushing darkness. But they were utterly alone, high in an unfamiliar, unforgiving alpine wilderness, with no supplies, no light, and the chilling mystery of Boone's fate hanging heavy between them. Had he escaped with the creature's help? Been taken to some unknown fate? Was the creature still nearby?

As they scanned the desolate saddle, searching for any sign of Boone, any indication of which way he might have gone, Nora pointed silently towards a large, flat rock near the edge of the pass. Etched into its surface, fresh and unmistakable, were three parallel lines. Boone's signal. He had been here. And he had moved on. But which way? And was he alone?

The whispers of the lost miners seemed to echo on the wind sweeping across the pass. They had followed a desperate path, found clues buried in time, and emerged into a new, uncertain landscape, still bound to the mystery, still caught between worlds. Finding Boone, understanding his fate and the creature's paradoxical actions, felt like the next crucial step. But survival, once again, was the most pressing imperative. They needed shelter, water, a way down from this exposed height before the mountain claimed them as it had claimed so many others before.

Chapter 18: The Roof of the World

The wind was a physical entity on the high mountain pass, a scouring, relentless force that tore at their clothes, numbed exposed skin, and shrieked through the jagged rock formations like the tormented spirits Nora's legends spoke of. It drove the mist in swirling eddies, revealing tantalizing, terrifying glimpses of the world spread out below – immense, shadowed valleys plunging into unseen depths, opposing ridges serrated against the bruised twilight sky, glaciers clinging grimly to the highest peaks under a perpetually overcast ceiling. They were infinitesimally small specks adrift on the roof of the world, spat out from the mountain's gut into a realm of brutal, alpine indifference.

Elise huddled behind a low outcrop of wind-scoured granite, trying desperately to regain her breath, trying to stop the violent shivering that shook her entire frame. The transition from the stagnant, subterranean darkness to this exposed, wind-blasted height was profoundly disorienting. Relief at reaching breathable air warred with the stark terror of their absolute isolation and vulnerability. They had escaped the immediate clutches of the guardians, the suffocating darkness of the caves, but they had emerged into a different kind of peril – exposure, exhaustion, starvation, and the vast, unforgiving indifference of high-altitude wilderness.

Nora knelt beside the flat rock bearing Boone's cryptic signal – three parallel lines scratched fresh into the lichen-covered surface. Her expression was intent, focused, her weariness momentarily overshadowed by the immediate puzzle. She ran her fingers lightly over the grooves, then examined the surrounding windswept ground, patches of thin, gravelly soil clinging between outcrops.

"He was here," she stated unnecessarily, her voice thin against the wind's roar. "Not long ago. The marks are fresh, dust barely settled." She pointed towards the ground leading away from the rock, angling slightly northwards along the ridge crest. "Tracks… faint here. Wind scours them quickly. But his boot print… see?"

Elise crawled closer, peering where Nora indicated. Preserved in a small patch of damp, sheltered grit was the partial imprint of a heavy lug sole, unmistakably Boone's. And beside it, fainter but discernible, was the edge of something much larger – the splayed, outer toe impressions of a Stick-shí'nač foot. They were still together.

"Which way did they go?" Elise asked, scanning the desolate ridge line disappearing into the mist in both directions. North or South? Descend east back towards AO Hollow (unthinkable)? Or west, down into the unfamiliar drainages beyond?

Nora rose slowly, her gaze sweeping the surrounding terrain, reading the subtle contours, the patterns of wind deposition, the direction the hardiest vegetation leaned. "North," she decided finally, pointing along the ridge crest. "The tracks lead that way, towards that lower saddle." She indicated a dip in the ridge perhaps half a mile distant. "From there… perhaps a way down the western slope. Sheltered from this wind, maybe. Leading away from the Hollow Ground."

It was as good a guess as any. Trusting Nora's instinct, they pushed themselves upright, legs trembling, bodies protesting every movement. Standing fully exposed to the wind again was brutal. It snatched the breath from their lungs, hammered against their bodies, threatening to tear them from their precarious footing.

"We need shelter," Nora stated urgently, her voice raised against the gale. "Soon. Cannot survive the night up here like this."

They began moving north along the ridge, hunched low against the wind, moving from rock outcrop to rock outcrop, seeking minimal protection where they could. Progress was painfully slow. The ground was uneven, littered with sharp stones hidden by patches of tough alpine grass and low-growing heather. Visibility was often reduced to less than fifty feet by the swirling mist, creating a disorienting, claustrophobic feeling despite the vast open space around them. Elise felt dizzy, lightheaded, likely from a combination of altitude, exhaustion, and lack of food.

Every few minutes, they paused, scanning the ground for further sign of Boone and his immense companion. They found occasional faint impressions – Boone's boot scuffing against rock, a single, deep toe imprint where the creature had stepped on softer ground – always leading northwards along the ridge. The creature's stride was immense, covering ground effortlessly where Elise and Nora struggled. Boone's prints seemed uneven, sometimes dragging, confirming his wounded state. There was still no clear indication of coercion or assistance – just two disparate beings moving together through this desolate landscape. The mystery of their relationship, their destination, only deepened.

What conversation, Elise wondered, could possibly pass between a haunted, grieving tracker and the ancient guardian whose kin were responsible for his deepest trauma? Was Boone a prisoner? A reluctant patient? An ambassador? Or simply… prey being led to a final, inevitable end? The lack of answers was maddening, adding another layer of psychological torment to their physical ordeal.

As they traversed a particularly exposed section of the ridge, the wind gusting with renewed ferocity, Elise stumbled, her foot catching on a loose rock. She cried out, pitching forward, only Nora's quick reflexes, grabbing the back of her jacket, prevented her from tumbling down the steep, mist-shrouded eastern slope towards the unseen depths of the valley below. Elise clung to Nora, heart pounding, gasping for breath, the near-fall leaving her trembling violently.

"Careful, Child," Nora admonished gently but firmly, helping her regain her footing. "The mountain demands attention. Your thoughts wander."

Elise nodded mutely, ashamed of her lapse. Nora was right. Grief, speculation, fear – they were luxuries they couldn't afford. Survival required absolute focus on the immediate: the next step, the next handhold, the next breath. She forced herself to push aside the swirling questions, the haunting memories, concentrating only on placing her feet carefully, maintaining balance against the wind, following Nora's steady lead.

They reached the lower saddle Nora had aimed for perhaps an hour later, as the last vestiges of usable light were being swallowed by the encroaching twilight and the thickening mist. The wind was slightly less ferocious here, buffered by the surrounding rock formations, but the cold felt even deeper, seeping into their bones. The tracks – Boone's and the creature's – led clearly downwards from the saddle, descending a steep, scree-filled gully slicing into the western slope.

"Down there," Nora confirmed, peering into the gloomy depths of the gully. "Looks treacherous. But sheltered from the worst of the wind, perhaps."

The descent into the gully was a controlled slide as much as a climb. Loose rock shifted and tumbled underfoot, echoing alarmingly in the confined space. They moved slowly, crab-wise, using hands as much as feet, trying desperately not to trigger a larger rockfall. Darkness fell completely within the gully's depths, forcing Elise to rely on her headlamp again, the weak beam casting long, distorted shadows that made the loose rocks seem to writhe like living things.

After descending perhaps two hundred feet, the gully walls widened slightly, and Nora stopped near a shallow overhang, a place where the rock face curved inwards, offering a small pocket of relative protection from the wind and the worst of the dripping moisture filtering down from above.

"Here," Nora declared, her voice echoing slightly off the rock. "We rest here for the night. Cannot risk moving further in the dark on this loose ground."

It wasn't much – a cramped space maybe ten feet wide and five feet deep, the floor uneven rock – but it was shelter. They collapsed onto the cold ground, huddling together instinctively for warmth, pulling Nora's blanket over both of them. The darkness felt absolute now, the silence broken only by the whisper of wind around the edges of the overhang and the occasional clatter of a distant pebble dislodged somewhere higher up the gully.

Elise fumbled in her pack, retrieving the last energy bar. She broke it in half, handing one piece to Nora. They ate in silence, the dense, sugary substance feeling like gravel in their mouths, doing little to satisfy the deep, gnawing hunger but providing a desperately needed sliver of energy. They shared the last few sips of water from Elise's canteen, the metal tasting cold against her lips. Tomorrow, finding a reliable water source would be critical.

Sitting there in the cold darkness, leaning against the unyielding rock, exhaustion weighing her down like lead, Elise felt the full weight of their situation settle upon her. They were alive, yes. Out of the caves, away from the immediate threat of the creatures. But they were stranded high in an alpine wilderness, miles from help, with no food, failing light sources, inadequate clothing for the plummeting nighttime temperatures, and no way to signal for rescue. Their survival depended entirely on Nora's ability to navigate them downwards, find water, perhaps find sustenance, before exposure or starvation claimed them. And hanging over everything was the unresolved fate of Boone, and the chilling knowledge that Kestrel's hunt likely continued, methodically sweeping the vast wilderness.

"We lost so many," Elise whispered into the darkness, the words barely audible above the wind's moan.

Nora sighed, a long, weary sound. "The mountain takes its due," she replied softly. "Always has. Those who come seeking, those who trespass, those who disrespect... sometimes they pay the price. Graves, with his hidden agenda. Jules, with his eagerness overriding caution. Levi, paying a debt he felt he owed. Boone..."

her voice caught slightly, "…seeking answers he perhaps finally found, though not the ones he expected."

"And us?" Elise asked, shivering. "What price do we pay?"

"We survived," Nora stated simply, though her tone held little triumph. "We carry the story. That is its own burden. Its own price." She shifted, pulling the blanket tighter. "Now, we must focus on living, Elise. One breath, one step, one sunrise at a time. Grieve the lost, yes. But do not let the grief paralyze you. We owe them survival."

Her words, pragmatic and wise, offered a sliver of focus in the overwhelming darkness. Survive. One step at a time. Elise clung to that thought, forcing down the despair, the fear, the paralyzing questions.

She must have drifted into an exhausted, hypothermic stupor rather than true sleep. She became vaguely aware of Nora shifting beside her, murmuring softly in Lushootseed, perhaps prayers, perhaps just words to keep herself awake, alert. The cold deepened, biting through their layers, numbing fingers and toes. Elise curled into a tight ball, trying to conserve warmth, drifting in a grey limbo between consciousness and oblivion, haunted by fragmented images – glowing symbols, falling stones, Levi's face, Boone's receding back.

Sometime later – minutes or hours, she couldn't tell – a sound pulled her back towards awareness. Not wind. Not rockfall. A low, rhythmic sound, seeming to come from far below, echoing faintly up the gully.

Thump… thump… thump…

Like a distant drumbeat. Or… a colossal heartbeat?

Elise's eyes snapped open, straining against the darkness. Nora had gone utterly still beside her, head cocked, listening intently.

Thump... thump... thump...

It was slow, incredibly deep, resonating through the rock itself, felt as much as heard. It seemed to align with the Resonance she had felt in the caves, but more focused now, more rhythmic, almost... purposeful?

"What is that?" Elise whispered, her voice trembling.

Nora didn't answer for a long moment, her face tight with concentration, perhaps even fear. "The Heart," she breathed finally. "The Heart of the Mountain. Beating."

Was it geological? Seismic activity? Or something else? Something alive? The sound was deeply unsettling, primal, suggesting immense power slumbering deep beneath them, the same power that fueled the sanctuary, the Resonance, perhaps the guardians themselves. Was it waking? Reacting to their presence, their escape? Or was it entirely natural, its timing merely a coincidence designed to fray their already shattered nerves?

Thump... thump... thump... The sound continued, slow, inexorable, a deep pulse from the earth's core echoing up through the darkness. It felt like a reminder that even here, on the surface, exposed to the wind and sky, they were still profoundly within the mountain's influence, still subject to its ancient rhythms and potentially its judgment.

They huddled together in the cramped rock shelter, listening to the mountain's heartbeat, feeling smaller, more insignificant than ever before. The wind howled outside, the darkness pressed in, and the vast, cold, indifferent wilderness waited. Survival felt like a fragile, flickering candle flame against an immense, encroaching storm. Morning, and the daunting descent that awaited them, seemed terrifyingly far away.

Chapter 19: Descent and Discovery

The deep, rhythmic thumping from the heart of the mountain eventually faded with the first, almost imperceptible lightening of the eastern sky, receding back into the subsonic realm, leaving behind only the howl of the wind and a lingering sense of profound unease. Elise and Nora hadn't slept, huddled together against the numbing cold, listening to the earth's pulse, feeling like insignificant microbes clinging to the flank of some vast, slumbering beast. The experience solidified Elise's reluctant acceptance of realities far beyond her scientific training – this mountain, this region, pulsed with energies and perhaps even consciousness that defied conventional explanation.

Dawn arrived not as a bright promise, but as a slow, grudging dilution of the oppressive darkness. The mist still clung stubbornly to the ridges and valleys below, but visibility improved slightly, revealing the terrifying steepness of the gully they needed to descend and the vast, rugged expanse of the western Olympic slopes stretching out before them. It was a landscape of immense scale and brutal beauty, utterly devoid of any sign of human presence.

They pushed themselves stiffly upright, bodies protesting violently against the cold, the stiffness, the deep ache of exhaustion and hunger. Every movement was an effort. Their hands were numb, feet felt like blocks of ice inside their damp boots. Hypothermia was no longer a distant threat, but a very real possibility if they couldn't find shelter and warmth soon.

"Water," Nora stated, her voice hoarse, pointing further down the gully where the terrain seemed to level out slightly, suggesting the presence of a stream or seep. "And sun. We need to get below the mist, find sun on the eastern slopes if possible."

The descent was treacherous, arguably more dangerous than the climb down the Crevice had been. The loose scree shifted constantly underfoot, threatening to send them tumbling. They moved with agonizing slowness, testing every foothold, using their hands for balance, sometimes resorting to sliding down short sections on their backsides, dislodging showers of rock that echoed alarmingly down the gully. Elise's focus narrowed to the immediate – the next step, the next hand placement, the desperate need to stay upright. The memory of the Heart-Chamber, the Kestrel conspiracy, even Boone's fate, receded into the background, overshadowed by the sheer, primal imperative to keep moving downwards without falling.

After what felt like hours, the angle of the gully finally eased. The rock walls widened, giving way to sparse, hardy vegetation – clumps of alpine heather, twisted dwarf willows clinging to crevices. And, blessedly, the sound of trickling water grew louder. They stumbled upon a small seep emerging from the rock face, forming a tiny, ice-fringed pool before disappearing back underground.

They fell upon the water source gratefully, breaking the thin layer of ice with numb fingers, scooping the frigid water into their cupped hands, drinking deeply despite the aching cold it sent through their bodies. It tasted clean, pure, life-giving. They refilled their canteens, the simple act feeling like a major victory.

While resting briefly by the seep, scanning the terrain below, Nora pointed again. "Look. Smoke."

Elise followed her gaze. Far below, maybe a mile or two distant down the slope, nestled in a pocket of dense timber near what looked like the main stem of a creek, a thin, almost invisible plume of grey smoke rose lazily into the misty air. Not the thick, angry smoke of the wildfire they had escaped, but the gentle plume of a campfire, or a cabin chimney.

Hope surged again, fierce and desperate. People? A ranger station? A remote cabin? Could it possibly be… rescue? Or was it another trap? Kestrel, lying in wait? Or something else entirely?

"Too small for Kestrel basecamp," Nora assessed, her voice cautious. "Too deliberate for wildfire remnant. Could be... hunters? Backpackers? Or..." she hesitated, "...someone who knows these woods well. Someone hiding."

The ambiguity was agonizing. Approaching the smoke source felt like walking towards a potential ambush, yet ignoring it, pushing onwards into the unknown wilderness with no supplies, felt equally perilous.

"We need to investigate," Elise decided, the potential reward – shelter, food, perhaps communication – outweighing the risk in her exhausted, desperate state. "But carefully. Very carefully."

They began moving downslope again, aiming towards the source of the smoke, but diverting from the direct path, using the contours of the land and the available tree cover to approach indirectly, maximizing concealment. Their progress was slow, hampered by dense undergrowth and the need for absolute quiet. Every snapped twig, every dislodged stone, felt like a betrayal, potentially alerting whoever was down there to their presence.

As they drew closer, maybe half a mile away, the terrain leveled slightly, opening into stands of larger timber – fir, hemlock, scattered cedar. The scent of woodsmoke grew stronger, mingling with the damp, earthy smell of the forest floor. They began to hear sounds – the distinct, rhythmic chop of an axe splitting wood, echoing clearly in the quiet air. Someone was definitely there, actively working.

Moving with excruciating slowness now, crouching low, using tree trunks and dense ferns for cover, Elise and Nora crept towards the edge of a small clearing surrounding the source of the smoke. Peering through the final screen of foliage, Elise's breath caught in her throat.

Nestled in the clearing was a small, rustic log cabin, sturdier-looking than Whis Elem's but clearly old, weathered by decades of mountain winters. Smoke curled invitingly from its stone chimney. Neatly stacked cords of firewood lined one wall. And standing near the woodpile, rhythmically swinging a heavy axe, splitting rounds of wood with practiced efficiency, was a figure.

Not Kestrel. Not Stick-shí'nač. A man. Tall, lean, clad in worn jeans, a faded plaid flannel shirt despite the cold, and a thick wool cap pulled low over his brow. His back was mostly towards them, but something about his posture, the economy of his movements, the way he seemed utterly at home in this remote wilderness setting, felt... familiar.

Then he paused, setting the axe aside, and turned slightly to wipe sweat from his brow with the back of his glove. Elise saw his profile. Weathered face. Strong jawline shadowed by several days' worth of stubble. Eyes narrowed slightly as he scanned the surrounding woods, a habitual vigilance.

"Boone?" Elise whispered, disbelief warring with a surge of overwhelming, impossible hope.

It couldn't be. Boone was gone. Taken by the elder in the fissure beneath the sanctuary. Dead. Yet... the resemblance was uncanny. The build, the posture, the way he moved.

Nora gripped Elise's arm hard, her eyes wide, fixed on the figure. She too recognized him, or the ghost of him.

Could they be hallucinating? Driven by grief and exhaustion to see phantoms? Or had Boone somehow, miraculously, survived the encounter with the elder? Escaped? Found his way here? It seemed impossible. The fall in the fissure, the sounds of struggle...

Just as Elise was convincing herself it was a trick of the light, a cruel hallucination, the man turned fully, picking up another log, preparing to split it. And Elise saw his face clearly.

It *was* Boone. Alive. Standing there in the quiet clearing, chopping wood as if it were just another ordinary day in the woods. He looked thinner, perhaps, gaunt beneath the stubble. There were fresh, healing scratches on his visible cheek and neck. He moved slightly stiffly, favoring one side. But it was him. Unmistakably.

Overwhelming relief washed over Elise, so potent it made her dizzy. Tears sprang to her eyes, blurring her vision. He was alive. He had made it.

"Boone!" she cried out, stumbling out from behind the trees into the clearing, heedless of caution now, driven only by the desperate need to confirm the miracle.

Boone spun around instantly at the sound of her voice, dropping the log, his hand automatically reaching for the heavy hunting knife sheathed at his belt, his body tensing into a defensive crouch, eyes narrowed, instantly assessing the threat. His reaction was primal, ingrained, the response of a man living constantly on the edge.

Then his eyes focused on Elise, then on Nora emerging cautiously behind her. Recognition dawned, followed by utter, slack-jawed astonishment. He straightened up slowly, lowering his hand from the knife, his face a mask of disbelief.

"Doc? Nora?" he breathed, his voice rough, incredulous. "You… you made it out?" He took a hesitant step towards them, then another, his eyes scanning them, taking in their ragged appearance, their exhaustion. "How…? The caves… the elder… I thought…"

"We thought *you* were gone!" Elise sobbed, rushing forward, closing the distance between them. She stopped just short of throwing her arms around him, suddenly awkward, unsure of the protocol for reuniting with someone you believed dead after surviving impossible horrors together. "The fissure… we heard the fight… then silence."

Boone ran a hand over his face, a gesture of profound weariness and lingering shock. "Yeah," he said grimly. "Wasn't much of a fight. More like… bein' tossed around like a rag doll." He touched his side gingerly. "Cracked a few ribs, I think. Knocked the wind outta me. When I came to… it was gone. Just… darkness. Took me hours to find my way out of that damned fissure, followin' what little sign you two left." He shook his head, still looking stunned. "Never thought I'd see daylight again. Let alone… see you two."

"But the creature?" Elise pressed. "The elder? It just… left you? After wounding you?" It made no sense.

Boone frowned, a flicker of confusion crossing his features. "Wounded me?" He looked down at his side, then back at Elise. "It didn't wound me, Doc. Not deliberately. Tossed me around, sure. Pinned me down. Roared in my face till I thought my head would explode." He shuddered at the memory. "But the ribs… that was from hittin' the wall when I tried to dodge. It… it held back. Coulda snapped my neck like a twig. Coulda torn me apart. But it didn't." He looked genuinely bewildered. "After… after it roared for a while, like it was ventin', it just… backed off. Gave me this long look… couldn't read it at all… then turned and disappeared back into the passage, towards the river cavern."

Elise and Nora exchanged glances, equally baffled. The elder, wounded by Boone's shotgun blast, enraged, had cornered him… and then simply let him go? Why? Had Boone's defiance, his willingness to fight despite the odds, earned some kind of grudging respect? Or was it related to the death of the other creature in the river – perhaps the elder's rage spent, its sense of 'balance' restored, leaving Boone no longer the primary target? Or was the motivation something far stranger, connected to the Resonance, the sanctuary, Boone's own long history with the valley?

"And the other one?" Elise asked hesitantly. "The one that fell in the river?"

Boone's face darkened. "Didn't see it again. River took it. Fast." He looked towards the creek flowing past the cabin clearing. "Water runs deep in these mountains. Takes things. Doesn't always give 'em back." The implication was clear. Their desperate act had likely been fatal for the creature. The thought left a sour taste in Elise's mouth, complicating the relief of their own survival.

"So you followed our tracks?" Nora asked, bringing them back to the present. "Found this place?"

Boone nodded. "Saw your sign back on the pass. Followed you down the gully. Lost your trail for a bit in the timber, then… smelled the smoke." He gestured towards the cabin. "Found this old place yesterday evening. Trapper's cabin, maybe? Built solid, ages ago. Door was rotten, busted in. Place was empty, dusty. But the hearth was good, chimney draws clear. Found some dry wood stacked inside. Figured… figured it was as good a place as any to hole up, try to recover, figure out the next move." He looked at them again, exhaustion evident beneath the surface resilience. "Never figured my next move would be seein' you two walk outta the woods."

The reunion felt surreal, improbable. Three survivors, reunited against all odds in a forgotten cabin deep in the wilderness, linked by shared trauma and the impossible secret they carried.

"Levi?" Boone asked quietly after a moment, his gaze searching their faces, already guessing the answer from their expressions.

Elise shook her head, fresh tears welling. "He didn't make it, Boone," she whispered. "Infection… and the climb… He… he stayed behind. Bought us time."

Boone closed his eyes briefly, absorbing the news. He cursed softly under his breath, a sound of weary grief, not surprise. He likely knew Levi's chances had been slim. Another casualty added to the tally. Another sacrifice made.

He opened his eyes, the grief settling into grim resolve. "Right," he said heavily. "So… it's just us three then." He looked from Elise to Nora, then scanned the surrounding woods again, the hunter's instinct reasserting itself. "Question is… for how long? Kestrel knows you two got out. They'll be lookin'. And," his gaze grew distant, troubled, "whoever left that rope in the vent shaft… someone else knows about these passages. Knows how to get in and out. Maybe Tallsalt," he glanced at Nora, "maybe… somethin' else."

The mystery of the rope, the question of other players, added another layer of complexity to their already perilous situation. But for now, finding Boone alive felt like a miracle, a desperately needed infusion of strength and practical skill into their depleted party.

"First things first," Boone decided, turning back towards the woodpile, picking up his axe with a familiar, comforting solidity. "Need more wood before dark. Need water boiled. Need to figure out how hurt we all really are." He looked at Elise, a flicker of the old, pragmatic tracker returning. "And you, Doc… you look like you got stories to tell. About glowing caves, maybe? About why that elder let me walk away?"

Elise met his gaze, saw the questions burning there, the need to understand. She nodded slowly. Yes, there were stories to tell. Stories of the Heart of the Mountain, of Project Chimera, of buried files and frozen bodies. Stories that might explain everything, or nothing at all. Sharing the burden, finally, felt like the only way forward. Here, in this remote cabin, reunited with Boone, allied with Nora, perhaps they could finally begin to piece together the Hollow Truth, and figure out how to survive carrying its immense, dangerous weight. The respite might be temporary, the threats still closing in, but for the first time in a long while, Elise didn't feel entirely alone in the vast, whispering wilderness.

Chapter 20: Scars of the Mountain, Scars of the Mind

The flickering firelight cast dancing shadows across the rough-hewn log walls of the small cabin, a welcome bastion against the deepening twilight outside. The scent of woodsmoke mingled with the earthy aroma of drying herbs hanging from the rafters and the faint, metallic tang of blood from the cuts Elise was carefully cleaning on Boone's face and hands. Nora sat quietly by the hearth, tending a pot of water boiling over the flames, occasionally adding herbs whose fragrance filled the small space – willow bark for pain, perhaps, yarrow to cleanse wounds, Elise guessed, recognizing some from Whis Elem's teachings.

The atmosphere was subdued, heavy with exhaustion and the ghosts of the fallen, yet underscored by a fragile sense of relief, of reunion against impossible odds. Finding Boone alive felt like finding an anchor in a storm-tossed sea. His presence, his pragmatic competence, his sheer stubborn refusal to be broken by the horrors they had faced, lent a desperately needed strength to their ragged trio.

As Elise dabbed antiseptic from her depleted first-aid kit onto a nasty gash above Boone's eye – likely from his collision with the fissure wall – he recounted his encounter with the elder Stick-shí'nač after she and Nora had fled.

"Pinned me down like a damn butterfly," Boone said, his voice low, gravelly, wincing as the antiseptic stung. "Felt its breath on my face… smelled like wet earth and… ozone, almost. Like right before lightning strikes." He shuddered involuntarily. "Roared right over me, sound went through my bones, shook my teeth loose, felt like. Thought that was it. Then… it just stopped."

He frowned, still clearly bewildered by the memory. "Looked at me. Real hard. Like it was… readin' somethin'. Then it let out that howl… the one that sounded like pure grief. And then… just backed off. Turned around and walked away, back towards the river cavern passage. Didn't even look back."

"It knew," Nora murmured from the hearth, her voice soft but certain. "It knew its kin had fallen in the river. Perhaps… perhaps it saw no need for further death. Or perhaps," her gaze grew distant, "it saw something in your spirit, Boone. Resilience. Respect, maybe, even in the fight. The guardians… their ways are not always about simple vengeance."

Boone snorted softly, unconvinced by the mystical explanation but unable to offer a better one. "Whatever the reason, I didn't stick around to ask questions. Soon as it was gone, I checked my ribs – felt like hell, but nothin' punctured – grabbed my light, and started followin' your tracks outta that fissure before it changed its mind." He shook his head. "Climbin' out… that was rough. Found my shotgun where you said. Empty. Figured you two kept goin', hoped like hell you'd find a way down."

"We found the Crevice," Elise explained quietly, finishing the bandage on his forehead. "An old loggers' route. Straight down." She didn't elaborate on the terror of that descent, the darkness, the failing lights. The shared experience needed no detailed recounting.

Boone nodded grimly. "Figured as much. Saw the signs on the pass. Followed you down the gully." He looked around the small cabin. "Led me here. Lucky break."

"Maybe not just luck," Nora countered gently. "This place… it offers refuge to those who approach with need, not greed. Perhaps the mountain guided you."

Boone didn't argue, just accepted a mug of hot, herb-infused water from Nora, cradling it in his scraped hands. The warmth seemed to seep into him, easing some of the tension in his shoulders.

Now it was Elise's turn. As darkness fully enveloped the cabin outside, the only light the flickering fire and the single, precious tallow candle Nora had produced and lit, Elise recounted their own journey after Boone's disappearance. She described the impossible architecture of the sanctuary, the ethereal light, the feeling of ancient presence, the eerie silence. She spoke of the adolescent creature, its tentative curiosity, the near-communication shattered by Levi's delirious shot. She detailed the terrifying attack, the falling stones, Levi being taken then inexplicably left behind, Boone's charge drawing the elder away.

Boone listened intently, his expression shifting from disbelief to grim understanding as she described the chaos. He closed his eyes briefly when she recounted Levi's final moments, his sacrifice at the base of the fissure. "Damn fool," he muttered, but the words held affection, respect, not condemnation. "Paid his debt, I guess."

Then Elise moved on to the deeper secrets, the core of the Hollow Truth she now carried. She described the hidden passage behind the rockfall, the miners' chamber, the desperate logbook entries chronicling their descent into madness and death, the corroboration of the Resonance, the whispering stones. She explained finding Miller's Bible, the implication that Kestrel or Project Backwoods had silenced human witnesses decades ago.

She recounted their discovery of the hidden Kestrel lab, the frozen body of 'Echo', the evidence of horrific experimentation dating back to the late 80s, the connection to Aris Thorne and the mysterious Volkov. She described the adolescent creature's apparent grief, its fearful retreat.

And finally, she spoke of the Heart-Chamber. The pulsing crystals, the glowing carvings telling millennia of history, the overwhelming Resonance, the hints of extraterrestrial contact buried deep in Stick-shí'nač lore and glyphs. She described the impossible stone doorway opening, the feeling of being invited or compelled into the source of the power, the subsequent sensory overload and retreat. She explained finding Boone's scratch marks, his discarded shotgun, the ambiguous tracks leading out onto the high pass.

As she finished, silence filled the small cabin, thick and heavy. Boone stared into the fire, processing the torrent of impossible information, his face pale beneath the firelight, his expression unreadable. Nora sat quietly, seemingly unsurprised by the deeper revelations, the existence of the Heart-Chamber and the forbidden stories aligning perhaps with the most esoteric layers of Tallsalt cosmology.

"So," Boone said finally, his voice rough, "Graves wasn't just chasin' Bigfoot. Kestrel… they're after somethin' else entirely. Alien tech? The power source? And the creatures… they're just… collateral damage? Or maybe… guardians of somethin' even they don't fully understand?" He shook his head, rubbing his temples. "Makes my head spin."

"It changes everything," Elise agreed quietly. "Kestrel's motives aren't just scientific curiosity or even resource exploitation. It's about… control. Control of potentially world-altering technology or energy. Control of the narrative, burying decades of illegal operations, disappearances, unethical research. They'll stop at nothing to protect that secret." She recounted the encounter with the unmarked helicopter, the managed fire line, the containment crews, the chilling debriefing, the confirmation they were loose ends.

"Which means they're still hunting us," Boone concluded grimly. "This cabin… it's shelter for now. But they'll keep looking. Expanding their search grid. Using tech we can't even guess at." He looked at Elise. "And that proof you carry… the memory card, the logbook page… that makes you target number one."

"I know," Elise admitted. "I hid the main files back in the caves, before we found you. But I kept this." She patted the hidden pocket in her jacket. "Enough to be dangerous, I guess."

"Dangerous is right," Boone muttered. He fell silent again, staring into the flames, the weight of their situation pressing down. Three survivors against a ruthless, technologically advanced shadow organization, possessing knowledge that could rewrite history or trigger global catastrophe, stranded in a wilderness potentially still patrolled by ancient, powerful beings whose motives remained terrifyingly opaque.

"We need a plan," he said eventually, looking from Elise to Nora. "Staying here long-term ain't it. They'll find us eventually. Trying to hike out conventionally… risky. Roads will be watched. Towns watched. Kestrel's got eyes everywhere."

"Whis Elem…" Elise began, "she suggested… learning. Understanding. Trying to find a way to communicate, maybe even mediate…"

Boone cut her off with a harsh laugh. "Meditate? With them? Doc, did you forget they tore Jules apart? Used David Chen's bones for nesting material? Tried to crush us with standing stones? Yeah, the elder let me walk away, for reasons I sure as hell don't understand. And yeah, maybe the young one felt bad about Echo. But that don't make 'em trustworthy allies! They're wild, powerful, unpredictable. One wrong move, one misunderstood signal – like Levi's shot – and they turn lethal. Trying to 'mediate' sounds like a good way to end up as another skull in their collection." His fear, his trauma, his pragmatic survival instinct recoiled from the idealistic path Whis Elem had suggested.

"Boone has a point," Nora conceded sadly, though Elise sensed her own inclination leaned towards Whis Elem's view. "Direct communication… is fraught with peril. Misunderstanding runs deep between our kinds, after centuries of conflict and fear. And Kestrel… they are the immediate fire burning at our backs. Dealing with them must be the priority, perhaps."

"But how?" Elise asked desperately. "We can't fight them head-on. Exposing them through official channels seems impossible, they'll just discredit us or silence us."

Boone leaned forward, poking the fire thoughtfully, his eyes narrowed in calculation. "Maybe... maybe we don't fight Kestrel head-on. Maybe we fight fire with fire. Or rather... secrets with secrets." He looked up, a hard glint in his eyes. "You said Graves' files mentioned Kestrel wasn't the first. Project Backwoods. Army involvement. Government cover-up goin' back decades."

Elise nodded. "Yes. The files I hid, the logbook, the stuff in the Backwoods substation... it all points to a long history, probably originating in the Cold War."

"Right," Boone continued, thinking aloud. "So Kestrel... they ain't operating in a vacuum. They inherited this mess, this secret, from someone higher up. Government agencies. Military intelligence. People who likely still have an interest in keepin' that lid clamped down tight. Maybe Kestrel is just... the current contractor, the deniable asset doin' the dirty work."

"What are you suggesting?" Elise asked, intrigued by his line of reasoning.

"I'm suggestin'... maybe Kestrel has enemies," Boone said slowly. "Or rivals. Within the government, maybe. Other agencies who resent their secrecy, their budget, their methods. Or maybe... foreign powers who'd love to get their hands on whatever Kestrel's protecting or exploiting in that valley." He looked at Elise intently. "That Russian name in the lab – Volkov? What if Kestrel's cleanup wasn't perfect? What if evidence exists, not just buried in caves, but in old government archives, forgotten military bases, maybe even overseas, that could expose not just Kestrel, but the whole damn fifty-year cover-up?"

The idea was audacious. Instead of trying to leak their fragmented proof to an unprepared public, maybe they could leak it *strategically* to Kestrel's hidden rivals, triggering an internal conflict, a shadow war that might expose the entire conspiracy from within, or at least distract Kestrel long enough for Elise and Nora to disappear more permanently.

"How would we even find such evidence?" Elise asked, daunted by the scale of the suggestion. "Let alone leak it without getting caught?"

"Don't know yet," Boone admitted. "But it feels… like a direction. Something active. Something that uses Kestrel's own paranoia against them." He glanced towards the hidden proof Elise carried. "That memory card… the logbook page… maybe combined with whatever's in those Backwoods files you found… it might be enough. Enough to light a fuse, if delivered to the right place, the right person."

He suggested a new plan, tentative, dangerous. Use Nora's network again, not just for survival, but for intelligence. Try to identify potential weak points in the Kestrel/government secrecy apparatus – disgruntled former agents, rival departments, forgotten archives accessible through back channels. It would require immense caution, sophisticated tradecraft neither Elise nor Boone truly possessed, relying heavily on Nora's contacts and their ability to move undetected.

"It's still incredibly risky," Elise cautioned, though the idea held a certain appeal – turning the tables, using information as a weapon. "One mistake, one intercepted message…"

"Everythin's risky now, Doc," Boone countered grimly. "Sittin' here is risky. Walkin' out is risky. This… at least feels like fightin' back on our own terms, using our heads, not just runnin'."

Nora remained thoughtful. "Using knowledge as a weapon… can cut both ways," she warned. "Unleashing such secrets could cause chaos far beyond Kestrel. Are we prepared for that?"

"We're already living in the chaos, Nora," Boone argued. "Kestrel created it. Maybe exposing it is the only way to eventually find balance again."

The debate hung in the air, heavy with consequence. Fight Kestrel directly? Try to understand and mediate with the Stick-shí'nač? Or attempt Boone's strategy of igniting a shadow war by leaking secrets to unseen rivals? Each path felt fraught with peril, each carrying immense ethical weight.

As the fire burned low, casting long shadows that danced like spirits on the cabin walls, Elise felt the weight of the decision settle upon her. Whis Elem's path felt right, aligned with respecting the creatures and the ancient balance. But Boone's pragmatism, his assessment of Kestrel as the immediate, relentless threat, felt undeniably true. And his idea… using Kestrel's own secrecy against them… it held a certain dark appeal, a potential route to justice for the fallen, even if it risked wider instability.

Perhaps, she realized, the paths weren't mutually exclusive. Perhaps understanding the Stick-shí'nač, learning their ways, was necessary *in order to* effectively combat Kestrel, to protect the sanctuary from the *human* threat. Perhaps Boone's tactical approach and Whis Elem's wisdom could coexist, informing each other.

"Okay," Elise said finally, meeting Boone's intense gaze, then Nora's calm one. "Let's explore Boone's idea. Let's see if Nora's network can gather any intelligence on Kestrel's structure, potential rivals, old Backwoods connections. Let's identify potential targets for the information we have." She paused, adding a crucial condition. "But we do it carefully. We don't release anything that could directly pinpoint the sanctuary or endanger the creatures unnecessarily. Our first priority is stopping Kestrel's immediate plans, their Sanitization Protocol. Exposing the deeper truth about the Stick-shí'nač themselves… that needs more thought. More understanding. Maybe," she echoed Whis Elem, "the world isn't ready."

It was a compromise, an attempt to balance the immediate need for action against Kestrel with the long-term ethical considerations regarding the Stick-shí'nač. Boone nodded slowly, accepting the constraint. Nora inclined her head, acknowledging the difficult balance.

A fragile consensus was reached. Their new mission: gather intelligence, identify Kestrel's vulnerabilities, and prepare to use their fragmented, dangerous knowledge as a weapon, aiming it strategically not just for survival, but for disruption, hoping to trigger a conflict within the shadows that might consume the hunters themselves. It felt like walking into a minefield blindfolded, but it was a direction.

As they banked the fire and prepared for an uneasy, watchful rest, Elise felt a strange sense of clarity amidst the exhaustion and fear. The scars of the mountain, the trauma inflicted by the guardians, were deep, undeniable. But the scars left by Kestrel, by human greed and secrecy, felt somehow more insidious, more poisonous. Addressing those scars, fighting back against the human darkness, felt like the necessary next step on her journey as a Child of Two Worlds. The listening would continue, the respect would remain, but the time for passive observation was over. The hunt, in a different, more strategic form, was back on.

Chapter 21: Threads in the Shadows

The days following their reunion in the isolated cabin settled into a tense rhythm of recovery, planning, and low-level reconnaissance, underscored by the constant, gnawing awareness of their precarious position. Boone's cracked ribs healed slowly, the pain a persistent reminder of the elder Stick-shí'nač's terrifying power and inexplicable restraint. Elise's exhaustion began to recede, replaced by a sharp, focused energy fueled by their new, desperate plan. Nora, the quiet center of their fragile unit, moved with her usual efficiency, tending to their needs, her deep knowledge of the forest providing sustenance and security, while her eyes held the watchful wisdom of someone navigating multiple invisible currents.

They couldn't stay at Boone's discovered cabin. It felt too exposed, too easily discoverable if Kestrel expanded their search grid systematically. Using Nora's intricate knowledge of the less-traveled paths and hidden places within her ancestral territory, they relocated, moving cautiously south and west, further away from AO Hollow and the known Kestrel activity near the park boundaries. Their new base became a series of temporary, shifting camps – a dry overhang beneath a waterfall, a forgotten hunter's blind deep in an alder thicket, eventually settling for a slightly longer period in a small, dry cave system Nora knew, hidden high on a ridge overlooking a sparsely populated river valley.

This new location offered relative security – difficult access, multiple escape routes, good vantage points – but also proximity, albeit still measured in miles of rough terrain, to small towns, logging roads, and potentially, fragments of the outside world's communication network. From here, they began the incredibly risky process of pulling at the threads of the Kestrel conspiracy, guided by Elise's fragmented knowledge from the buried files and Boone's increasingly sharp strategic thinking.

"Alright, Doc," Boone said one evening, huddled near the small, smokeless fire they risked inside the cave mouth, sketching rough organizational charts in the dirt with a stick based on Elise's recollections. "Project Backwoods. Forest Service, Army, maybe CIA or someone similar involved back in the 70s. Their goal was observation, suppression. Then it morphed into Kestrel's Project Chimera, overseen by... who? Still government? Or is Kestrel fully private now, gone rogue with the knowledge?"

"I don't know," Elise admitted, frustration clear in her voice. "The files I saw... the transition memo... it implied Kestrel Foundation oversight, but the original authorization, the secrecy protocols... they felt governmental. Maybe Kestrel is a cut-out, a deniable entity funded through black budgets?"

"Makes sense," Boone nodded grimly. "Keeps the politicians' hands clean if things go sideways. Like they did with Goliath. Like they did with Echo. Like they did with us." He tapped the dirt. "So, Backwoods operatives... some likely rotated out, retired over the years. Some might have died, like the guy in the substation. Some might have been... silenced, if they knew too much or objected." He looked at Elise. "And some might still be around. Old soldiers, old forest rangers, intelligence spooks haunted by what they saw in these woods decades ago."

"Finding them would be like finding needles in a continent-sized haystack," Elise argued. "Their records would be classified, buried deep."

"Maybe," Boone conceded. "But people talk. Especially years later. Especially if they carry guilt, or resentment." He glanced at Nora. "Your network, Nora... any whispers? Old stories from elders about strange military types asking questions back in the day? Or locals who worked on those secret bases, maybe saw things they shouldn't have?"

Nora considered it, her gaze distant. "There are always stories on the edges," she said slowly. "Rumors of men who came asking about the Stick-shí'nač, showing strange photos, offering money for guidance into forbidden valleys. Most were turned away.

Some... were perhaps listened to, for a price, by those less concerned with the old ways." She frowned. "And yes, tales of the hidden bases during the Cold War. My uncle... he once stumbled upon a fenced area near Mount Jupiter while hunting, was aggressively turned back by men in unmarked uniforms. He never went near there again. Said the air felt... wrong."

"Mount Jupiter?" Boone's eyes sharpened. "That's south of here. Known seismic activity in that region too, right Doc?"

Elise nodded. "Minor tremors, usually. Part of the Cascadia subduction zone complex. Why?"

"Resonance," Boone said thoughtfully. "Maybe Kestrel, or Backwoods, had listening posts near geologically active zones, trying to understand the source? Or maybe trying to communicate *using* it?" The idea was outlandish, but fit the pattern of strangeness. "Could be a place Kestrel missed in their cleanup. Worth checking archives, if we can risk it."

Their intelligence gathering became a multi-pronged, incredibly cautious effort. Nora used her contacts, dispatching discreet inquiries through trusted channels within the Tallsalt and neighboring tribal communities, seeking elders' memories, hunters' observations, any anomalies related to specific locations or time periods linked to Backwoods or Kestrel activity. The process was slow, reliant on trust and oral tradition, yielding fragments rather than hard data, but potentially invaluable context.

Elise and Boone focused on the digital realm, a terrifying prospect given Kestrel's likely surveillance capabilities. They established a strict protocol. Using the burner laptop, powered by a small, foldable solar panel Boone had scavenged and repaired, they only ever connected to the internet from unpredictable locations, miles from their current camp, usually public Wi-Fi hotspots in small towns they hiked near under cover of darkness or poor weather. They used layers of VPNs, anonymizing browsers like Tor, and constantly changing encrypted email accounts for any necessary communication tests or dead drops. Each connection felt like holding their breath underwater, lasting only minutes, downloading targeted information quickly, then wiping the connection logs and physically moving before any signal could be reliably traced.

Elise focused her searches, guided by the names and project codes from the files. She searched declassified government archives online, university research databases, obscure geological survey reports, looking for mentions of Project Backwoods, Dr. Aris Thorne, Dr. Ivan Volkov, or anomalous environmental data related to AO Hollow or other suspected sites like Mount Jupiter. Most searches hit dead ends, classified walls, or returned sanitized, useless information. But occasionally, a crack appeared. A heavily redacted environmental impact statement from the late 70s briefly mentioning 'geotechnical instability' necessitating restricted access near the Elwha mine site. A footnote in an obscure seismology paper referencing unexplained 'low-frequency resonance patterns' detected by temporary arrays near Mount Jupiter in 1975, data subsequently classified. A single, tantalizing hit on Aris Thorne in an archived university staff directory from the 1970s, listing him as a visiting scholar in 'Primate Ethology and Cryptozoology' – the latter term raising Elise's eyebrows – before his record vanished from subsequent years. Small fragments, but they corroborated the hidden history.

Boone, surprisingly adept at navigating the shadier corners of the internet, focused on different angles. He searched dark web forums, whistleblower sites (approached with extreme caution, assuming Kestrel monitored them), looking for any leaked documents, any chatter related to black budget projects, private military contractors operating in the Pacific Northwest, or unexplained disappearances linked to Kestrel's known (though limited) public activities. He found mostly noise, conspiracy theories, dead ends. But he also found whispers – rumors of a shadowy foundation involved in 'biological asset recovery', hints of clashes between private security outfits and federal agencies in remote areas, mentions of advanced sonic or electromagnetic tech being tested in wilderness zones. Again, nothing concrete, but suggestive patterns emerged, hinting at Kestrel's operational methods and potential rivalries.

They compiled their findings meticulously in Elise's notebook, cross-referencing, looking for overlaps, trying to build a coherent picture from the scattered puzzle pieces. It felt like trying to map a hidden continent based on driftwood and distant birdsong.

Their precarious existence was punctuated by moments of sharp fear. One afternoon, while Elise was cautiously using the Wi-Fi at a small roadside café miles from their camp, the connection suddenly dropped. At the same moment, a nondescript utility van pulled slowly into the parking lot, two men inside watching the café entrance intently. Elise didn't wait. Leaving her half-finished coffee, she slipped out the back door, disappearing into the adjacent woods, heart pounding, convinced her digital precautions had failed, that they had traced her signal. She spent hours hiking back to camp through rough terrain, paranoia riding her shoulder, convinced every shadow held an agent. Whether it was a genuine near-miss or coincidence, the incident forced them to become even more cautious, reducing their online activity to absolute minimums.

Another time, scouting a potential new campsite further west, Boone found undeniable evidence of recent Kestrel presence – discarded military-grade ration wrappers (different from their own expedition supplies), faint tracks from specialized all-terrain boots, and most disturbingly, a tiny, camouflaged electronic sensor device attached high on a tree overlooking a game trail, likely part of Kestrel's expanding surveillance network. They retreated immediately, the discovery confirming Kestrel wasn't just searching randomly; they were deploying assets, actively monitoring movement corridors even outside the primary quarantine zone.

And sometimes, reminders of the other watchers surfaced. Faint, resonant hums felt deep in the earth at odd hours. A series of massive, unidentifiable tracks found crossing a muddy creek bed far from AO Hollow, heading purposefully westwards. One evening, huddled near their cave entrance, they heard it – a distant, mournful howl echoing from the high ridges, answered moments later by another, further away. Not wolves. The sound was deeper, richer, carrying that same bone-vibrating quality Elise remembered from the elder's grief-stricken cry. The guardians were active, communicating, perhaps responding to the increased human intrusion, their presence a wild card in the deadly game being played out in their territory.

Despite the dangers and setbacks, their fragmented intelligence slowly began to coalesce around one potential lead, emerging from the confluence of Nora's network and Elise's archival digging. Nora's contacts reported persistent rumors, dating back years, about an old, supposedly decommissioned Cold War radar station hidden deep in the forests southwest of Mount Olympus. Locals occasionally saw strange lights there at night, or encountered unusually aggressive 'security personnel' warning them away from the perimeter, even though the site was officially listed as abandoned federal property. Concurrently, Elise found heavily redacted budget documents from the late 1970s referencing 'Special Project - Site Sierra' (matching the protocol name from the Backwoods transition memo) involving significant upgrades to remote 'atmospheric monitoring facilities' in the Olympic region, upgrades whose funding trail abruptly vanished into classified Kestrel Foundation accounts in the early 1980s.

Site Sierra. The name felt significant. A remote Cold War facility, secretly maintained or reactivated by Kestrel? Could this be where they took Goliath after capture? Where Echo was experimented on? Could it hold central archives, biological samples, evidence Kestrel couldn't easily sanitize or relocate?

"It fits," Boone mused, studying the location on Elise's map. "Remote. Defensible. Existing infrastructure they could repurpose secretly. Close enough to the AO for transport, but far enough to be outside the immediate quarantine zone." He traced a potential route. "Getting there... won't be easy. Rough country. And you can bet Kestrel guards it tighter than Fort Knox if it's still active."

"We need confirmation," Elise insisted. "We can't risk approaching a potentially active Kestrel base without knowing what we're walking into."

Nora offered a possibility. "There is an old hunter," she said thoughtfully. "Man of the Klallam people, related to my mother's side. Lives alone, deep in the woods near the Sol Duc River, closer to that area. Knows those ridges better than anyone alive. Avoids outsiders. But... he respects the old ways. And he has no love for the government that took his ancestral lands." She paused. "He might know something about Site Sierra. Might have seen things over the years. If anyone could get close enough to observe without being detected, it would be him. His name is Ish."

Making contact with this reclusive hunter, Ish, felt like their next logical step. A potential source of direct, eyewitness intelligence about Site Sierra, bypassing the risks of digital surveillance or direct confrontation. It required another journey, deeper into unfamiliar territory, relying once again on Nora's network and guidance.

They debated the risks. Ish might refuse to speak with them. He might inadvertently lead Kestrel to them. The journey itself would be perilous. But the potential reward – confirmation and actionable intelligence about a hidden Kestrel facility – was too great to ignore. If Site Sierra held the keys to understanding Kestrel's operations, potentially even biological evidence or records Kestrel thought long buried, it could be the leverage they desperately needed.

As they prepared to leave the relative safety of their cave hideout, packing their dwindling supplies, checking their worn gear, Elise felt a familiar mix of fear and resolve. Every step forward felt like deeper entanglement, higher stakes. They were pulling at threads woven over decades, threads connecting government secrets, corporate greed, ancient guardians, and forgotten victims. Each thread potentially led to answers, but also risked unraveling the entire fragile tapestry, bringing the full weight of Kestrel's power, or the guardians' wrath, down upon them. Yet, the alternative – silence, waiting, letting the Hollow Truth remain buried – felt like a betrayal they could no longer afford. The whispers from the past were growing louder, demanding attention, and the path towards the solitary hunter Ish, near the rumored secrets of Site Sierra, felt like the only way to truly begin answering their call.

Chapter 22: The Hermit of Sol Duc

The journey towards the Sol Duc valley, seeking the elusive Klallam hunter named Ish, felt like descending into another layer of the Olympic wilderness, wilder and more remote than the areas they had traversed since escaping the Crevice. Nora led them on paths that seemed barely to exist – faint game trails winding through colossal stands of ancient rainforest, riverbanks choked with impenetrable salmonberry thickets, steep ridges draped in mist where the silence was broken only by the mournful cry of a distant raven or the roar of unseen waterfalls crashing in deep canyons below.

They moved with heightened caution, acutely aware that they were venturing into territory less familiar even to Nora, closer to areas potentially frequented by the Stick-shí'nač outside their core sanctuary, and simultaneously deeper into the potential search grid Kestrel might be establishing around rumored sites like the abandoned radar station, Site Sierra. Every shadow seemed deeper here, every snapped twig more alarming. The feeling of being watched was a constant companion, though whether by human eyes, guardian eyes, or simply the ancient, indifferent awareness of the primordial forest, remained unsettlingly ambiguous.

Their supplies were critically low. The last energy bar was gone, their diet reduced to foraged roots Nora identified, edible but bitter ferns, and the occasional small trout Boone managed to catch with a makeshift line and hook in the icy streams. Hunger became a dull, constant ache, sharpening their senses but also fraying their nerves, making rational thought feel like swimming against a current of fatigue and gnawing emptiness. Elise felt her body weakening, the hard-won physical recovery threatening to slip away under the relentless strain.

After four days of grueling travel, following Nora's intricate navigation through the complex drainages feeding the Sol Duc River, they finally reached the area Ish was said to inhabit – a secluded side valley, high up, shielded by steep ridges, known historically to the Klallam as a place of spiritual significance and difficult access.

"He will be wary," Nora warned as they approached the valley floor, moving slowly through stands of immense Sitka spruce and western hemlock whose canopy formed a perpetual twilight. "Ish values his solitude. He does not welcome outsiders, especially those carrying the scent of trouble."

"How do we approach him?" Elise asked, feeling acutely aware of her own otherness, her connection to the world that had likely caused Ish's ancestors, and perhaps Ish himself, great harm.

"We do not approach directly," Nora instructed. "We make our presence known respectfully. Wait for him to acknowledge us. Or turn us away."

Following Nora's lead, they found a small, clear stream bubbling through mossy rocks near the center of the valley floor. Here, Nora performed a simple ritual. She gathered smooth stones from the stream bed, arranging them in a specific pattern on a large, flat boulder near the water – a traditional Klallam signal, she explained, indicating respectful visitors seeking counsel. Then, she sat quietly on the boulder, facing upstream, her posture conveying patience, deference. Elise and Boone found spots nearby, imitating Nora's quiet waiting, trying to project calm they didn't feel.

They waited. An hour passed. The only sounds were the gurgle of the stream, the sigh of wind high in the ancient trees, the occasional call of a forest bird. Elise fought against impatience, against the urge to call out, to search for Ish's dwelling. Trust the process, she reminded herself. Trust Nora's wisdom.

Finally, a figure emerged silently from the dense woods across the stream, moving with a quiet grace that blended seamlessly with the shadows. He was older than Elise had expected, perhaps in his late seventies or even eighties, but lean and wiry, his face a roadmap of deep wrinkles etched by sun, wind, and time. He wore practical, patched canvas clothing and carried a long, beautifully crafted wooden bow, unstrung, resting easily in his hand. His eyes, dark and piercingly sharp, scanned the three visitors on the opposite bank, lingering longest on Elise, the obvious outsider. This had to be Ish.

He didn't speak immediately. He simply stood, observing them, his presence radiating a quiet, grounded authority, a deep connection to this place that felt immensely powerful, utterly unshakeable. Elise felt suddenly self-conscious, acutely aware of her torn clothes, her grimy face, the fear that likely still lingered in her eyes.

After a long moment that stretched Elise's nerves taut, Ish finally spoke, his voice low, rough, like stones rubbing together, yet carrying clearly across the stream. "The singing grandmother sends greetings?" He looked directly at Nora.

Nora inclined her head respectfully. "Whis Elem remembers you, Uncle Ish. She sends prayers for your continued health."

Ish nodded slowly, accepting the connection. His gaze shifted back to Elise, then to Boone. "You travel with heavy shadows," he observed flatly. "The scent of fear… and blood recently shed… clings to you. Trouble walks with you." It wasn't a question.

"We seek knowledge, Uncle," Nora replied carefully. "Guidance. About the watchers on the mountain. And about… the other intruders. The ones with machines and dark jackets."

Ish's eyes narrowed almost imperceptibly. He remained silent for another long moment, studying them, his gaze seeming to penetrate beneath their ragged exteriors, assessing their intentions, their spirits. Elise held her breath, sensing this was a critical juncture. His cooperation, his knowledge, could be vital. His rejection could leave them utterly stranded.

"The mountain guards its secrets fiercely," Ish said finally, his voice low. "And those who disturb its sleep... often find only sorrow." He paused, his gaze sweeping across the silent forest around them. "But the balance... it feels... wrong lately. The whispers on the wind are troubled. The guardians," he used a Klallam term Elise didn't recognize but understood implicitly, "are restless. Their ancient anger stirs." His eyes returned to Elise. "And the other intruders... the ones with cold eyes and hidden weapons... their presence is a poison spreading through the roots."

He seemed to reach a decision. "Come," he said simply, turning back towards the woods. "My camp is near. We will speak. But choose your words carefully. Truth is a sharp edge in these times."

Relief washed over Elise, quickly followed by renewed apprehension. They had been accepted, granted audience. But Ish's words held warning. He knew of the guardians, felt the disturbance, recognized the threat posed by Kestrel. Sharing their story, asking for his help, required navigating a delicate path between revealing too much and not enough.

They followed Ish across the stream, stepping carefully on submerged stones, then along a barely visible path leading deeper into the woods. He moved with surprising speed and silence for his age, forcing them to hurry to keep up. After perhaps ten minutes, they arrived at his camp. It wasn't a cabin, but a remarkably well-camouflaged shelter built against the base of a colossal, ancient cedar tree. Walls were formed from woven cedar bark panels and tightly packed moss, blending almost perfectly with the surrounding forest floor. A low doorway covered by a hide flap led inside. A small, smokeless fire pit nearby held glowing embers, radiating warmth. It was a place of profound simplicity, utterly integrated with the environment.

Ish gestured for them to sit on smooth logs arranged near the fire pit. He disappeared briefly inside the shelter, emerging with dried salmon strips and a small pouch of potent-smelling herbs, which he added to a kettle of water already heating over the embers. He offered them the salmon, which Elise and Boone accepted gratefully, tearing into the chewy, salty flesh with ravenous hunger.

As they ate, Ish watched them, his silence more appraising than awkward. When they had finished, he poured the steaming herbal tea into three chipped enamel mugs, handing one to each of them. The tea was strong, bitter, but warming.

"Now," Ish said, sipping his own tea slowly. "Tell me of the heavy shadows you carry. Tell me why the guardians hunt you, and why the poison-bringers follow."

Taking a deep breath, Elise began, choosing her words with care, aided by occasional clarifications or cultural context from Nora. She spoke of the Kestrel expedition, framed initially as ecological research. She described the escalating strangeness – the silence, the tracks, the sounds. She recounted Boone's story of his lost brother, linking the past to the present. She mentioned Jules' disappearance, hinting at violence without detailing the nest. She spoke of the technological failures, the sense of being herded. She described the clear sighting on the ridge, confirming the creatures' reality. She recounted Graves' increasingly erratic behavior, the confrontation, his death during the escape attempt (omitting the specific cause, attributing it vaguely to the climb and the creature's presence). She told of Levi's sacrifice, their desperate journey through the caves.

Throughout her narrative, she deliberately omitted the most explosive secrets – the hidden sanctuary, the Heart-Chamber, the extraterrestrial hints, the contents of Graves' files proving Kestrel's long conspiracy and horrific experiments, the miners' logbook, the hidden evidence she carried. She presented their story as one of survival against unknown creatures and a mission gone terribly wrong, hinting at Kestrel's negligence and potential cover-up without revealing the full depth of their monstrosity or the true nature of the Stick-shí'nač civilization. It felt like a necessary deception, protecting the deepest secrets while still conveying the essence of their peril and their need for information about Kestrel.

Ish listened impassively, his ancient eyes revealing nothing, sipping his tea, occasionally adding a twig to the embers. When Elise finished, the silence stretched again, thick with unspoken questions.

"You saw the Sa'qellema'?" Ish asked finally, using a specific Klallam name for the creatures, one that perhaps carried nuances beyond the more generic 'Stick-shí'nač'. "Felt their power? Walked their hidden paths?"

"Yes," Elise confirmed simply.

"And Kestrel," Ish continued, his gaze sharpening. "The poison-bringers. You believe they hunt you now to… silence you? To protect their failed mission?"

"Yes," Elise said. "And perhaps… to protect older secrets. We found evidence… of earlier intrusions. Military projects, perhaps. From decades ago." She kept it vague, testing his reaction.

Ish nodded slowly, his expression grim. "Project Backwoods," he murmured, confirming Boone's suspicion and Elise's fragmented findings. "Yes. My father, his brothers… they knew of it. Soldiers moving secretly in the deep woods, building hidden camps, asking questions about the Sa'qellema'. Taking photographs from the air. Setting strange machines that hummed in the earth." He spat contemptuously onto the ground. "They thought their secrets were well kept. But the mountain sees all. And the people of the forest… we listen."

"What happened to them?" Elise asked urgently. "Project Backwoods?"

Ish shrugged, a gesture encompassing decades of rumor and tragedy. "They angered the guardians, I think. Pushed too far. There were… disappearances. Men vanished from locked camps. Equipment found smashed by impossible strength. Strange sicknesses afflicted those who spent too long near the humming machines." He looked towards the direction of the abandoned radar station Nora had mentioned. "Site Sierra, they called one place. High on the ridges overlooking the Sol Duc. Active for years, lights seen, guarded fiercely. Then... suddenly silent. Empty. The government said the project ended, the site decommissioned due to budget cuts, geological instability." He snorted softly. "More lies. Something happened there. Something broke free, perhaps. Or something broke *them*."

"Is the site still guarded?" Boone asked, leaning forward intently. "Is Kestrel using it now?"

Ish frowned thoughtfully. "I have not been that high on those ridges for many seasons. My legs are old." He paused. "But hunters I trust... they say the silence there feels... wrong. Not empty, but... watchful. They have found strange tracks nearby sometimes, not Sa'qellema', but... metal? Machines? And occasional lights still seen at night, low to the ground, moving erratically. Some say Kestrel uses it as a dumping ground, perhaps. For failed experiments? Broken machines? Or bodies?" The implication was chilling.

A dumping ground? Or an active, hidden facility? They needed to know.

"Uncle Ish," Nora said respectfully, "we believe Kestrel plans further... disruption. Perhaps near Site Sierra. Perhaps related to the Resonance, the power you spoke of. We need to know what is there. We need to anticipate their next move, find a way to stop them before more harm is done."

Ish regarded her gravely. "Seeking Kestrel's secrets is like digging for roots near a hornets' nest. You risk disturbing far more than you intend."

"We understand the risk," Elise stated firmly. "But doing nothing feels like a greater danger now. To us, to the balance you spoke of, maybe even to the guardians themselves if Kestrel's 'Sanitization Protocol' is real."

Ish studied their faces again – Elise's desperate resolve, Boone's grim determination, Nora's quiet strength. He seemed to weigh their sincerity, their potential, against the dangers. Finally, he gave a slow, decisive nod.

"Very well," he said. "I cannot go with you. My time for climbing high ridges is past. But I can offer guidance. And perhaps… a warning."

He spent the next hour sharing his knowledge, sketching rough maps in the dirt with a stick, describing landmarks, hidden trails, potential hazards near Site Sierra. He confirmed the location of the old radar station complex, nestled in a high basin, difficult to approach unseen. He spoke of strange magnetic anomalies in the area, compasses spinning wildly, radios failing – corroborating the miners' logbook and their own experiences near AO Hollow, suggesting the Resonance was strong there too. He warned of treacherous terrain, sudden weather shifts, and the increased likelihood of encountering unsettled guardians in that region, disturbed perhaps by Kestrel's lingering presence or the echoes of past conflicts.

His most crucial piece of guidance, however, was tactical. "Kestrel watches the obvious approaches," he stated. "The old access road, the main ridge lines. They use machines that see heat, that hear movement from afar." He pointed towards a deep, shadowed canyon system on Elise's topographical map, west of Site Sierra. "But they likely do not watch the deep ravines as closely. Especially those with… difficult air." He tapped a specific narrow canyon. "This one… the Klallam call it 'Stinkwater Canyon'. Not poison, but… sulfurous springs deep within. The air is heavy, unpleasant. Few animals use it. Kestrel's machines… perhaps they avoid it too? It offers a hidden path, approaching Site Sierra from the west, below the main ridge. Dangerous footing, bad air… but perhaps, unseen."

A hidden route, exploiting Kestrel's likely technological blind spots. It was exactly the kind of intel they needed.

As dusk began to settle again, casting long shadows across the small clearing, Ish offered them shelter for the night, sharing more of his smoked salmon and potent tea. He asked few questions about their time in the sanctuary, seeming to understand that some experiences were too profound, too dangerous, to be easily articulated. But his eyes held a deep, abiding curiosity, and a warning.

"You carry the scent of the Heart-Chamber now," he told Elise quietly, as they prepared to rest. "The guardians... they will know you. Some, like the elder perhaps, might show restraint, recognizing the... change in you. Others, angered by the intrusion, the deaths... they may see only a target. Tread carefully. Listen always. And remember," his gaze was piercing, "you cannot control the power you witnessed. Seek only to understand, and perhaps, to guide it away from conflict. Trying to wield it... that way lies madness, like the miners before you."

His words resonated deeply, reinforcing the perilous path Elise felt compelled to follow. Understanding, not control. Mediation, not manipulation.

That night, huddled in the surprising warmth and security of Ish's unique shelter – a shallow cave behind the cedar tree, lined with furs and woven mats – Elise felt a fragile sense of progress. They had found an ally, gained crucial intelligence, identified a potential target in Site Sierra, and discovered a possible hidden route. The odds still felt impossibly stacked against them, Kestrel's resources vast, the guardians' presence an unpredictable variable. But they had a direction, a strategy, however desperate.

As she drifted into an exhausted sleep, the last image in her mind was not of terror, but of the intricate carvings she had seen in the Heart-Chamber, telling millennia of history. She felt bound to that history now, a reluctant participant in the latest, perhaps final, chapter of the long, secret war between humanity and the ancient guardians of the Hollow Ground. The path led towards Site Sierra, towards Kestrel's hidden scars, and potentially, towards a confrontation that could determine the fate of more than just their own small group of survivors.

Chapter 23: Stinkwater Canyon

The air in Stinkwater Canyon hung thick and heavy, tasting metallic on the tongue, carrying the unmistakable, cloying stench of sulfur. It wasn't overpowering enough to be immediately debilitating, but it burned Elise's nostrils, made her eyes water, and left a constant unpleasantness at the back of her throat. Ish hadn't exaggerated; the air here felt fundamentally wrong, stagnant, leeched of the clean, pine-scented vitality of the surrounding forests. The narrow canyon floor was choked with sickly-looking vegetation – stunted, yellowing ferns, slimy patches of algae clinging to perpetually damp rocks, skeletal remains of alder trees that seemed to have withered from the roots up. The small stream that carved through the canyon ran sluggishly, its water stained a disconcerting reddish-orange in places, coated with a greasy film near the edges.

"Place feels cursed," Boone muttered, pulling the collar of his jacket higher, trying vainly to filter the unpleasant air. He moved stiffly, his cracked ribs clearly protesting the strenuous two-day trek from Ish's camp to the canyon mouth, but his eyes constantly scanned their surroundings, alert for any sign of Kestrel patrols or guardian presence.

"Not cursed," Nora corrected quietly, moving with her usual steady grace despite the oppressive atmosphere. "Just… wounded. Unbalanced. The springs deep within release poisons from the rock. Life struggles here." She pointed to faint game trails near the canyon wall, noticeably avoiding the watercourse itself. "Animals pass through, but do not linger."

That, Elise realized, was the strategic advantage Ish had offered. Kestrel's thermal imagers would struggle to differentiate body heat signatures against the background geothermal activity hinted at by the sulfurous springs. Their seismic sensors might be confused by the natural instability of the canyon walls and the constant trickle of water. And the Stick-shí'nač themselves, deeply attuned to the natural balance, likely avoided this 'wounded' place unless absolutely necessary. Stinkwater Canyon offered a corridor of relative concealment, a back door approach towards the suspected Kestrel facility at Site Sierra, precisely because it was inhospitable.

Their progress, however, was slow and miserable. The canyon floor was a treacherous obstacle course of slick, algae-covered rocks, deep pools of stagnant, foul-smelling water, and dense thickets of the unhealthy-looking vegetation that snagged their clothes and scraped their skin. They tried to stick to the slightly higher ground near the canyon walls, following the faint animal trails, but often the passage narrowed, forcing them back towards the sickly stream or requiring difficult scrambles over rockfalls.

The oppressive atmosphere weighed on them, amplifying their exhaustion, shortening tempers. The constant smell of sulfur induced a low-level nausea in Elise. Boone's breathing seemed more labored here, the bad air likely irritating his injured ribs. Even Nora's usual stoicism seemed strained, her face etched with a deeper weariness as they pushed deeper into the canyon's gloomy depths.

They traveled for most of the day, following the winding course of the canyon as it climbed gradually upwards, cutting deeper into the flank of the mountain ridge where Site Sierra supposedly lay hidden. According to Ish's directions and Elise's map consultations, they should be approaching the area directly west of the abandoned radar station complex. Their plan was to find a concealed vantage point, observe the site, confirm Kestrel activity, and hopefully identify security patterns, potential weaknesses, or signs of the 'Sanitization Protocol' preparations they feared, before deciding on their next move. Attempting direct infiltration felt suicidal without more information.

Late in the afternoon, as the already dim light within the canyon began to fade towards twilight, Nora held up a hand, signaling a halt. She tilted her head, listening intently, her expression suddenly sharp with alarm.

"What is it?" Boone whispered, instantly tensing, raising his shotgun.

"Voices," Nora breathed. "Human voices. Ahead. Around the next bend."

Elise's heart leaped into her throat. Kestrel? Had they anticipated this route? Were they patrolling even this desolate canyon? Or was it someone else? Lost hikers? Rangers?

"Get down," Boone ordered curtly, gesturing towards a dense thicket of withered rhododendrons clinging to the canyon wall. They scrambled into the concealing foliage, crouching low, peering cautiously around the upcoming bend.

The voices grew slightly louder, echoing strangely off the canyon walls. Male voices, speaking English, calm, professional, punctuated by the crackle of a radio.

"…perimeter sweep confirms negative contact, Sector Gamma," one voice reported, the sound carrying clearly in the still air. "No thermal signatures, no seismic anomalies detected within the canyon past Checkpoint Delta."

"Roger that, Gamma Lead," another voice crackled back over the radio. "Maintain position. Overwatch reports possible seismic spike near Vent Shaft Alpha – could be geological, could be interference. Proceed with caution if investigating. Kestrel Actual out."

Kestrel. Unmistakably. They were here. Patrolling. Using code names, checkpoints, referencing ventilation shafts – likely those connected to the Site Sierra facility itself. Ish's 'hidden' route wasn't entirely unwatched.

Elise, Boone, and Nora remained frozen in the thicket, hardly daring to breathe. Two figures emerged around the bend, moving slowly down the canyon towards them, perhaps fifty yards away. They wore dark, weatherproof tactical gear, carried short-barreled carbines held at the ready, and moved with the efficient, wary posture of trained operatives. They scanned the canyon walls, the stream bed, their eyes missing little. One carried a sophisticated sensor device, occasionally pausing to take readings.

They were Kestrel field agents. Experienced, well-equipped, alert. And heading directly towards their hiding place.

Panic tightened its icy grip on Elise. There was nowhere to run, nowhere deeper to hide in the narrow confines of the canyon at this point. If the sensor operator detected them... confrontation was inevitable. And against two armed, trained Kestrel agents, their chances were virtually nil.

Boone slowly, silently raised his shotgun, his face grim, preparing for the worst. Nora subtly shifted her grip on her axe. Elise fumbled for her pistol, her fingers numb, useless.

The two agents continued their slow approach, sweeping the area methodically. Twenty yards away now. Fifteen. The lead agent paused, raising the sensor device, aiming it towards the thicket where they hid. Elise held her breath, bracing for the inevitable shout of alarm, the muzzle flashes...

Then, something happened that defied all expectation.

From high on the canyon rim directly above the two agents, a single, large rock detached itself and plummeted downwards. It wasn't a massive boulder like the one that had nearly taken Graves, but substantial enough, maybe fifty pounds. It fell with startling speed, crashing onto the rocks just behind the second agent with a sharp crack that echoed through the canyon.

Both agents spun around instantly, weapons raised, startled by the sudden rockfall. "What the hell?" the lead agent exclaimed, scanning the rim above. "Did you see where that came from?"

"Negative!" the second agent replied, also peering upwards. "Damn unstable walls in this sector. Could have been anything."

But as they were distracted, looking upwards, a shadow detached itself from a deep cleft in the canyon wall *behind* them, a place Elise hadn't even registered as a potential hiding spot. It moved with impossible speed and silence across the narrow canyon floor.

It was the adolescent Stick-shí'nač.

Before the Kestrel agents could react, before they even realized the threat wasn't from above but behind, the adolescent was upon them. It didn't roar, didn't use weapons. It moved with a blur of controlled, devastating force. One massive arm swept out, catching the second agent across the back, sending him crashing face-first into the rock wall with sickening force, crumpling unconscious. The other arm shot out, grabbing the lead agent's carbine, ripping it from his grasp with contemptuous ease, snapping the weapon in half over its knee like a dry twig.

The lead agent, momentarily disarmed and stunned, fumbled for his sidearm. But the adolescent was faster. It grabbed him by the front of his tactical vest, lifted him bodily off the ground as if he weighed nothing, and slammed him hard against the opposite canyon wall. The agent let out a strangled cry, then went limp, sliding down the rock face, clearly incapacitated, possibly dead.

It was over in less than five seconds. Brutal. Efficient. Shockingly swift.

The adolescent stood panting slightly in the center of the narrow canyon floor, surrounded by the two downed Kestrel agents. It looked down at the broken carbine pieces, nudged one with its massive foot, then looked towards the thicket where Elise, Boone, and Nora remained hidden, frozen in stunned disbelief.

Its dark eyes seemed to find theirs through the foliage. It held their gaze for a long moment. There was no menace in its expression now, no fear like they'd seen in the lab. Only… acknowledgment? A silent message? Then, it let out a soft, low grunt, almost a sigh, turned, and melted back into the deep shadows of the cleft it had emerged from, vanishing as silently as it had appeared.

Silence returned to the canyon, broken only by the trickle of the stream, the distant hiss of sulfurous springs, and the ragged gasps of the three hidden observers. Elise felt dizzy, her mind struggling to process what she had just witnessed.

The adolescent creature… it had deliberately intervened. It had ambushed the Kestrel agents. It had neutralized them with calculated, non-lethal (perhaps?) force. And it had seemingly done so to protect… them? The intruders? The ones whose companion had shot at it in the sanctuary? It defied all logic, all previous experience.

"Did… did you see that?" Boone stammered, lowering his shotgun slowly, his face pale with astonishment.

Nora nodded, her eyes wide with awe. "It protected us," she whispered. "The young one… it chose a side."

"But why?" Elise asked, bewildered. "After everything? After the gunshot? After we invaded their home?"

"Perhaps," Nora mused, her gaze distant, thoughtful, "it understands more than we know. Perhaps it recognizes the greater threat. Kestrel. The poison-bringers. An enemy to its people, spanning generations, as the lab proved. Perhaps… it sees us not just as intruders, but as… potential allies? Or at least, fellow enemies of its enemy?"

The idea of an alliance, however tentative, however fragile, with these ancient beings felt both ludicrous and profoundly significant. Could the adolescent's action be a signal? An opening? A deliberate step towards the kind of mediation Whis Elem had spoken of?

"Or maybe," Boone interjected, his pragmatic skepticism returning, "it just hates Kestrel more than it hates us right now. Maybe it saw an opportunity to take out two of their soldiers, and we just happened to be nearby." He looked towards the downed agents warily. "Question is, what do we do now?"

Leaving the agents here, potentially injured but alive, meant risking them reporting the encounter, revealing the creature's presence outside the quarantine zone, potentially escalating Kestrel's response. Finishing them off felt unthinkable, a descent into the very ruthlessness they despised in Kestrel. Searching them for intelligence seemed necessary, but incredibly risky – they might regain consciousness, or other patrols might be nearby.

"We disarm them completely," Elise decided quickly, forcing herself into practical action. "Take their radios, any comms devices, weapons, sensor gear. Destroy what we can't carry. Leave them… incapacitated but alive. We can't afford prisoners, and we can't become murderers." It felt like a messy compromise, but the only ethical option. "Then we get out of this canyon, fast, before more show up."

Working quickly, nerves still jangling from the encounter, they emerged from the thicket. The two agents remained unconscious, though Elise confirmed both were still breathing. They stripped them of their weapons, radios, sophisticated sensor equipment, sidearms, knives, even spare ammunition clips. Boone methodically smashed the radios and sensor devices against rocks, rendering them useless. They couldn't carry the carbines, so Boone field-stripped them, scattering the essential components into the dense undergrowth, ensuring they couldn't be easily reassembled. They took the sidearms and ammunition – more firepower might be needed. They also quickly searched the agents' pockets and pouches, finding small encrypted data pads (useless without passwords, but potentially valuable if crackable later), basic med kits (which they gratefully confiscated), and laminated maps marked with Kestrel operational grids and patrol routes for this sector.

This last find was gold. "Look at this," Boone breathed, spreading one of the maps on a rock. "Site Sierra marked clear as day. Patrol routes. Sensor placements. Checkpoints." He pointed to a location marked 'Vent Shaft Alpha' – likely the one they had used to enter the mine. "They knew about the shaft access." He then traced the Stinkwater Canyon route. "But Ish was right. Patrols seem lighter in here. Marked hazardous. They were likely just doing a routine sweep when they stumbled onto us… or when the young one stumbled onto them."

The map confirmed Site Sierra's location, high on the ridge above them. It also confirmed the area was actively monitored, though perhaps imperfectly. And it provided potential routes to approach the facility while avoiding marked patrol paths.

"Okay," Elise said, tucking the confiscated map securely away. "We have what we need. Let's move. We need to find a way up to that ridge, get eyes on the site, but stay hidden."

Leaving the two unconscious Kestrel agents where they lay – a calculated risk, but one they had to take – they quickly moved deeper into the canyon, away from the scene of the encounter. They followed the canyon for another half mile, the sulfurous smell gradually lessening, the air feeling slightly cleaner. As Ish had predicted, the canyon eventually began to climb steeply again, branching into smaller, overgrown ravines leading up towards the main ridgeline.

They chose the most promising-looking ravine, one choked with dense forest cover offering concealment, and began the arduous ascent out of Stinkwater Canyon, leaving behind the scene of the adolescent guardian's shocking intervention. Elise's mind reeled, trying to process the implications. Had the creature acted alone? Or on the elder's instruction? Was it a strategic alliance? A warning? Or simply an unpredictable act by a being whose motives remained fundamentally alien?

Whatever the reason, the encounter had shifted the balance again. They now possessed Kestrel weapons, Kestrel intelligence, and the terrifying, hopeful knowledge that at least one of the guardians might perceive them as something other than enemies to be exterminated. The scars of the mountain, the scars of the mind – they remained deep. But now, interwoven with the fear and grief, was a fragile, complex thread of potential connection, a whisper of understanding echoing in the silent, wounded heart of the Hollow Ground. The path towards Site Sierra felt more dangerous than ever, but also, somehow, more purposeful.

Chapter 24: Site Sierra

Climbing out of Stinkwater Canyon felt like ascending from one layer of purgatory to another. The air grew cleaner, losing the acrid bite of sulfur, but the terrain became brutally steep, a near-vertical scramble through tangled roots, loose rock, and dense, dripping rhododendron thickets that clawed at their already ragged clothes. Every upward step was an agony for Elise's exhausted muscles, a sharp reminder of Boone's injured ribs, a testament to Nora's quiet, relentless endurance. The captured Kestrel map, studied during brief, breathless pauses, confirmed they were approaching Site Sierra from the west, using the ravine Ish had suggested, hoping to bypass the primary sensor grids and patrols guarding the more obvious approaches from the south and east.

The knowledge of the adolescent Stick-shí'nač's intervention hung heavy between them, largely unspoken. Boone, pragmatic as ever, focused on the immediate tactical advantage – the captured weapons, the map, the confirmation of Kestrel activity – but Elise saw the flicker of profound confusion, even awe, that sometimes crossed his face when he thought she wasn't looking. How did you reconcile a creature capable of ripping a man from a cliff face with one that deliberately neutralized armed opponents to seemingly protect you? Nora remained inscrutable, accepting the event with the same quiet gravity she accepted the rising sun or the falling rain, perhaps seeing it as another manifestation of the mountain's unpredictable power, the shifting balances her ancestors understood. For Elise, the incident was a paradigm shift, forcing her to confront the possibility of complex motivations, alliances, perhaps even a form of interspecies diplomacy, however crude or desperate, playing out in this hidden conflict. The Stick-shí'nač weren't just guardians or monsters; they were actors with agency, making choices, their relationship with humanity potentially far more nuanced than simple hostility.

As they neared the ridgeline, the forest began to thin, giving way to sparser stands of wind-stunted subalpine fir and exposed rock formations draped in mist. The air grew colder again, carrying the sharp scent of altitude and impending twilight. They moved with extreme caution now, staying low, using every available scrap of cover, knowing they were entering the immediate vicinity of an active, clandestine Kestrel facility. The silence here felt different – not the living quiet of the deep woods, nor the resonant pulse of the Heart-Chamber, but a tense, watchful stillness, heavy with the potential for human surveillance.

Finally, crawling the last few yards through dense, low-growing juniper, they reached a vantage point Nora had selected – a rocky outcrop concealed by gnarled trees, offering a commanding, if mist-shrouded, view of the high alpine basin nestled just below the main ridge crest where Site Sierra lay hidden.

Elise slowly raised her confiscated binoculars, scanning the basin below. At first, she saw only rolling waves of grey mist clinging to the rocky terrain and sparse clusters of stunted trees. Then, as the mist swirled and momentarily thinned, the structures came into view, confirming Ish's stories and the map's markings.

It wasn't a single building, but a scattered complex of low, weathered structures, designed perhaps to blend into the landscape or minimize visibility from the air. The most prominent feature was the decaying geodesic dome of the old Cold War radar installation, its white panels stained and cracked, looking like a skeletal skull half-buried in the tundra. Clustered around it were several smaller, windowless buildings constructed from concrete or corrugated metal, some appearing derelict, others showing subtle signs of recent maintenance – newer antennae bristling from rooftops, faint heat signatures shimmering around exhaust vents visible even through the mist (confirming Kestrel was indeed using the site), security cameras mounted discreetly under eaves. A high chain-link fence, topped with razor wire and bearing faded 'US Government Property - No Trespassing' signs likely dating back decades, enclosed the central compound, though sections of it looked damaged or poorly maintained. Outside the fence, almost hidden amongst rocks and trees, were darker shapes that might have been camouflaged sensor arrays or automated defense emplacements.

The whole place radiated an aura of decay, neglect, and repurposed secrecy. It looked less like a high-tech Kestrel command center and more like… exactly what Ish had suggested. A dumping ground? A forgotten outpost? A place where old secrets, and perhaps old mistakes, were left to fester. Yet, the signs of recent activity, the heat signatures, the cameras, indicated it wasn't entirely abandoned. Someone was here. Kestrel was using it, for something.

"See any movement?" Boone whispered, hunkered down beside Elise, scanning the compound with his own set of binoculars, also confiscated from the agents.

"No personnel visible outside," Elise replied, keeping her voice low. "But lights are on in that rectangular building near the dome. And look…" She pointed towards a larger, hangar-like structure set slightly apart from the main compound, near the edge of a steep drop-off. "That heat signature is significant. Like… generators running? Or heavy machinery?"

Boone focused his binoculars on the hangar. "Could be. Or…" his voice grew grim, "could be incineration. Sanitization Protocol, remember? Getting rid of evidence? Bodies?"

The thought sent a chill through Elise, colder than the alpine wind. Was that Kestrel's purpose here? Not active research, but disposal? Erasing the physical remnants of their decades of disastrous meddling – old equipment, failed experiments, compromised personnel, perhaps even the remains of Goliath or Echo moved here for final destruction?

"We need a closer look," Boone stated decisively. "Need to know what they're doing in that hangar. Need to see how many personnel are on site, assess their defenses."

"Approaching the fence line directly… suicide," Nora murmured, scanning the perimeter with her keen eyes. "Cameras obvious. Others… hidden, likely. Pressure plates? Seismic sensors?"

"The map," Elise pulled out the agent's laminated map they'd taken. "It shows patrol routes, sensor blind spots… but it might be outdated. Or deliberately misleading." She traced a finger along the western edge of the compound, near the hangar. "This area… backs up against that steep drop-off. Marked 'Unstable Slope - Minimal Patrol Coverage'. It might be our best approach vector."

Boone studied the map, then the terrain below. "Risky. Climbing down that slope in the dark, bypassing whatever sensors *are* there… But yeah, might be the only way to get close without triggering alarms."

Their plan coalesced, desperate and fraught with peril. Wait for full darkness. Use the cover of the steep, unstable western slope to bypass the main fence perimeter. Approach the hangar structure from the rear, hoping for weaker security, less surveillance. Observe. Gather intelligence. Identify the nature of Kestrel's activity. And perhaps, if an opportunity presented itself, find a way to disrupt it, sabotage it, find leverage. Direct confrontation was out of the question; stealth and cunning were their only weapons.

The hours leading up to full darkness were agonizingly slow, spent huddled amongst the rocks, shivering, hungry, nerves stretched taut. The mist thickened as night fell, swallowing the basin below in an impenetrable grey shroud, occasionally parting to reveal the faint, isolated lights glowing within the Kestrel compound, emphasizing their isolation, their otherness. The wind howled, a constant reminder of their exposure.

Finally, under the cloak of a moonless, starless night, they began their descent. Moving with infinite caution, guided by Nora's near-supernatural ability to navigate by feel and sound, they picked their way down the steep, treacherous slope west of the compound. Loose rock shifted underfoot, threatening to betray their position with every step. They froze frequently, listening intently for any sound from the compound below – voices, vehicles, alarms – but heard only the relentless moan of the wind.

Reaching the base of the slope, perhaps fifty yards from the rear wall of the large hangar structure, they took cover in a dense cluster of stunted, wind-blasted firs. The heat radiating from the hangar was more noticeable here, carrying the faint, unpleasant smell of burning fuel, chemicals, and something else… something organic, deeply unsettling, like… burning flesh?

Elise felt nausea rise in her throat. Boone's face was grim in the faint ambient light. Incineration. Disposal. It seemed increasingly likely.

"Need to get closer," Boone whispered, his eyes fixed on the hangar wall. "See if there are windows, vents… any way to see inside."

Leaving Nora concealed as lookout, Boone and Elise began a low crawl across the rocky, uneven ground towards the rear of the hangar. They moved agonizingly slowly, testing each handhold, careful not to dislodge pebbles, staying absolutely silent. The tension was unbearable. Every shadow seemed to hold a hidden camera, every gust of wind felt like it carried their scent towards unseen sensors.

They reached the base of the hangar wall – cold, corrugated metal, vibrating slightly from machinery running inside. They crept along the wall, searching for any opening. Most of the structure was windowless, solid. But near one corner, set high up near the roofline, was a louvered ventilation shaft, faint light and the low hum of machinery escaping from within.

"Boost me up," Boone whispered, cupping his hands.

Heart pounding, Elise braced herself, and Boone, surprisingly light despite his size and injuries, used her clasped hands as a step, reaching upwards, grabbing the edge of the ventilation housing. He carefully, silently, peered through the louvers into the hangar's interior.

He remained there for a full minute, motionless, observing. Then he lowered himself back down beside Elise, his face pale, his eyes wide with horror and disbelief.

"What?" Elise whispered urgently. "What did you see?"

Boone swallowed hard, struggling for words. "It's… it's not just disposal, Doc," he finally rasped, his voice shaking slightly. "It's… worse." He took a deep breath. "They've got one. Alive."

Elise stared at him, uncomprehending. "Alive? One of…?"

Boone nodded grimly. "Yeah. A Stick-shí'nač. Chained up. In a cage. Looks… young. Maybe the adolescent we saw? Or another one?" His voice dropped lower, filled with disgust. "And they're… they're working on it. Kestrel scientists. Lab coats. Needles. Taking samples. Attaching… probes." He shuddered. "It's sedated, mostly. But it's fighting back sometimes. Roaring. Thrashing. And the smell… they *are* burning something. Discarded tissue samples, maybe? Or… mistakes?"

The horror of it washed over Elise, cold and sickening. Live capture. Vivisection. Unethical experimentation on a sentient being, just like Echo decades before, but happening *now*. Kestrel hadn't learned; they had escalated. Was this the 'Asset Recovery' mentioned in the files? Had they managed to capture one during the chaos after the fire, or perhaps even before?

"And… something else," Boone added, his eyes haunted. "There's… equipment. Heavy drilling machinery. Set up near the back. Looks like they're preparing to drill… down. Deep into the rock beneath the hangar."

Sanitization Protocol. Not just incinerating evidence, but potentially drilling deep to deploy a biological agent, or perhaps a localized explosive, to collapse the passages leading to the sanctuary, burying the secret forever, eliminating the creatures at their source. They were actively preparing the final phase.

"We have to stop them," Elise said, her voice trembling with a mixture of rage and terror. "We have to…"

Before she could finish, a blinding beam of light stabbed through the darkness, pinning them against the hangar wall. A voice, amplified, metallic, cut through the wind.

"Subject Holloway! Subject Boone! Freeze! Do not move! You are contained! Cease resistance!"

Floodlights flared on around the perimeter of the hangar, bathing the entire area in harsh, unforgiving white light. Figures emerged from the shadows – Kestrel operatives, clad in black tactical gear, helmets down, weapons raised, forming a closing cordon around them. They had been spotted. The approach hadn't been stealthy enough. Or perhaps, Kestrel had anticipated their target, laid a trap.

Boone instinctively raised the confiscated Kestrel sidearm, pushing Elise behind him. Nora, alerted by the lights and commotion, emerged from the trees nearby, axe held ready, placing herself protectively near them.

They were surrounded. Outnumbered. Outgunned. Trapped between the horrific experiments within the hangar and the closing circle of Kestrel agents outside. There was no escape route, no cover, nowhere to run.

The amplified voice boomed again. "Drop your weapons! Hands visible! Comply immediately! Failure to comply will be met with lethal force! This is your only warning!"

Boone hesitated, his gaze flicking between the closing agents, the hangar door, Elise and Nora beside him. Fight? Surrender? Either option felt like a death sentence.

But as he weighed their impossible choices, a new sound began to rise, cutting through the wind and the amplified commands. A low, deep, resonant hum, starting almost subliminally, then rapidly building in intensity, vibrating through the ground, through the metal walls of the hangar, through the very air around them. It was the Resonance. Stronger than Elise had ever felt it outside the Heart-Chamber. Focused. Intentional.

The Kestrel agents faltered, looking around in confusion, some clutching their helmets as if experiencing sudden pressure or pain. The lights flickered violently. Electronic devices on their gear sparked, sputtered, went dark.

And then, from the deep woods surrounding the basin, from the high ridges overlooking Site Sierra, came an answering call. Not a single voice, but a chorus. Deep, mournful howls blending with sharp, angry barks and resonant, earth-shaking hums. The sound echoed off the mountains, building into a terrifying symphony of ancient power unleashed.

The Stick-shí'nač. They were here. Not just one or two. Many. Drawn perhaps by the Resonance, by the captive's distress calls, by the long-festering wound Kestrel had inflicted upon their sacred mountain.

The Kestrel agents reacted with disciplined panic, shifting their aim from the cornered humans towards the surrounding darkness, firing warning shots into the trees, shouting into dead radios. But their technological advantages – night vision, communications, perhaps even energy weapons Elise hadn't seen – seemed to be failing under the onslaught of the Resonance.

And then, the first massive shadow detached itself from the tree line near the hangar and charged into the light. Followed by another. And another. The guardians had arrived. Not to rescue the humans, perhaps, but to reclaim their own, to deliver judgment upon the desecrators, to unleash the wrath of the forest upon Site Sierra.

Caught between the closing Kestrel cordon and the charging Stick-shí'nač, bathed in the failing floodlights and the rising cacophony of roars, gunfire, and resonant power, Elise realized their desperate gamble hadn't just led them to Kestrel's secrets; it had potentially ignited the final, catastrophic battle for the Hollow Ground. And they were standing directly in the crossfire.

Chapter 25: Crossfire

The world dissolved into chaos. Harsh floodlights sputtered, casting strobing, disorienting shadows across the basin as the Kestrel agents' technology buckled under the intensifying Resonance. The air vibrated, thick with the overlapping roars of the charging Stick-shí'nač, the sharp crackle of failing radios, the panicked shouts of the human operatives, and the deep, earth-shaking hum that seemed to emanate from the very rock beneath their feet.

Elise pressed herself flat against the cold metal wall of the hangar, Boone shielding her partly with his own body, Nora crouched low beside them, axe held ready. They were caught, utterly exposed, in the deadly no-man's-land between two warring forces, neither of which likely held any regard for their survival.

The Kestrel agents, momentarily thrown into disarray by the technological failure and the sudden, terrifying appearance of multiple nine-foot-tall behemoths charging from the darkness, reacted with trained, albeit panicked, discipline. They formed ragged firing lines, laying down suppressing fire with their conventional firearms – carbines, sidearms – towards the advancing Stick-shí'nač. Bullets ricocheted off the rocky ground, pinged against the metal hangar walls, shredded foliage, the sounds sharp and deadly against the primal roars.

The guardians absorbed the initial volley with horrifying resilience. Elise saw bullets strike thick fur and muscle, staggering the creatures momentarily, eliciting roars of pain and fury, but failing to bring them down immediately. Their dense musculature, thick hides, perhaps even the strange resonance affecting the area, seemed to offer them unnatural protection against standard ballistics. They closed the distance with terrifying speed, covering ground in immense, fluid strides, long arms swinging, massive hands balled into fists or reaching out with claw-like intent.

The first clash was brutal, primal. A Stick-shí'nač, likely the adult male Elise recognized from the river cavern encounter, slammed into the Kestrel line near the hangar corner. It didn't use weapons, just sheer kinetic force and overwhelming strength. It swept one agent aside with a blow that sent him cartwheeling through the air like a broken doll, his scream cut short by the impact against distant rocks. It grabbed another agent's carbine, tore it from his grasp, and used it as a club, smashing it against the man's helmeted head with devastating force. The agent crumpled instantly.

Other creatures hit the line moments later. Chaos reigned. Agents fired desperately at close range, some scoring hits, eliciting roars of pain, but often being overwhelmed before they could reload or retreat. The creatures moved with blurring speed, their power devastating. Elise watched in horror as one lifted an agent bodily and hurled him against the chain-link fence with enough force to buckle the metal posts. Another simply stomped down hard, crushing equipment and limbs underfoot.

But the Kestrel agents, despite their technological disadvantages and the sheer terror of their adversaries, fought back fiercely. They were highly trained, likely veterans of unseen conflicts, perhaps equipped with specialized ammunition or tactics designed for just such a contingency, even if their leadership had underestimated the scale of the threat. They inflicted wounds. One Stick-shí'nač stumbled back, clutching a heavily bleeding shoulder, roaring in agony after taking a concentrated burst of fire. Another went down, collapsing heavily onto the rocky ground, possibly felled by a lucky headshot or a specialized round. The battle wasn't entirely one-sided; it was a desperate, bloody mêlée under the flickering, dying lights.

Caught in the middle, Elise, Boone, and Nora could only huddle against the hangar wall, praying to remain unnoticed amidst the larger conflict. Stray bullets whizzed past, thudding into the metal wall near their heads. The ground shook with the impact of falling bodies, both human and guardian. The noise was deafening, overwhelming.

"We need to move!" Boone yelled over the din, pulling Elise lower as debris showered down from a nearby impact. "Get inside the hangar! Might be the only cover!"

The hangar? Where Kestrel scientists experimented on a live captive? It felt like jumping from the frying pan into the fire. But Boone was right. Staying pinned against the outer wall was suicide.

Watching for a lull in the fighting near their corner, Boone made the decision. "Now! Go!"

He pushed Elise forward, towards a small personnel door set into the hangar wall a few yards away, providing covering fire with the confiscated Kestrel sidearm, firing quick, unaimed shots towards the general chaos to discourage immediate attention. Nora followed Elise closely, helping her stay low.

The personnel door was unlocked, likely left open during the initial Kestrel response. Elise threw it open and stumbled inside, Nora right behind her. Boone fired one last shot, then dove in after them, slamming the heavy metal door shut just as a burst of automatic fire stitched across the exterior wall where they had been moments before.

They found themselves in a small antechamber or storage area, dimly lit by flickering emergency lights. The sounds of the battle outside were slightly muffled now, but still terrifyingly close. The air inside was thick with the chemical stench and the smell of burning organics they had noticed earlier, stronger now, making Elise gag. Ahead, another door, likely leading into the main hangar space where Boone had seen the captive creature, stood slightly ajar.

"Check the area!" Boone ordered, his voice tight, adrenaline overriding his injuries. He moved quickly, checking corners, ensuring the antechamber was clear. Nora stood guard at the door they had just entered, peering through a small reinforced window slit, reporting on the escalating chaos outside.

"They're falling back," Nora reported grimly. "Kestrel. Towards the main buildings. The guardians… they are relentless. Tearing through them." Her voice held a mixture of fear and perhaps, a grim satisfaction at seeing the 'poison-bringers' face the consequences of their actions.

Elise, meanwhile, cautiously pushed open the inner door, peering into the main hangar space. The scene within was one of controlled horror. Banks of fluorescent lights, also flickering under the influence of the Resonance, illuminated a large, open area. Along one wall were makeshift laboratory stations – tables cluttered with computers (screens dark now), microscopes, centrifuges, chemical containers. Along the other wall stood rows of large, empty cages, similar to the ones in the abandoned mine lab, but newer, cleaner. In the center of the room, dominating the space, was the cage Boone had described.

Constructed from thick, reinforced steel bars, it held a single occupant: a Stick-shí'nač. It was smaller than the adults fighting outside, likely the adolescent Boone had suspected, though confirming its identity was impossible amidst the shadows and its current state. It was slumped against the bars, head bowed, thick leather and metal restraints binding its wrists and ankles to heavy chains bolted to the floor. Electrodes were crudely patched onto its scalp, wires snaking towards a bank of dead monitoring equipment. Its dark fur was matted, patchy, showing signs of neglect or perhaps the effects of drugs. It breathed in shallow, ragged gasps, occasionally letting out a low, mournful whimper that tore at Elise's heart. It looked utterly broken, defeated.

Standing near the cage, seemingly oblivious to the battle raging just outside the hangar walls, were two figures in white lab coats, hastily packing equipment into metal cases. One was a stern-looking older man with thinning grey hair, the other a younger woman with sharp features and cold eyes. They moved with urgent efficiency, focused entirely on securing their research materials, their data, before attempting evacuation. They were Kestrel scientists, the ones Boone had seen experimenting on the captive. Their callous disregard for the life in the cage, for the battle unfolding outside, was chilling.

"Bastards," Boone growled, peering over Elise's shoulder, taking in the scene. His hand tightened on his pistol.

"Wait," Elise cautioned, pulling him back slightly. "Direct confrontation is suicide. Two of them, maybe armed under those coats. And getting the creature out... look at those restraints."

The chains looked incredibly thick, the locks complex. Freeing the adolescent, even if they could somehow overpower the scientists, seemed impossible without specialized tools or codes they didn't possess.

But as they watched, hidden in the doorway, the situation inside the hangar shifted again. The intensifying Resonance, which had crippled Kestrel's external tech, seemed to be affecting the internal systems as well. Lights flickered more violently. Equipment sparked. And suddenly, the electronic locking mechanisms on the cage door hissed, sputtered, and then, with a loud *clunk*, disengaged. The heavy cage door swung partially open.

The two scientists spun around, startled, their faces paling as they realized the containment had failed. The adolescent creature lifted its head slowly, its deep-set eyes focusing, despite the sedation, on the open door, on the two humans in lab coats who represented its tormentors.

A low growl started deep in its chest, rising in pitch and volume, transforming from a whimper of pain into a building roar of pure, unadulterated fury. The sedation was wearing off, or perhaps the sheer rage, combined with the resonant energy filling the hangar, was overriding its effects.

" containment breach! Sedation protocol!" the older male scientist yelled, fumbling for a large syringe gun lying on a nearby table.

But the adolescent was already moving. With surprising speed despite its weakened state and the heavy restraints still partially attached to its wrists, it surged towards the open cage door. It swiped one massive hand, catching the table, sending equipment, syringes, and vials crashing to the floor.

The younger female scientist screamed, stumbling backwards. The older man raised the syringe gun, trying to aim, but the creature slammed into him, sending him flying across the room to crash heavily against the far wall, where he lay still.

The adolescent stood panting in the center of the hangar, momentarily free but still hampered by the dangling chains. It looked around, disoriented, enraged, its gaze falling on the remaining scientist, the woman, who stood paralyzed with terror near the main hangar door leading outside.

It gathered itself, preparing to lunge, its roar echoing deafeningly in the confined space. This was it. Primal vengeance about to be unleashed.

Elise felt frozen, horrified, yet unable to intervene. This felt like a tragically inevitable consequence of Kestrel's own actions.

But then, something unexpected happened. Nora stepped out from the antechamber doorway into the main hangar, placing herself deliberately between the enraged adolescent and the terrified scientist. She held up her hands, palms outwards, in a gesture of peace, of calming.

"Easy now, Young One," Nora called out, her voice surprisingly calm, carrying over the creature's ragged breathing, pitched in a low, soothing tone Elise hadn't heard her use before. She spoke partly in English, partly in Lushootseed, the words flowing together in a melodic, almost chanting rhythm. "The hurt is great. The anger is strong. But more violence... solves nothing. They are beaten. Your kin fight outside. Let... let the anger pass."

The adolescent creature paused, its head tilted, seeming momentarily confused by Nora's presence, by her calm demeanor, her lack of fear, the strange cadence of her words. It growled again, low and warningly, but the immediate killing rage seemed to falter slightly. Its gaze shifted from the terrified scientist, to Nora, then towards the main hangar door, where the sounds of the battle outside still raged, though perhaps beginning to lessen slightly.

It seemed torn. The urge for immediate vengeance warred with... what? Confusion? Pain? A dawning awareness of the larger conflict? Or perhaps Nora's words, her energy, resonated in a way Elise couldn't comprehend?

Taking advantage of the creature's hesitation, Elise made a split-second decision. Forget Kestrel, forget the proof, forget escape. The immediate priority was preventing more death, de-escalating the horror unfolding before them. She grabbed the arm of the terrified female scientist, who seemed rooted to the spot.

"Come on!" Elise hissed urgently. "Move! Now! While it's distracted!"

She practically dragged the numb, unresisting scientist back towards the antechamber, pulling her through the doorway just as Boone slammed it shut again, throwing his weight against it, expecting the adolescent to charge after them.

But no impact came. Peering back through the window slit, they saw the adolescent creature still standing uncertainly in the center of the hangar, looking from the closed antechamber door, to the unconscious form of the male scientist, then back towards the main hangar doors leading outside. It let out another low, mournful sound, then turned and lumbered towards the main doors, dragging its broken restraints, disappearing into the chaos of the ongoing battle beyond, perhaps seeking its kin, perhaps simply seeking escape from the place of its torment.

Silence fell in the antechamber, broken only by the ragged breathing of the three humans and the distant, fading sounds of conflict outside. They had survived again, miraculously spared by the adolescent creature's hesitation and Nora's incredible courage. But they were still trapped, deep within a Kestrel facility under siege by enraged guardians, with a terrified, potentially hostile Kestrel scientist now added to their desperate equation. The crossfire might have momentarily passed over them, but the battle for Site Sierra, and their own survival, was far from finished.

Chapter 26: Loose Ends

The silence in the small antechamber felt brittle, fragile, like a thin sheet of ice over churning black water. Outside, the sounds of the battle – the roars, the gunfire, the crashing impacts – were gradually receding, replaced by an eerie quiet punctuated by sporadic, distant shouts and the crackle of flames from somewhere beyond the hangar, suggesting the Stick-shí'nač had either overwhelmed the Kestrel defenders or the conflict had moved elsewhere within the compound. Inside, the only sounds were their own ragged breaths and the low, whimpering sobs coming from the Kestrel scientist Elise still held firmly by the arm.

The woman – perhaps in her late thirties, blonde hair escaping a severe bun, her white lab coat stained with chemicals and fear – finally seemed to snap out of her paralysis. She looked wildly from Elise's grim face, to Boone leaning heavily against the door, pistol still ready, then to Nora standing stoically nearby, axe held loosely but radiating quiet menace. Panic flared anew in her eyes.

"Who... who are you?" she stammered, trying to pull her arm free from Elise's grasp. "What's happening? Where are the security teams?"

"Security teams look a little busy right now," Boone growled, nodding towards the door leading outside. "Seems your 'assets' got loose."

The woman's eyes widened further in terror and comprehension. "The Subjects... they breached containment?" She looked towards the inner door leading to the lab where the adolescent had been held. "Subject Omega... it got out?"

"Omega?" Elise repeated, the clinical designation chilling her despite the circumstances. "Is that what you called him? After

'Goliath' and 'Echo'?" The names, the sequence, hinted at a long, systematic program.

The scientist flinched at the mention of the other names, her face paling further. "How do you know those names?" she whispered, suspicion warring with fear. "Who sent you? Are you... Internal Audit? Oversight Committee?" She seemed to grasp at straws, trying to fit them into her known Kestrel hierarchy.

"Let's just say we're severely disgruntled former consultants," Boone said dryly. "The ones Kestrel left for dead back in AO Hollow."

Understanding, and a new kind of terror, dawned on the scientist's face. "Holloway... Boone..." she recognized the names from mission briefings, perhaps. "You... survived?" She stared at them as if seeing ghosts. "They said... the reports said... wildfire... exposure..."

"Reports lie," Elise stated flatly. "Just like the reports about Goliath's 'post-mortem findings' likely omitted the part where Kestrel captured him alive after killing his mate. Just like the reports on Echo probably didn't mention keeping her alive for neurological experiments for over a year before she finally succumbed. Just like the reports on David Chen conveniently ignored the fact his remains ended up in a nesting site." Each revelation struck the scientist like a physical blow, stripping away the layers of sanitized denial Kestrel cultivated.

The woman crumpled slightly, leaning against the wall for support, her professional composure shattering completely. "You... you know?" she whispered, horrified. "How?"

"We found your scars, Doctor..." Elise deliberately left the name blank, prompting.

"Allen," the scientist supplied numbly, seeming resigned now, the fight gone out of her. "Dr. Lena Allen. Xenobiologist."

"We found your scars, Dr. Allen," Elise repeated. "The lab beneath the Elwha mine. Echo's body. Miller's Bible. We found Graves' files. We know about Project Chimera. We know about the Sanitization Protocol. We know Kestrel didn't just stumble upon these creatures; they've been hunting them, experimenting on them, covering it up for decades. And leaving a trail of bodies – human and guardian – in their wake."

Dr. Allen closed her eyes, seeming to shrink under the weight of the accusations, the truth laid bare. "I... I didn't know the full history," she murmured weakly, though it sounded like a feeble excuse. "I was assigned to Chimera Phase Two eighteen months ago. Focused on neuro-mapping, cognitive assessment... trying to understand the Resonance potential. Omega... the juvenile... was captured six months ago during... during a fire containment operation near the Quinault." Another lie, Elise suspected; the Quinault disappearances were likely targeted captures. "They told me... the research was vital. National security implications. Understanding the threat... potentially harnessing the abilities..."

"Harnessing?" Boone spat the word with contempt. "You mean weaponizing? Controlling?"

Allen flinched. "There were... theoretical applications discussed. Bio-resonance amplification. Psychic interface potential. But my work was purely analytical..."

"Analytical work done on a terrified, captive sentient being while your colleagues likely planned to 'sanitize' the entire species after extracting what they needed?" Elise countered coldly. "Don't try to justify it, Doctor. We saw the setup here. The incinerator. The drilling equipment Boone spotted. This wasn't just research; it was preparation for extermination and erasure."

Dr. Allen offered no defense, tears beginning to stream down her pale cheeks. Whether they were tears of guilt, fear, or self-pity, Elise couldn't tell, and frankly, didn't care.

"What now?" Boone asked gruffly, glancing towards the outer door again. The sounds of conflict seemed to have died down almost completely. An ominous silence was settling over Site Sierra. "We can't stay here. Kestrel survivors will regroup. Or the guardians might come back for her," he nodded towards Allen. "Or us."

"Her knowledge…" Elise looked at Allen thoughtfully. "She knows Kestrel protocols, personnel, facility layouts, maybe access codes? She could be… useful." The idea felt distasteful, using this compromised scientist, but pragmatism dictated they needed any advantage they could get.

"Useful how?" Boone countered. "We can't exactly take her with us. She's Kestrel. Probably got tracking implants up the wazoo. And even if she cooperated, where do we go?"

"We need to disable whatever Kestrel was planning here," Elise insisted. "The drilling. The incinerator. Buy time. Create chaos. Then… maybe use her knowledge to find a secure way out of this compound, away from the main access points Kestrel will be watching."

It was a desperate plan, relying on the cooperation of a terrified enemy scientist and navigating a facility potentially still crawling with hostile guardians or regrouping Kestrel forces.

"Dr. Allen," Elise addressed the weeping scientist directly, her voice hard. "You have two choices. You can stay here and wait for your colleagues to return – assuming they survived – and face whatever consequences Kestrel imposes for this containment breach and security failure. Given their protocols regarding witnesses and failures, I doubt it will be pleasant." Allen visibly paled further. "Or," Elise continued, "you can help us. Help us disrupt whatever final phase Kestrel was enacting here. Help us find a way out, away from both Kestrel and the guardians. Cooperate, and maybe, just maybe, you walk away from this. Maybe you even get a chance to expose Kestrel yourself, anonymously, later. Your choice."

Allen looked from Elise's determined face, to Boone's menacing presence, to Nora's silent judgment. She seemed to weigh her options, the terror of Kestrel's internal discipline likely warring with the immediate fear of the creatures outside and the uncertain threat posed by these survivors. After a long, trembling moment, she nodded numbly. "Okay," she whispered. "Okay. What… what do you need?"

"First," Boone said, taking charge of the tactical side, "that drilling equipment. Where is it controlled from? How do we disable it? Permanently."

Allen hesitated, then seemed to realize defiance was pointless. "The main drilling controls… are in the Geo-Monitoring dome," she pointed vaguely towards the direction of the old radar structure. "But the primary power conduit runs through… through the sub-level access tunnel connecting this hangar to the main lab complex. Severing that conduit should shut down the heavy machinery, including the deep drill and the main incinerator feed."

"Sub-level tunnel?" Boone raised an eyebrow. "Show us."

Keeping low, moving cautiously, they forced Allen to lead them out of the antechamber, back into the main hangar. The adolescent creature was gone. The body of the male scientist lay sprawled near the far wall. The cage stood empty, door ajar, dangling chains a testament to the recent captivity. The air still hummed faintly with residual Resonance, less intense now but still palpable.

Allen led them towards the rear of the hangar, near where Boone had spotted the drilling equipment being set up. Behind stacks of crates and machinery components, almost hidden, was a heavy steel hatch set into the concrete floor. Allen manipulated a locking wheel, similar to the one on the lab door in the mine, and pulled the heavy hatch open, revealing a dark opening and metal rungs descending into blackness.

"Tunnel connects to the main complex basement levels," Allen explained nervously, avoiding Boone's eyes. "Contains power conduits, data lines, environmental controls. Runs beneath the entire compound."

"Perfect," Boone grinned mirthlessly. "A rat run." He glanced at Elise and Nora. "Alright. New plan. We go down. Find the main power conduit Allen mentioned. Sever it – axe should do the trick," he nodded to Nora, "or maybe find a junction box we can sabotage. Create a major power outage. Chaos. That should disrupt their drilling, their systems, maybe cover our escape."

"Escape how?" Elise asked.

"Tunnel likely has other access points," Boone reasoned. "Maintenance hatches, emergency exits, maybe connects to older drainage systems. We find another way out, somewhere away from the main gates, away from where they expect us." He looked at Allen. "You know the layout down there?"

Allen nodded weakly. "I've... seen schematics. Used the tunnels occasionally. It's... a maze. Some sections are collapsed. Some flood during heavy rains. But yes, there are other hatches. One near the old meteorological station, outside the main fence line to the north…"

"Good enough," Boone decided. "Alright. Allen, you lead. Nora, you watch our back. Doc, you stick with me. Let's move. And Doctor Allen," his voice hardened, "any tricks, any attempt to alert your friends... Nora deals with you. Understand?"

Allen swallowed hard, nodding again, clearly terrified of both Boone's overt threat and Nora's silent, imposing presence.

Descending the metal rungs into the sub-level tunnel felt like plunging back into the familiar nightmare of subterranean darkness. The air here was stale, smelling of concrete dust, dampness, and electrical ozone. Emergency lights flickered weakly along the ceiling, casting long, unreliable shadows. Pipes and thick bundles of cables lined the walls of the narrow concrete passageway. Water pooled on the floor in places.

Allen led them hesitantly through the dimly lit maze, occasionally consulting faded diagrams bolted to the tunnel walls. The silence down here was profound, broken only by their own footsteps splashing through puddles and the distant, rhythmic hum of machinery – likely generators or ventilation systems still functioning somewhere within the main complex. There was no sign of pursuit, no immediate indication Kestrel knew they were down here.

After navigating several junctions, Allen pointed towards a section of the tunnel wall where thick, heavily insulated cables, wider than a man's arm, emerged from a conduit and ran along heavy-duty brackets towards the main complex. "That's it," she whispered. "Primary power feed from the backup generators to the hangar and the deep-core drilling rig."

Nora stepped forward without a word, hefting her axe. Assessing the thickest cable, she took careful aim and swung. The axe bit deep into the heavy insulation with a shower of sparks, followed by a loud, buzzing *CRACK* as she severed the conductors within. Lights flickered violently throughout the tunnel, then plunged into near-absolute darkness as the emergency backup systems struggled to compensate. A distant whining sound, perhaps the drilling equipment or generators powering down, echoed through the tunnel, followed by an abrupt, heavy silence.

"Good work," Boone breathed in the darkness, flicking on one of the confiscated Kestrel flashlights – brighter and more reliable than their own failing headlamps. "That should slow 'em down."

"Now," Elise urged, "the exit. Which way, Allen?"

Allen, disoriented by the sudden darkness and the power failure she had helped cause, pointed nervously down a side passage. "That way… towards Met Station B access hatch… maybe half a kilometer…"

They moved quickly now, guided by Boone's flashlight beam, splashing through puddles, stumbling over unseen debris. The darkness felt absolute, the silence broken only by their own movements and the distant, unsettling drip of water somewhere in the maze.

They reached the designated side passage and followed it as it sloped upwards. After several minutes, they saw it – a circular metal hatch set into the ceiling at the top of a short flight of concrete steps. A locking wheel, similar to the others, secured it.

"This leads outside the main perimeter fence," Allen confirmed, her voice trembling. "Near the old weather station building. Usually less guarded."

Boone quickly scaled the steps and began working on the wheel lock. It turned more easily than the others, likely used more recently for maintenance access. With a final grunt, he spun the wheel, disengaging the locks. He pushed upwards. The heavy hatch groaned open, revealing… grey, misty daylight. Freedom.

"Go! Go!" Boone urged. Elise scrambled up the steps, pushing Allen ahead of her, emerging thankfully into the cold, damp air of the surface world. Nora followed right behind. Boone took one last look back into the darkness of the Kestrel tunnels, then climbed out, pulling the heavy hatch shut behind them, though not locking it.

They found themselves in a dense thicket of fir and hemlock, about a hundred yards outside the main Site Sierra perimeter fence, near a small, dilapidated wooden structure that was likely the old meteorological station Allen mentioned. The main compound was hidden from view by the trees and the rolling terrain. The air here was free of the hangar's stench, carrying only the clean scent of rain-washed forest. There was no immediate sign of Kestrel patrols. For the moment, they seemed to be clear.

But what now? They had survived the battle, disrupted Kestrel's immediate plan, and escaped the compound. But they were still fugitives, deep in hostile territory. They had a terrified, unreliable Kestrel scientist with them. And they possessed knowledge that made them targets of immense value and danger.

Elise looked at Boone, at Nora, then at the trembling Dr. Allen. The immediate crisis had passed, but the larger struggle remained. Exposing Kestrel, protecting the sanctuary, finding a way to navigate the complex truth they carried – the path forward felt more uncertain than ever. They had bought themselves time, perhaps, but the long shadow of Project Chimera, and the ancient guardians of the Hollow Ground, stretched far, promising no easy escape, no simple resolution. They were loose ends, adrift in a secret war, their survival dependent on choices yet to be made in the heart of the whispering wilderness.

Chapter 27: Tangled Threads

The sudden immersion in the cold, mist-laden air of the high ridge felt like a physical blow after the stale confinement of the sub-level tunnels. Elise gasped, pulling the thin, damp air deep into her lungs, the scent of wet fir and alpine earth a stark, welcome contrast to the lingering metallic tang of ozone and decay from the Kestrel facility. They had made it out. Alive. Unseen, for the moment. But the fragile bubble of relief was instantly pierced by the cold reality of their situation, as tangible and biting as the wind whipping around the rocky outcrop where they crouched, concealed within a dense thicket just yards from the maintenance hatch.

Below them, partially obscured by swirling mist and the ragged silhouettes of wind-blasted trees, lay the silent, brooding complex of Site Sierra. No sirens wailed, no alarms blared. The chaotic sounds of battle had ceased entirely, replaced by an unnerving, almost watchful stillness. Had the Stick-shí'nač simply overwhelmed the Kestrel defenders and melted back into the woods? Or had Kestrel managed to repel the attack, regroup, and were now silently locking down the perimeter, hunting for the intruders who had sabotaged their systems and witnessed their secrets? The lack of activity felt more menacing than open conflict.

Beside Elise, Boone scanned the compound through the confiscated Kestrel binoculars, his expression grim, lines of pain etched around his eyes and mouth as his injured ribs protested the cramped position. Nora knelt nearby, utterly still, her senses seemingly extended into the surrounding forest, listening for sounds Elise couldn't perceive, her hand resting lightly on the handle of her axe.

And between them huddled Dr. Lena Allen, the Kestrel xenobiologist. Her initial terror had subsided into a state of numb shock, punctuated by uncontrollable shivers that had little to do with the cold. Her lab coat was torn and stained, her severe bun had collapsed into a messy tangle of blonde hair, her eyes darted nervously between her captors and the silent compound below. She was a prisoner, a liability, and potentially, their only source of crucial intelligence.

"See anything?" Elise whispered to Boone, keeping her voice low.

Boone lowered the binoculars slowly. "Nothing moving outside. Lights still off in the main buildings, hangar included. Power's definitely cut. But…" he frowned, raising the binoculars again, focusing on the old geodesic radar dome, "…thought I saw… yeah. Faint heat signature near the base of the dome. Maybe a small backup generator? Or… body heat? Someone hiding? Or waiting?"

The uncertainty prickled at Elise's nerves. They couldn't stay here. This close to the facility, near an access hatch Kestrel surely knew about, was asking for trouble. They needed to put distance between themselves and Site Sierra, find safer cover, and then figure out their next move.

"We need to go," Elise stated quietly but firmly. "Now. Before they realize the hatch was used, before daylight makes us easier targets."

Boone nodded curtly. "Which way? Back down into Stinkwater? Or try traversing this ridge?"

Nora pointed north, along the ridge line, away from the direction they had ascended the ravine from. "That way. Follow the ridge away from their likely patrol routes. Leads towards older forest, more cover. There's a hanging valley Ish mentioned… might offer shelter, water."

"Alright," Boone agreed. "Allen," he addressed the scientist, his voice hard, devoid of sympathy, "you walk between us. No signals, no sudden moves. You try anything, anything at all… Nora will handle it." He didn't need to elaborate. Allen nodded mutely, her eyes wide with fear.

Getting Allen to move cohesively with them proved difficult. She was clearly not accustomed to rugged terrain or physical hardship. She stumbled frequently on the uneven ground, her lab shoes offering little grip, her breathing quickly becoming ragged. Elise found herself alternating between frustration at the scientist's hindrance and a grudging flicker of empathy. Allen was a product of Kestrel's sterile, controlled environment, suddenly thrust into a brutal wilderness survival scenario after witnessing horrors that likely shattered her own scientific worldview. Yet, any empathy was tempered by the image of Echo on the gurney, of the adolescent 'Omega' chained in the cage. Allen was complicit, however much she might rationalize her role.

They moved as quickly as Allen's faltering pace allowed, pushing northwards along the exposed ridge, the wind tearing at them, the mist swirling, sometimes reducing visibility to mere yards. Boone took point, using the Kestrel map and his own instincts to pick a path, constantly scanning ahead and checking their back trail. Elise stayed close to Allen, ready to grab her if she stumbled, while Nora brought up the rear, her movements silent, watchful.

After perhaps an hour of tense, difficult progress, the ridge began to descend slightly, leading them into stands of larger timber, offering blessed relief from the worst of the wind. The ground became softer underfoot, carpeted with needles and moss. Here, Boone called a halt, finding a small, sheltered depression amongst a cluster of ancient, moss-covered boulders.

"Need to rest," he stated, leaning heavily against a boulder, breathing hard, favoring his injured side. "And we need answers." He turned his gaze towards Allen, his eyes cold. "Alright, Doctor. Talk. Everything you know. Sanitization Protocol – what is it, exactly? Timeline? Method?"

Allen shrank back under his stare, wrapping her arms around herself. "I... I don't know everything," she stammered. "I wasn't involved in... operational planning. My focus was Omega... the juvenile subject."

"Don't bullshit me, Allen!" Boone snapped, taking a menacing step closer. "You were in that hangar. You saw the drilling equipment. You smelled the incinerator. What were they planning?"

"It... it was designated Protocol Zero," Allen whispered, avoiding his eyes, staring at the ground. "Activated only under catastrophic containment failure or imminent exposure risk. Like... like tonight." She shuddered. "Phase One was incineration of all compromised biological materials, data logs, physical evidence within Site Sierra. Phase Two... involved the deep-core drill."

"Drilling for what?" Elise pressed urgently. "To collapse the tunnels? Seal the sanctuary?"

Allen shook her head numbly. "Worse. The drill wasn't just for collapse. It was... for deployment."

"Deployment of what?" Boone demanded.

"A biological agent," Allen choked out, tears welling again. "Genetically engineered mycorrhizal fungus. Highly aggressive strain. Designed to spread rapidly through subterranean root networks and ecosystems. It... it consumes organic material. All of it. Leaves only sterilized rock and mineral dust behind."

Elise felt sick. A bio-weapon. Designed to sterilize the entire underground ecosystem, eradicate the Stick-shí'nač, their sanctuary, their food sources, everything, leaving no trace, nothing for future discovery. It was genocide, packaged as 'sanitization'.

"The target wasn't just Site Sierra," Elise realized with horror. "It was the source. The Heart-Chamber. The energy signatures Kestrel detected... they must have mapped the passages leading there, planned to drill down and introduce the fungus near the source, let it spread outwards through the network."

Allen nodded miserably. "The estimated propagation time… weeks, perhaps months, to achieve full sterilization of the primary AO Hollow system and associated passages. Irreversible. Untraceable, eventually. Presented as a novel bioremediation technique for hypothetical 'cave-borne pathogens' if any external questions were ever asked."

"And the timeline?" Boone pushed. "When were they planning to drill? To deploy?"

"I don't know the exact schedule," Allen insisted, twisting her hands nervously. "It required specific seismic stability conditions, final authorization codes from Kestrel Command based on risk assessment. But… the equipment was being prepped. Calibrated. They were close. Maybe days away. Tonight's breach… it likely triggered emergency activation protocols. If any senior personnel survived, if they can regain power and control… they might try to initiate deployment immediately, before pulling out."

The urgency slammed back into Elise. Sabotaging the power conduit hadn't just bought them time; it might have temporarily halted planetary-scale ecocide. But if Kestrel could restore power, if key personnel escaped the guardians' wrath… the threat remained imminent.

"We need to get word out," Elise said desperately. "Warn someone. But who? Who would believe us? Who could possibly stop Kestrel?"

Boone looked thoughtful, recalling their earlier conversation. "Rivals," he murmured. "Maybe that's still the play. If Kestrel is about to unleash something this catastrophic, maybe even their government overseers – assuming they still have some – would balk. Or maybe a rival agency would see an opportunity to step in, seize control, expose Kestrel's recklessness." He looked at Allen.

"Who *does* Kestrel answer to? Is there an oversight committee? A funding source we can trace?"

Allen hesitated, torn between ingrained secrecy and self-preservation. "Officially... Kestrel is private, funded by anonymous endowments, focused on 'sensitive environmental research'," she recited the standard cover story. "But... unofficially... there have always been whispers. Links to... certain factions within DARPA. Advanced Energy research programs. Possibly... older intelligence directorates still operating off-book since the Cold War." She shook her head. "It's heavily compartmentalized. Even senior scientists like me... we only see our small piece. We don't get the full picture. Director Thorne... he seemed to bridge the gap between the science and... the other side."

"Aris Thorne," Elise mused. The name kept recurring, a central figure spanning decades. "Where is he now? Is he still involved?"

Allen looked surprised. "Director Thorne? He... he disappeared two years ago. Officially retired, health reasons cited. But the internal rumors... suggested he clashed with the new operational directorate over the direction of Project Chimera. He argued against Phase Two, against live capture protocols after Omega was taken. Said it was too reckless, violated ethical parameters he'd tried to establish after... after Echo." Her voice dropped. "Some whispered he was silenced. Others thought he simply vanished, went deep off-grid."

Thorne, the potential conscience of Kestrel, gone missing after opposing the very escalation they were now facing. Was he dead? Or in hiding? Could *he* be the key? Could he possess proof, contacts, a way to expose Kestrel from the inside?

"Find Thorne," Boone said decisively, seizing on the new possibility. "If he's alive, if he opposed this madness... he might be our best bet. An insider witness. Someone credible."

"Find him how?" Elise asked, the task feeling monumental. "He could be anywhere in the world."

"Maybe not," Boone countered. "He knew these woods. Knew the secrets. Maybe he didn't go far. Maybe he's hiding somewhere close by, watching, waiting." He looked at Allen again. "Did Thorne have any... personal connections? Family? Colleagues he trusted? Any research sites he favored outside Kestrel facilities?"

Allen frowned, thinking hard. "He was... solitary. Divorced years ago, no children I know of. His work was his life." She paused. "But there was... one place he mentioned sometimes. Almost nostalgically. An old university research station, way up in the northern Cascades, near Mount Baker. Used for high-altitude atmospheric studies back in the 70s and 80s. Officially defunct now, handed over to the Forest Service, but mostly abandoned. Thorne did some early, independent atmospheric resonance research there, before Kestrel fully recruited him. Said the natural energy fields were... unique."

Northern Cascades. Miles away, different mountain range entirely. But remote, abandoned, potentially holding unique energy signatures Thorne was interested in. It felt like a plausible place for a brilliant, disillusioned scientist to disappear, to continue his work off the grid, perhaps even monitor Kestrel from afar.

"It's a long shot," Elise admitted. "Based on whispers and nostalgia."

"Got any better ideas, Doc?" Boone challenged. "Feels more concrete than trying to find mythical rival agencies or hoping the guardians develop a sudden urge to testify before Congress."

He was right. Finding Thorne, if he was alive and willing to help, offered the most direct path to potentially stopping Kestrel and corroborating their story. It required another perilous journey, crossing from the Olympics to the Cascades, evading Kestrel surveillance all the way, finding an abandoned station in another vast wilderness. But it felt like a tangible goal, a thread of hope in the overwhelming darkness.

"Okay," Elise agreed. "We try to find Thorne. But first… we need to get out of the Olympics safely. We need supplies. We need to make sure Kestrel isn't right on our heels."

They rested for another hour, finishing the last of their water, the gnawing hunger a constant reminder of their dwindling resources. Boone used the time to study the confiscated Kestrel map again, planning a potential route westwards, towards the coast, towards areas with more roads, small towns where they might risk resupplying or finding temporary transport, before attempting the difficult crossing to the Cascades.

As they prepared to move out, Nora, who had been silently scanning the surrounding woods, suddenly stiffened. "Company," she breathed, nodding subtly towards a dense thicket downslope.

Elise and Boone froze, instantly alert, weapons coming up. Peering through the trees, Elise saw them – two figures, moving slowly, cautiously up the slope towards their position. Not Kestrel agents; their movements were less tactical, more… searching. They wore worn hiking gear, carried heavy packs. One held a GPS unit, consulting it frequently, looking confused. Lost hikers? Or…

Then Elise recognized the faded logo on one of the backpacks. A defunct logging company insignia she remembered seeing on trucks back in Bluffs End. These weren't hikers. They looked like… locals. Perhaps hunters, or people searching for something specific in these remote woods.

Boone cursed under his breath. "Just what we need. Witnesses." He looked torn between warning them off and avoiding contact altogether.

Before they could decide, Dr. Allen, perhaps seeing an opportunity, or simply driven by residual Kestrel protocols about preventing 'witness contamination', made a sudden, foolish move. She stumbled deliberately out from behind the boulders, waving her arms weakly. "Help!" she cried out, her voice thin but carrying. "Help us! We're lost!"

"Allen, no!" Elise hissed, grabbing for her, but it was too late.

The two figures below stopped, startled, peering upwards towards the sound. They exchanged glances, then began moving cautiously towards the source of the cry, towards Elise, Boone, Nora, and Allen, their expressions wary but concerned.

They were about to have company. And in their current situation, any contact with the outside world, however well-intentioned, felt like tripping a wire, potentially exposing them, alerting Kestrel, unraveling their fragile chance of escape. Allen's desperate act, born perhaps of fear or ingrained protocol, had just thrown another dangerous variable into their already impossible equation.

Chapter 28: Uninvited Guests

The two men approaching through the thinning timber moved with the cautious competence of people familiar with rough country, but their body language lacked the sharp, tactical edge of Kestrel operatives. They wore sturdy, well-worn hiking boots, canvas pants layered against the damp chill, and faded jackets bearing no insignia except the grime of the trail. One carried a sturdy hunting rifle slung over his shoulder, the other leaned heavily on a carved wooden hiking staff. As they drew closer, navigating the uneven slope, their faces became clearer – middle-aged, deeply lined, eyes narrowed with a mixture of concern and ingrained backcountry suspicion. They looked like exactly what Boone had initially guessed: local hunters, perhaps, or maybe prospectors still searching for forgotten claims in these remote hills.

"Allen, get back here!" Boone hissed, pulling the scientist roughly back behind the cover of the boulders, his face tight with anger at her reckless move. "You trying to get us all killed?"

"They can help us!" Allen protested, her voice high-pitched with panic and misplaced hope. "They have supplies! Maybe a radio!"

"Or maybe they report us to the authorities, who report us to Kestrel, you idiot!" Boone snarled back, keeping his voice low. "Now shut up and stay down!"

Elise watched the approaching men with dread coiling in her stomach. Allen's cry for help had irrevocably changed the situation. Running now would look suspicious, potentially hostile. Hiding might work if the men passed by, but if they came directly to investigate the shout, confrontation seemed unavoidable. And any interaction carried immense risk. These men might be harmless locals, but they were also witnesses. Witnesses Kestrel might feel compelled to silence if they learned too much.

"Hello?" the man with the rifle called out as they reached the base of the small rise where Elise's group huddled. His voice was rough, carrying a distinct local accent. "Heard someone yellin'. You folks alright up there?" He squinted upwards, trying to peer through the trees and mist.

Boone exchanged a quick, desperate look with Elise and Nora. No choice now. Projecting cautious non-aggression was their only play. "Stay put," he murmured to the women, then slowly stood up from behind the boulder, keeping his confiscated Kestrel sidearm holstered but visible, his shotgun held loosely at his side, muzzle pointed safely downwards.

"Evenin'," Boone called back down, his voice calm, attempting a tone of weary backcountry camaraderie. "Yeah, that was… uh… my associate." He nodded vaguely towards where Allen was hidden. "Took a nasty fall back there. Twisted her ankle bad. Little disoriented." He deliberately downplayed Allen's panic, framing it as injury-induced confusion.

The two men below exchanged glances, their suspicion slightly easing, replaced by concern. They climbed the last few yards, stopping a respectful distance away, their eyes taking in Boone's rough appearance, the visible fatigue etched on his face, the modern pistol at his hip contrasting slightly with his otherwise rugged attire.

"Name's Chet," the man with the rifle said, extending a calloused hand cautiously. "This here's my cousin, Dale. We were trackin' elk up from the Bogachiel drainage. Didn't expect to find anyone this high up, 'specially this time o' year." His eyes flicked past Boone, trying to get a look at the others hidden behind the rocks.

Boone ignored the offered hand, keeping his own near his weapon, maintaining a cautious distance. "Boone," he replied curtly. "Me and my… colleagues… were doin' some geological survey work further east." He waved vaguely back towards the direction of Site Sierra, careful not to be too specific. "Got caught in some bad weather, equipment failed, got turned around tryin' to hike out." He kept the story simple, plausible, omitting any mention of Kestrel, creatures, or being chased.

"Geological survey?" Dale, the quieter one holding the hiking staff, frowned slightly. "Ain't much survey work happens up here anymore. Not since the park expanded. And you're a long way off any marked trails." His eyes held a shrewd curiosity.

"Yeah, well, tell that to the foundation payin' the bills," Boone grumbled, trying to sound like a disgruntled field worker. "Sent us into some damn rough country." He gestured towards the hidden women again. "Like I said, my partner twisted her ankle bad. We were tryin' to find shelter, maybe follow a creek down."

Chet and Dale seemed to accept the explanation, at least superficially. Backcountry accidents happened. People got lost. "You folks need help?" Chet asked, his tone shifting towards genuine concern. "Got a first aid kit. Some spare water. Our camp ain't too far back down the ridge, maybe two hours. Got a satellite phone there, might be able to raise the Ranger station if the signal holds."

A satellite phone. The offer hung in the air, tempting, dangerous. If it worked, it meant rescue, escape. But it also meant official reports, questions, drawing attention directly to their location, potentially alerting Kestrel through monitored emergency channels. And could they trust these men? Were they truly just helpful locals? Or could they be something else – Kestrel assets disguised as hunters? Or perhaps even... lookouts for the guardians themselves, human allies protecting the valley? Elise's mind spun with paranoia, every interaction feeling like a potential trap.

"Appreciate the offer," Boone said slowly, carefully weighing the risks. "But the sat phone... doubt you'll get signal this deep in, 'specially with this weather." He was trying to politely refuse, avoid deeper entanglement. "Maybe just... point us towards the easiest route down towards the Hoh or the Bogachiel? We can manage from there, slow-like."

Chet frowned, looking Boone up and down again, perhaps sensing the evasion. "You sure? Your lady looked pretty bad off from the sound of her yell. And you folks look rode hard and put away wet. No offense."

Just then, Allen, perhaps sensing the conversation wasn't going the way she hoped, whimpered loudly from behind the rock. "Please… my ankle… I think it's broken!" she cried out, injecting genuine pain into her voice, though Elise suspected the injury, if any, was minor.

Chet and Dale exchanged worried glances. "See?" Chet said to Boone. "She needs help. Look, our camp ain't far. Got shelter, hot food, heavy-duty first aid. Least let us splint her ankle proper, give you folks a hot meal. We can try the phone from camp, maybe hike out to better signal tomorrow if need be." His offer seemed genuine, motivated by the unwritten code of the backcountry – you help those in trouble. Refusing now would seem deeply suspicious.

Boone hesitated, clearly hating the idea of accepting help, of being indebted, of potentially walking into another unknown situation. He glanced back at Elise and Nora. Elise gave a tiny, almost imperceptible shake of her head – too risky. But Nora's expression was harder to read. She seemed to be studying Chet and Dale intently, not just their appearance, but their energy, their connection to the place, perhaps. After a long moment, Nora gave a slow, deliberate nod towards Boone. *Trust them,* the gesture seemed to say. *Or at least, risk trusting them.*

Caught between Elise's caution and Nora's surprising endorsement, Boone seemed to make a reluctant decision. "Alright," he sighed, lowering his shotgun slightly further. "Alright. Appreciate it. Lead the way."

The tension lessened fractionally. Chet nodded, relief evident on his face. "Good deal. Just take it slow followin' us. Trail gets slick down there."

Elise and Nora helped Allen to her feet, the scientist leaning heavily on Elise, exaggerating her supposed ankle injury. As they stepped out from behind the boulders, Chet and Dale got their first clear look at the rest of the party – two women, one clearly Native, both looking as exhausted and battered as Boone, and one seemingly injured academic or scientist. Their expressions registered surprise, perhaps, but no overt alarm or recognition. They seemed to accept the cover story, at least for now.

They began the slow descent, following Chet and Dale along a winding game trail leading down from the ridge into the denser forest below. Boone kept a close eye on the two men ahead, while Nora subtly watched their back trail. Elise focused on supporting Allen, whose occasional winces and complaints seemed designed to maintain the injured facade, while simultaneously scanning the woods, her own senses still on high alert.

The hunters' camp, when they reached it after an hour of careful descent, was well-established but unobtrusive, tucked into a sheltered grove of ancient cedars beside a clear, fast-flowing creek. A sturdy canvas tent was pitched beneath the trees, smoke rising from a well-built rock fire ring nearby, carrying the welcome scent of coffee and frying bacon. Packs leaned against trees, gear neatly organized – rifles cleaned and propped safely, fishing rods leaning nearby, animal snares drying on a branch. It looked exactly like the camp of experienced, respectful backcountry users. Nothing immediately screamed Kestrel or hidden agendas.

Chet immediately set about tending to Allen's 'injured' ankle, producing a remarkably well-stocked first-aid kit. He was surprisingly gentle, knowledgeable, wrapping the ankle firmly but not too tightly, improvising a supportive splint from sticks and bandanas. Dale, meanwhile, offered them steaming mugs of strong cowboy coffee and thick slices of freshly fried bacon and bannock cooked over the fire. The food tasted impossibly good, the coffee searingly hot and restorative. Elise devoured her portion gratefully, feeling warmth return to her core for the first time in what felt like days.

As they ate and drank, conversation remained cautious, superficial. Chet and Dale asked general questions about their supposed survey work, the failed equipment, the bad weather. Boone and Elise offered vague, consistent answers, sticking to the cover story, careful not to reveal too much about their route, their true origins, or the specifics of their 'ordeal'. They learned Chet and Dale were cousins, loggers by trade during the week, passionate hunters and fishermen on weekends, exploring these remote drainages for trophy elk and rumored hidden trout streams their grandfather had told them about. They seemed genuine, ordinary men seeking escape and challenge in the wilderness.

Yet, Elise couldn't shake a lingering unease. Their appearance felt... too coincidental. Their camp location, while logical for hunters, placed them directly along a potential escape route from Site Sierra. Was it possible they weren't Kestrel, but something else? Watchers for the guardians, perhaps? Human allies, like Ish, tasked with monitoring the edges of the territory, reporting intrusions? Nora seemed relaxed, interacting easily with the men, sharing stories of tracking elk in similar terrain, but Elise caught her occasionally casting sharp, assessing glances towards them when she thought they weren't looking.

After they finished eating, Chet retrieved the satellite phone from his pack – a bulky, older model, but functional-looking. "Alright," he said. "Let's see if we can raise some help for you folks." He powered it on, extended the antenna, and moved towards a small rise near the edge of the clearing, seeking better signal.

Elise, Boone, and Nora watched intently, holding their breath. If the call went through, what would happen? Would rescue crews arrive? Would Kestrel intercept the signal, pinpoint their location precisely? Would Chet and Dale's story of finding lost surveyors hold up under official scrutiny?

Chet frowned at the phone's small screen. "Damn," he muttered. "Signal's weak here. Keep losing satellite lock." He shifted position, holding the phone higher, turning slowly. "Come on, you piece of junk…"

Suddenly, his body went rigid. He froze, hand lowering the phone slightly, head cocked as if listening intently to something beyond the forest sounds. Dale noticed his cousin's change in demeanor, looking up sharply from cleaning his rifle. "Chet? What is it?"

Chet didn't answer immediately. He slowly turned his head, scanning the dense woods surrounding the clearing, his eyes narrowed, his earlier friendly concern replaced by a sudden, intense alertness that mirrored Boone's own ingrained vigilance.

"Company," Chet breathed, his voice low, tight. "Somethin'… big… movin' out there. West side. Comin' this way."

Instantly, the atmosphere in the camp shifted from cautious hospitality to high alert. Boone snatched up his shotgun. Nora grabbed her axe. Dale chambered a round into his rifle. Even Dr. Allen seemed to shrink further into herself, sensing the change.

Elise's blood ran cold. Not Kestrel. Something else. Had the guardians followed them even here? Had their scent, their passage, drawn unwanted attention? Or was it unrelated – just a bear, an elk moving through?

"How big?" Boone asked Chet quietly, moving to stand beside him, scanning the woods in the direction Chet indicated.

"Big," Chet confirmed grimly. "Heavy steps. Breakin' branches like they ain't even there. Too heavy for elk. Too… deliberate for bear." He raised his rifle, clicking the safety off. "Get ready."

They waited, frozen in a tense tableau, straining their ears over the gurgle of the creek and the crackle of the fire. The sounds grew closer – the heavy, rhythmic crashing through undergrowth, the snap of large branches, punctuated by low, guttural grunts. It was unmistakably something immense, powerful, and moving directly towards their camp.

Elise fumbled for her pistol again, her hand shaking. After everything, after escaping the caves, finding Boone, finding temporary refuge… was it all for nothing? Were they about to face the guardians' wrath again, here, with these unsuspecting hunters caught in the crossfire?

Then, the creature burst into the clearing.

But it wasn't a Stick-shí'nač.

It was a grizzly bear. A monstrous one, larger than any Elise had ever seen, easily rivaling a small vehicle in sheer bulk. Its fur was thick, grizzled brown, matted with mud and debris. A deep, ragged scar ran across its snout, pulling one lip back in a permanent snarl. Its small eyes, burning with pain, fury, and something that looked disturbingly like unnatural hunger, fixed on the humans around the fire. It let out a deafening roar, a sound thick with aggression and agony, and charged.

This wasn't a guardian defending territory. This felt… wrong. Unbalanced. Like the 'wounded' places Nora and Ish had spoken of, but concentrated, mobile, enraged. Had Kestrel's activities, the Resonance, the potential bio-agent, somehow affected the local wildlife, creating… something else? Or was this simply a desperate, starving bear in the wrong place at the wrong time?

There was no time to analyze. The charge was immediate, devastating. Chet and Dale reacted instantly, raising their rifles, firing almost simultaneously. The heavy caliber bullets slammed into the bear's massive chest, staggering it, eliciting another roar of pain. But incredibly, it didn't go down. It shook its massive head, ignoring the wounds, and kept coming, its momentum carrying it directly towards Chet.

Boone fired his shotgun, the buckshot tearing into the bear's flank, but having little apparent effect beyond enraging it further. Nora screamed a warning. Elise fired her pistol wildly, the small caliber bullets likely useless against the thick hide and muscle.

The bear slammed into Chet with the force of a freight train, swiping one massive paw armed with claws like railroad spikes. Chet cried out, his rifle flying from his grasp as he was thrown backwards against a tree, collapsing in a heap, unmoving.

The bear, ignoring the others now, focused its fury on the downed man, lowering its massive head, jaws wide, ready to savage its victim. Dale yelled his cousin's name, firing again, emptying his magazine into the bear's back, but the beast seemed impervious, driven by a terrifying, unnatural frenzy.

This was it. They were going to die here, torn apart not by the mythical guardians, but by a seemingly mundane, yet monstrously enraged, grizzly bear.

But just as the bear lunged towards the motionless Chet, another figure exploded from the dense woods on the far side of the clearing, moving with blurring speed. Taller than the bear, leaner than the elder Stick-shí'nač, but radiating an aura of coiled, dangerous power.

It was the adolescent guardian.

It hit the enraged grizzly broadside, tackling it with enough force to knock the massive bear off its feet, sending both creatures tumbling in a tangle of fur, claws, and roaring fury. They rolled across the clearing, crashing through the fire pit, scattering embers and equipment, locked in a truly titanic struggle. The Stick-shí'nač adolescent, though perhaps outweighed, possessed incredible strength and agility, dodging the bear's snapping jaws and raking claws, using leverage and precisely aimed blows to counter the bear's brute force. Its earlier hesitancy, its grief, were gone, replaced by focused, lethal combat instinct.

Elise, Boone, and Nora could only watch, stunned into inaction by the sheer primal violence unfolding before them. The adolescent wasn't fighting *for* them, Elise realized. It was fighting the bear because the bear was… wrong. Unbalanced. A manifestation of the sickness Kestrel had perhaps unleashed, a threat to the natural order the guardians, in their own way, sought to protect.

The fight was brief, brutal. The adolescent managed to get a grip on the bear's thick neck, using its immense strength to twist, forcing the bear's head back at an unnatural angle. There was a sickening crunch of bone, and the bear's struggles abruptly ceased. It lay still, its massive form suddenly inert.

The adolescent Stick-shí'nač rose slowly from the carcass, chest heaving, its dark fur spattered with bear blood. It shook its head, letting out a low, guttural sound, perhaps satisfaction, perhaps exhaustion. Then, it turned its gaze towards the remaining humans huddled near the ruined campsite.

Its eyes, deep-set and intelligent, met Elise's across the clearing. It held her gaze for a long, unreadable moment. Then, deliberately, it raised one blood-streaked hand, mimicking the gesture Elise had made in the sanctuary, palm facing outwards. A sign? Acknowledgment? Warning?

Before Elise could react, before Boone could raise his shotgun again, the adolescent turned and melted back into the forest, disappearing as silently and suddenly as it had arrived, leaving behind the dead bear, the unconscious Kestrel agents miles away, the dying fire, the injured hunter Chet, and three stunned survivors grappling with the impossible reality of their situation.

They had been saved, unexpectedly, terrifyingly, by one of the very beings they feared. The lines between friend and foe, guardian and monster, natural and unnatural, blurred completely, leaving only the stark imperative to survive the tangled threads of a conflict far deeper and stranger than any of them could have ever imagined.

Chapter 29: Echoes of Humanity

The silence that fell over the clearing after the adolescent Stickshí'nač vanished was absolute, save for the crackling hiss of the scattered embers from the destroyed fire pit and the low, pained groans coming from Chet, the injured hunter. The massive carcass of the grizzly bear lay like a small hillock near the center of the camp, its unnatural stillness a stark testament to the brutal, decisive power they had just witnessed. Steam rose faintly from its cooling body in the damp, cold air.

For a long moment, Elise, Boone, and Nora remained frozen, locked in a state of profound shock and disbelief. The sheer violence of the bear attack, followed by the utterly unexpected, almost surreal intervention of the adolescent guardian, had overloaded their already frayed senses, leaving them reeling, struggling to process the rapid cascade of events.

Boone was the first to break the spell, his ingrained survival instincts kicking back in. "Check Chet!" he ordered, already moving cautiously towards the injured hunter crumpled at the base of the cedar tree. "Nora, keep watch! Make sure that… that thing… is really gone. And make sure nothing else was drawn by the commotion."

Nora nodded grimly, her eyes scanning the surrounding woods with renewed intensity, axe held ready. Elise hurried after Boone, her first aid kit – now supplemented with supplies confiscated from the Kestrel agents – held ready.

Chet was alive, miraculously, but badly injured. The bear's glancing blow had clearly broken bones in his arm and shoulder, judging by the unnatural angle and the sharp cry of pain he emitted when Boone gently probed the area. Deep gashes from the creature's claws marred his chest and side, bleeding sluggishly through his torn jacket. He was conscious, but dazed, his eyes unfocused, likely concussed from the impact against the tree.

"Easy now, Chet," Boone murmured, his voice surprisingly gentle as he worked with Elise to cut away the blood-soaked fabric. "Easy. We gotcha."

Elise quickly assessed the wounds. The bleeding wasn't arterial, thankfully, but the gashes were deep, dirty, requiring immediate cleaning and dressing to prevent infection. The arm and shoulder needed stabilization. Working together with practiced efficiency honed by their shared ordeal, Elise cleaned the wounds as best she could with antiseptic wipes and precious filtered water, while Boone expertly fashioned a sturdy splint from straight tree branches and ripped strips of canvas from a discarded pack cover. They applied pressure bandages to the deepest cuts, trying to control the bleeding.

Throughout the process, Chet remained mostly passive, occasionally groaning, his eyes clouded with pain and confusion. He seemed only vaguely aware of what had happened, muttering fragments about "big bear… outta nowhere…"

Dale, the other hunter, had recovered from his initial shock and rushed over, his face pale, watching them work with horrified anxiety. "Is he… is he gonna be okay?" Dale asked, his voice trembling.

"He's tough," Boone replied noncommittally, tightening a bandage. "Lost some blood. Definitely broken bones. Head injury possible. Needs a doctor. Needs evacuation. Soon." He glanced up towards the sky, now rapidly darkening towards dusk. "Which ain't gonna happen tonight."

The reality of their situation slammed back in. They were miles deep in the wilderness, with a severely injured man requiring urgent medical care, dwindling supplies, failing light, and the knowledge that both Kestrel and potentially agitated Stick-shí'nač were active in the region. And their only potential communication device, Chet's satellite phone, lay smashed amongst the scattered embers of the fire pit, a casualty of the bear attack. They were cut off again, burdened with a casualty, their already desperate situation significantly worse.

"We need shelter," Nora stated firmly, returning from her perimeter check. "That thing... the young guardian... is gone. Tracks lead away fast, back towards the high country. No sign of others nearby, for now. But this camp... it smells of blood. It will draw scavengers. Maybe worse." She gestured towards the dark woods. "And the injured one... Chet... needs warmth, protection from the night."

The cabin. Boone's initial refuge. It was their only option nearby. It offered solid walls, a hearth for fire, relative defensibility compared to staying out in the open.

"Can we move him?" Elise asked doubtfully, looking at Chet's pale, pain-wracked face.

"We have to," Boone stated flatly. "Gonna hurt like hell. But staying here... he won't last the night."

Fashioning a makeshift stretcher or travois was impossible without more rope and time. They decided on the agonizingly slow method of carrying him, supported between Boone and Dale, while Elise carried the essential gear and Nora scouted ahead, clearing the path and watching for threats. Allen, the Kestrel scientist, was pressed into service carrying packs, her earlier terror now replaced by a sullen, fearful compliance, clearly realizing her survival was now inextricably linked to these rugged survivors she had likely been tasked, indirectly or directly, with containing or eliminating.

The journey back to the cabin, though likely less than two miles, felt endless. Chet cried out frequently as jolts of movement aggravated his injuries. Boone and Dale strained under his weight, their own exhaustion pushed to the absolute limit. Elise and Nora moved back and forth, assisting, clearing obstacles, scanning the deepening gloom. Every shadow seemed to hold menace, every rustle of leaves sounded like pursuit. The forest felt profoundly silent again, watchful, as if holding its breath after the recent violence.

They finally stumbled into the small clearing surrounding the cabin just as the last vestiges of twilight surrendered to full, moonless darkness. The cabin stood silent, a dark silhouette against the slightly lighter sky, feeling both welcoming and potentially ominous. Was it truly empty? Or had something else taken shelter there in their absence?

Boone cautiously approached the door, shotgun ready, while Nora circled around, checking the single small window, listening intently. After a tense moment, Nora gave a subtle nod. Clear.

Inside, the cabin felt cold, the embers in the hearth long dead. Working quickly by the dim light of Elise's fading headlamp and a spare flashlight from Chet's pack, they made Chet as comfortable as possible on the rough sleeping platform, covering him with salvaged blankets. Nora quickly rebuilt the fire, coaxing flames from dry tinder and kindling, the returning warmth and light feeling like a physical blessing against the encroaching darkness and despair. Boone secured the flimsy door as best he could, wedging a heavy log against it from the inside.

Dale, overwhelmed by his cousin's injury and the terrifying events, sank onto one of the stools near the fire, head in his hands. Allen huddled in the furthest corner, silent, watchful, her expression unreadable – was she reassessing her loyalties? Planning escape? Or simply numb with shock?

Elise checked Chet's wounds again in the firelight. He was stable, for now, but his breathing was shallow, his pulse rapid. The risk of infection, internal bleeding, shock… it was high. Without proper medical care, his chances remained grim.

As Nora brewed more of her potent herbal tea – likely adding something for pain relief for Chet – Elise found herself sitting beside Boone near the hearth, the two of them staring silently into the flames, processing the impossible events of the day.

"So," Boone said finally, his voice low, rough. "The kid saved us." He still sounded bewildered. "Attacked Kestrel agents. Fought off a damn grizzly bigger than my truck. Then just… walked away." He shook his head. "Don't make a lick of sense."

"Maybe," Elise offered tentatively, recalling Nora's earlier words, Whis Elem's wisdom, "it wasn't about *us*, not directly. Maybe it was about… balance. The bear felt wrong, unnatural. Maybe driven mad by something Kestrel did, or by the Resonance? The adolescent… maybe it was just restoring order? Protecting its territory from something sick, something unbalanced?"

Boone considered this. "Maybe," he conceded grudgingly. "But it chose *not* to attack *us* afterwards. Stood right there. Had us dead to rights. Coulda finished the job." He met Elise's eyes across the flickering firelight. "That hand gesture it made… like yours in the sanctuary… what do you think it meant?"

Elise hesitated. "I don't know. Acknowledgment? A warning? Maybe… maybe a truce? A recognition, like Nora said, that Kestrel is the bigger threat to both of us?" It felt like a wild leap, interpreting the actions of a fundamentally alien intelligence.

"A truce with nine-foot-tall bone collectors?" Boone scoffed, but the skepticism in his voice was less pronounced than before. He had witnessed the creature's power, its fury, but also its inexplicable restraint, its focused intervention against a common threat (the bear, and arguably, Kestrel). The lines were blurring, even for him.

"We have to consider it," Elise insisted quietly. "If there's even a chance… that they might see us differently now… that they might allow us passage, or even inadvertently help us against Kestrel… it changes things."

"Changes how?" Boone challenged. "We still gotta get out of here. Still gotta deal with Kestrel. Still gotta figure out what to do with…" he nodded towards Allen huddled in the corner, "…her. And the proof you carry."

The weight of their predicament settled heavily again. Finding Boone alive was a miracle. Surviving the bear attack, thanks to the adolescent guardian, was another. But their fundamental problems remained. They were trapped, injured, hunted, carrying explosive secrets.

"Allen," Elise said thoughtfully, looking towards the scientist. "She's the key right now. To understanding Kestrel's immediate plans. To finding weaknesses. We need her to cooperate. Fully."

Boone grunted. "She's scared. Might talk to save her own skin. But trust her? Not a chance. Kestrel trained her. Her loyalty might run deeper than fear."

"We have leverage," Elise pointed out. "We know about Echo. About Goliath. About the Sanitization Protocol. We know Kestrel silences failures and witnesses. Her best chance of survival, ironically, might be with us, helping us expose them."

They agreed to question Allen again in the morning, gently but firmly, using the knowledge they possessed to press for more details – about Site Sierra's defenses, Kestrel communication protocols, evacuation plans, known personnel, anything that might offer an advantage.

Nora rejoined them by the fire, handing them mugs of hot tea. She had been tending to Chet, who had drifted into a restless, pain-filled sleep. "He is strong," she said quietly, nodding towards the injured hunter. "But the mountain demands a price for survival. He will need much care." She looked towards Dale, who sat slumped, staring blankly at the floor. "And his cousin… carries heavy worry."

"Can we help them?" Elise asked, the question encompassing more than just medical aid. "Chet saved Allen, tried to help us. Now they're caught up in this because of us."

Nora met her gaze, her eyes holding ancient sorrow. "We help by surviving," she stated simply. "By finding a way out, for all who remain. But their path forward... may need to diverge from ours. Carrying our burdens... the knowledge, the pursuit... endangers anyone near us."

Elise understood. If they managed to stabilize Chet, find a way to signal for conventional rescue for him and Dale, it might be the kindest, safest option for the hunters. But it meant separating, Elise and Boone and Nora continuing their own perilous journey towards exposing Kestrel, carrying the secret alone.

As the fire burned lower, casting long, dancing shadows, Elise felt the immense complexity, the tangled threads of their situation. Human hunters caught in the crossfire. A Kestrel scientist turned reluctant captive. An ancient race of guardians exhibiting inexplicable behaviors ranging from lethal rage to protective intervention. A shadowy organization preparing potential ecocide. And three fugitives holding fragments of a truth that could save or destroy worlds.

She pulled out her battered field notebook, the only remaining repository of her journey, her observations, her copied fragments of proof. By the dim firelight, she began to write, not just documenting events, but trying to make sense of the contradictions, trying to find a pattern in the chaos. She sketched the Stick-shí'nač symbols she remembered, compared the behavior of the elder with the adolescent, cross-referenced Allen's reluctant admissions with the miners' logbook and Graves' files.

She wrote about the Resonance, speculating on its nature – geological energy, biological field, technological remnant? – and its apparent connection to both the creatures' abilities and Kestrel's interests. She wrote about the ethical tightrope – the need to stop

Kestrel versus the danger of exposing the Stick-shí'nač. She wrote about sacrifice – Levi's deliberate atonement, Boone's selfless diversion, the adolescent guardian's potentially protective intervention, even Chet's simple backcountry helpfulness that had drawn him into peril. Echoes of humanity, she thought, found in the most unexpected places, amidst monstrous actions and impossible beings.

Writing didn't provide easy answers. But it helped clarify the questions, solidify the stakes. It reinforced her conviction that understanding, not just survival, had to be the goal. Understanding Kestrel's full conspiracy. Understanding the Stick-shí'nač's complex reality. Understanding her own role, her own responsibility, as a witness caught between these colliding worlds.

Outside, the wind picked up again, moaning through the ancient trees. Elise shivered, drawing closer to the dying fire. The cabin felt like a tiny, fragile island in an immense ocean of darkness and danger. Morning would bring difficult choices, renewed risks. But tonight, huddled together, survivors of an impossible day, sharing warmth and weary companionship, they held onto a fragile thread of existence. The echoes of humanity, however faint, persisted even here, in the heart of the whispering wilderness, offering the barest glimmer of hope against the encroaching night.

Chapter 30: Diverging Paths

Dawn painted the small cabin window with streaks of pale, reluctant grey. The fire had died down to glowing embers, radiating a feeble warmth against the persistent chill that seeped through the log walls. Elise woke stiffly from a few hours of restless sleep on the hard floor, the familiar aches of exhaustion instantly reminding her of their precarious reality. Across the small room, Boone was already awake, silently checking the loads in the confiscated Kestrel pistol, his face set in grim lines. Nora sat beside the sleeping platform where Chet lay, monitoring the injured hunter's breathing, which seemed shallower, more ragged than the night before. Dale snored softly, curled up near the hearth, lost in temporary oblivion. Dr. Allen huddled in her corner, awake but motionless, eyes wide with residual fear and uncertainty.

The fragile peace of the shared sanctuary couldn't last. Decisions needed to be made, actions taken, before Kestrel regrouped or the guardians' inexplicable neutrality shifted back towards hostility.

"How is he?" Elise whispered, nodding towards Chet as she quietly accepted a mug of reheated herbal tea from Nora.

Nora shook her head slowly, her expression grave. "Fever climbs. Breathing is difficult. The wound on his side… looks angry." Infection was clearly setting in, compounding the trauma of broken bones and potential concussion. "Without proper medicine… soon…" She didn't need to finish the sentence.

"We need to get him out," Boone stated flatly, sliding the pistol back into its holster. "Forget the sat phone, it's smashed. Our only chance is hiking him down towards the ranger station near the Hoh River entrance. It's maybe… ten, twelve miles? Brutal terrain, but doable if we push hard." He looked at Dale, still asleep. "He'll need his cousin's help carrying him."

"And us?" Elise asked, knowing the implication.

Boone met her gaze squarely. "We ain't goin' with 'em, Doc. Can't. Our presence… it puts them in even more danger. If Kestrel intercepts them, finds us with them… they become liabilities too. Witnesses Kestrel might feel the need to silence. Best we split up. Let Dale get his cousin out, report him as a bear attack victim – which ain't entirely wrong," he added grimly. "Let them stick to a story Kestrel can accept. Gives them the best chance."

Elise hated the cold logic of it, the necessity of abandoning these civilians who had tried to help them. But Boone was right. Their knowledge, their very existence, was toxic. Anyone associated with them became a target. Splitting up offered the hunters the best chance of navigating the Kestrel quarantine and getting Chet the medical help he desperately needed without being dragged into the deeper conspiracy.

"Nora?" Elise looked towards the older woman, seeking her counsel.

Nora sighed, gazing towards the pale light filtering through the window. "It is the way," she agreed sadly. "Their path leads back towards the world of men. Ours… remains in the shadows. We cannot walk together safely." She looked at Elise, then Boone. "But splitting leaves us… weaker. More vulnerable."

"We'll manage," Boone said, though his voice lacked conviction. "We need to focus on the next step. Site Sierra. Thorne. We got the map intel from those agents. We got Allen," he glanced towards the scientist, who flinched under his gaze. "She gets us closer, tells us what she knows about security, layouts, Thorne's possible hideouts. Then… maybe we cut her loose too. Or maybe she becomes useful leverage."

The plan felt ruthless, pragmatic, born of desperation. Use Allen's knowledge, find Thorne, somehow disrupt Kestrel, all while evading capture and navigating the unpredictable presence of the Stick-shí'nač. It seemed impossibly complex, fraught with peril at every turn.

They woke Dale gently, explaining the situation, the need to get Chet to help immediately, the danger posed by Elise and Boone remaining with them. Dale, groggy at first, quickly grasped the severity, his face paling as he looked at his cousin's worsening condition. Fear warred with gratitude and confusion, but the urgency overrode everything else. He agreed readily to the plan.

While Boone and Nora carefully constructed a reinforced travois using sturdy branches, salvaged canvas, and sections of the precious rope they still possessed, Elise took Dr. Allen aside, towards the back of the cabin.

"Listen to me, Lena," Elise said, keeping her voice low but firm, using the scientist's first name deliberately, trying to foster a sliver of connection amidst the coercion. "Your survival depends entirely on your cooperation now. We know Kestrel protocols. We know what happens to agents involved in failed operations or security breaches. Helping us might be your only way out of this mess alive and with some chance of… redemption, maybe."

Allen looked up, her eyes filled with a mixture of fear and resentment. "Redemption? After what you've shown me… what I was part of…?" She shook her head. "There's no redemption. Only… consequences."

"Then help us mitigate the consequences," Elise pressed. "Help us stop the Sanitization Protocol. Help us find Aris Thorne. He tried to stop this, didn't he? Maybe he knows how. Tell us everything you know about Site Sierra's current status. Who's in charge now that Graves is gone? What are their communication methods? Evacuation plans?"

Allen hesitated, chewing her lip nervously, glancing towards Boone and Nora working on the travois. Finally, seeming to accept the grim reality of her situation, she began to talk, her voice low, rapid, spilling information perhaps withheld during their previous interrogations.

She confirmed Site Sierra was primarily a bio-containment and disposal facility now, research largely phased out after Thorne's departure and several earlier 'incidents'. The current site commander was a man named Marcus Thorne – Aris Thorne's estranged, more ruthlessly ambitious younger brother, ironically. Marcus Thorne answered directly to a shadowy Kestrel directorate known only as 'Quadrant'. Communications were heavily encrypted, routed through dedicated satellite uplinks via the main dome, likely offline now due to the power failure. Evacuation protocols involved designated helicopter landing zones north and south of the compound, but activation required specific authorization codes she didn't possess. The drilling equipment was indeed for deploying the sterilizing fungus, the final failsafe if containment of the 'asset' (Omega) or information about the sanctuary was irrevocably breached. She suspected Marcus Thorne, if he survived the Stick-shí'nač attack, would prioritize initiating Protocol Zero above all else, seeing it as both fulfilling his directive and erasing evidence of potential operational failures under his command.

As for Aris Thorne, Allen confirmed the rumors of his disappearance after vehemently opposing the live capture strategy and the development of the sterilization fungus. She didn't know his current whereabouts but mentioned he had always been deeply interested in the 'bio-resonance phenomenon', believing it held the key to understanding the Stick-shí'nač's unique abilities and potentially even their origins. He had apparently established small, off-grid monitoring stations years ago in areas known for anomalous energy readings – one near Mount Baker as she'd mentioned, another rumored to be somewhere in the remote coastal ranges near the Oregon border. If he was alive and hiding, those locations were the most likely bets.

The information was invaluable, confirming their suspicions, identifying the new antagonist in Marcus Thorne, highlighting the urgency of stopping Protocol Zero, and providing potential leads, however tenuous, to Aris Thorne's location.

By mid-morning, the travois was ready. Chet, delirious now, barely rousing, was carefully secured onto it. Dale, his face etched with worry but resolute, took his place at the front, ready to pull his cousin towards help.

The farewells were brief, laden with unspoken fears and uncertainties. "Good luck," Dale said to Boone, gripping his hand briefly. "Watch yourselves out there."

"You too," Boone replied gruffly. "Keep him warm. Keep movin'. Stick to the creek drainage, head west towards the Hoh road. Should hit ranger patrols eventually."

Nora offered Dale a small pouch of herbs. "For his fever," she instructed. "And for strength on your journey. May the ancestors guide your steps."

Dale nodded gratefully, tucking the pouch away. Then, with a final, worried glance back at the silent forest, he began the slow, arduous task of hauling the travois, disappearing down the faint trail leading away from the cabin clearing.

Elise watched them go, her heart heavy. Another divergence, another set of lives potentially endangered by their knowledge, their quest. She could only hope they made it, that Kestrel wouldn't intercept them, that Chet would survive.

Now, only four remained: Elise, Boone, Nora, and their reluctant captive, Dr. Allen. The cabin felt suddenly emptier, more vulnerable.

"Alright," Boone said, turning back, his focus shifting immediately to their next move. "Thorne. Mount Baker or the Oregon coast range. Long way from here either way. And Kestrel's likely lookin' for us between here and there." He looked at the map again, then at Allen. "Any Kestrel safe houses? Supply caches? Emergency transport options closer than Seattle?"

Allen shook her head. "Not that I was briefed on. Operations here were meant to be self-contained. Resupply was via helicopter to Site Sierra directly. If Thorne went off-grid, he'd likely avoid anything Kestrel-related."

"So we're on our own," Boone concluded grimly. "Means travelling light, fast, living off the land as much as possible. Which means…" he looked pointedly at Allen, "…you need to keep up. And be useful."

Their immediate plan was to head north, using Ish's knowledge and the Kestrel map to navigate the ridges and valleys west of Site Sierra, putting distance between themselves and the compromised area while angling towards potential routes leading out of the Olympics towards the northern Cascades. It was a journey of hundreds of miles through rugged wilderness, potentially taking weeks, all while evading Kestrel and avoiding further encounters with the guardians.

They spent the rest of the day preparing, reinforcing their own meager gear with salvaged items from the cabin and Chet's abandoned pack (a better compass, a small hatchet, fishing line, fire starter). Allen, stripped of her lab coat, looked absurdly out of place in ill-fitting spare clothes Boone provided. She remained sullenly cooperative, answering direct questions but volunteering little, her eyes constantly darting towards the surrounding woods. Trusting her was impossible, but her knowledge, particularly regarding Kestrel procedures and potentially recognizing their technology or personnel, was too valuable to discard, for now.

As dusk approached, they abandoned the cabin, melting back into the forest, heading north. The familiar rhythm of cautious movement, watchful silence, and gnawing uncertainty resumed. Elise walked beside Nora, leaving Boone to manage Allen just behind them.

"Do you think... we did the right thing?" Elise asked Nora quietly, the separation from the hunters weighing on her. "Letting them go alone?"

Nora walked in silence for a moment, her gaze scanning the path ahead. "Sometimes," she said finally, "the kindest path is the one that leads away from danger, even if it means walking alone for a time. Their burden was heavy enough without adding ours." She glanced back briefly towards where Allen stumbled behind Boone. "Some burdens, however, cannot be so easily set aside."

Elise understood. Allen was their burden now. And the knowledge they carried, the memory card hidden against Elise's skin, the logbook page, the secrets whispered by Whis Elem and Ish, the horrifying truth glimpsed in the frozen lab and the Heart-Chamber – these were burdens that bound the three of them together, driving them forward into the unknown, towards a confrontation that felt both terrifying and inevitable. The paths had diverged, but their own led inexorably deeper into the tangled web of secrets, survival, and the enduring, enigmatic presence of the guardians of the Hollow Ground. The hunt for Aris Thorne, and for a future free from Kestrel's shadow, had begun.

Chapter 31: The Hollow Truth

The thin air of the high ridge tasted of freedom and fear in equal measure. Behind them lay the violated secrecy of Site Sierra, the echoes of battle, the chilling evidence of Kestrel's monstrosity. Ahead lay the vast, indifferent wilderness of the Olympic Mountains, an expanse of mist-shrouded peaks and shadowed valleys that promised both refuge and potentially lethal hardship. They moved north along the rocky spine, away from the immediate contamination of the Kestrel facility, driven by adrenaline and the desperate need to put distance between themselves and the hornet's nest they had stirred.

Four figures now, silhouetted against the bruised pre-dawn sky: Boone, grim and watchful, moving with a painful stiffness but his senses sharp; Nora, the steady anchor, reading the terrain, her face etched with sorrow but her spirit unbroken; Elise, fueled by a volatile mix of terror, grief, and burgeoning resolve, clutching the fragmented proof that felt heavier than any physical burden; and Dr. Lena Allen, stumbling, terrified, a reluctant captive whose knowledge was both their greatest asset and their most dangerous liability.

The silence that had fallen over Site Sierra after the Stick-shí'nač assault felt profoundly unnerving. No alarms, no pursuing helicopters, no immediate sign of regrouping Kestrel forces. It was as if the entire compound held its breath, assessing the damage, dealing with its own internal chaos.

"Too quiet," Boone muttered, pausing behind a cluster of wind-blasted firs to scan their back trail with the binoculars. "They took heavy losses back there. But Kestrel doesn't just… quit. They'll be pulling back, securing the site, calling in reinforcements. And they'll be analyzing that power cut, the sabotage. They'll know someone got inside, got out. They'll assume it was us."

"The guardians… will they pursue?" Elise asked quietly, voicing the other fear that haunted their steps.

Nora scanned the immense landscape, her gaze distant. "Their rage was directed at the desecration of the site, the capture of the young one," she mused. "Perhaps… perhaps their immediate purpose was fulfilled. They reclaimed their own, punished the intruders within their territory. Whether their anger extends beyond those boundaries…" She shrugged slightly. "Their ways remain unknown. But I do not feel their focused presence behind us now. Only… the mountain watches."

The mountain itself felt like enough of an adversary. Their progress was slow, hampered by Allen's lack of stamina and inappropriate footwear, by Boone's injuries, by their own bone-deep exhaustion. Hunger gnawed relentlessly. Their water supply, replenished briefly at a high tarn, was already running low again. The cold intensified as the sunless day wore on, promising a brutal night ahead without shelter.

Allen, stumbling on loose scree for the third time, finally broke down, collapsing onto the rocky ground, sobbing uncontrollably. "I can't… I can't go on," she gasped between ragged breaths, tears freezing on her cheeks. "Leave me here. Just leave me. They'll find me eventually."

Boone regarded her with cold impatience. "Get up, Allen. Crying ain't gonna help. We leave you here, you freeze to death before Kestrel even bothers lookin'. You want to survive? You keep moving."

"Survive?" Allen laughed bitterly, a broken sound. "What's the point? Kestrel knows I failed. Knows I was compromised. Even if I get back, they'll… disappear me. Bury me alongside their other mistakes. And if *they* don't get me…" she cast a terrified glance back towards the direction of Site Sierra, "…*they* will."

"So you help us," Elise said, kneeling beside her, trying a different approach, keeping her voice steady despite her own exhaustion. "You help us survive, help us find Thorne, help us expose Kestrel. It's your only chance, Lena. Your only path to maybe making amends for… for Echo. For Omega."

The mention of the captive creatures seemed to strike a chord. Allen's sobbing subsided slightly, replaced by a look of profound guilt and despair. "Omega… I tried to keep the sedation levels low," she whispered, as if confessing. "Tried to… minimize the invasive procedures Marcus insisted on. But he wouldn't listen. He only cared about the Resonance data, the potential applications…" She looked up at Elise, her eyes pleading. "Aris… Dr. Thorne… he was different. He argued with Marcus constantly. Said we were provoking something ancient, powerful, that we didn't understand. Said the Resonance wasn't a tool to be harnessed, but a… a consciousness to be respected. He warned them this would happen."

"Where would he go, Lena?" Elise pressed gently. "The research station near Mount Baker? The Oregon coast range? You mentioned unique energy fields… Was he tracking something specific?"

Allen frowned, digging deep into her memory, perhaps seeing a chance to align herself with Thorne's apparently more ethical stance. "He was obsessed with… harmonic convergences," she said slowly. "Specific times, specific locations, where the natural earth resonance amplified, interacted with solar cycles, atmospheric conditions. He believed the Stick-shí'nač abilities, maybe even their consciousness, were tied to these peaks. He had charts… complex calculations based on seismic data, solar flare predictions, even obscure geological surveys." She paused. "There was one location he was particularly focused on lately, before he vanished. Not Baker, not Oregon. A remote caldera system deep in the Northern Cascades, known for anomalous magnetic readings and rare crystal formations. He called it… the 'Singing Caldera'. Believed it might be a major nexus point, maybe even another sanctuary like the one you described."

The Singing Caldera. Another piece of the puzzle, another potential destination. It felt more specific, more promising than the vague earlier suggestions.

"Can you find it on a map?" Boone asked sharply, pulling out their topographical charts.

Allen nodded hesitantly, leaning over the maps spread on the wind-swept rock, tracing a finger across the complex contours of the Cascades range, miles north of their current position. "Somewhere… in this region, I think. High altitude. Very remote."

"If Thorne is there," Boone mused, studying the map, "he'll be hard to reach. And likely well-hidden." He looked at Allen again. "Any Kestrel knowledge of this 'Singing Caldera'? Is it on their radar?"

Allen shook her head. "Not that I know of. Aris kept his resonance research highly compartmentalized, especially after his disagreements with Marcus. He might have considered it his personal… sanctuary. Or fallback point."

It was their best lead yet. Find Aris Thorne at the Singing Caldera. Potentially gain an expert ally, crucial intel, maybe even proof that could bring down Kestrel. But the journey there felt almost insurmountable.

"We still need supplies," Elise stated practicality. "We won't survive the trek north like this. We need to risk approaching civilization, just briefly."

Boone nodded grimly. "Agreed. There's a small highway crossing further west, near Lake Quinault. Old logging town nearby, Forks is further north. Might be able to resupply at a general store, maybe 'borrow' some gear from an unattended vehicle if we get desperate. Means crossing more open ground, risking exposure."

The plan solidified. Descend westwards, aiming for the Quinault region. Attempt a quick, low-profile resupply. Then swing north, using back roads and forest trails, heading towards the Northern Cascades and the Singing Caldera, hoping to find Thorne before Kestrel found them. Allen would accompany them as far as the resupply point; her fate after that remained an uneasy question mark.

The descent westwards was brutal, taking them down steep, forested slopes, across swift, icy rivers, through valleys choked with mist and silence. They moved cautiously, avoiding obvious trails, relying on Nora's guidance and Boone's tracking skills to navigate. Allen struggled constantly, her presence slowing them down, her fear a palpable drag on their already strained morale.

Late on the second day of descent, they finally reached the edge of the vast Quinault rainforest, the trees here even larger, older, than in the high country, draped in thick carpets of moss, creating a world of deep green shadows and profound quiet. They found a sheltered spot to make a cold camp, gnawing on the last edible roots Nora had gathered. Exhaustion was absolute.

As Elise was trying to find a comfortable position against a mossy log, intending to take the first watch, her hand brushed against the hidden pocket in her jacket. The notebook. The memory card. The logbook page. The weight of the proof, the Hollow Truth. It felt heavier than ever.

She pulled out the notebook, flicking on her dying headlamp one last time, needing to anchor herself in the story, the purpose, before succumbing to sleep. She reread her final entry, written in Whis Elem's cabin, her declaration of intent: *"...my journey into that mystery is not over. It has only just begun."*

She looked over at Boone, already asleep, slumped against a tree, pistol resting on his lap, his face looking younger, more vulnerable in repose. She looked at Nora, meditating quietly nearby, her connection to this ancient forest seemingly sustaining her where physical strength failed. She looked at Allen, huddled miserably, a prisoner of her own choices and circumstances. And she thought of Levi, of Jules, their faces fading but their sacrifices vivid.

The path ahead was terrifyingly uncertain. Finding Thorne was a long shot. Evading Kestrel felt like delaying the inevitable. Understanding the Stick-shí'nač, bridging the gap between worlds, seemed like a task beyond her capabilities.

But Nora's words echoed: *We help by surviving. We owe them survival.* And Whis Elem's: *Trust the balance, even when it feels most precarious.*

Perhaps survival wasn't about finding all the answers, or achieving some grand victory. Perhaps it was simply about enduring, witnessing, carrying the story forward, preserving the possibility of truth and balance in a world determined to pave over mysteries and silence dissent. Perhaps the Hollow Truth wasn't a burden to be exposed or buried, but a complex reality to be navigated, respected, and perhaps, eventually, understood.

She carefully tucked the notebook away. Her headlamp flickered, then died completely, plunging her into the soft, natural darkness of the rainforest night. She didn't feel the same panic as before. The darkness felt… different here. Less menacing. More like a blanket, ancient and protective.

She closed her eyes, listening. Not just for threats, but for the subtle language Whis Elem had tried to teach her. The drip of water from immense leaves. The rustle of a small creature in the duff. The sigh of wind high in the canopy. The distant call of an owl. And beneath it all, almost imperceptible, the faint, rhythmic pulse of the earth. The Resonance. Still there. A reminder of the deep power that permeated this land, the power the guardians protected, the power Kestrel sought to control.

She didn't know what the future held. Whether they would find Thorne, whether they would stop Kestrel, whether she would ever truly understand the Stick-shí'nač or her own place between their world and hers. But as she finally drifted towards sleep, a fragile sense of peace settled within her. She had survived. She carried the truth. And she was moving forward, not just fleeing, but seeking. Guided by loss, driven by purpose, walking a perilous path into the heart of an ancient mystery. The journey was far from over. The shadows in the timberline still held secrets, dangers, and perhaps, somewhere in the deep places, answers waiting to be discovered. The silence held, for now, but the echoes of the Hollow Ground would continue to resonate, shaping the path ahead.

Printed in Great Britain
by Amazon